"I am Tzaddi, governess t

he ever knew."

"Well, what is that to me, old woman? I have never seen the Prince and he has never seen me.

"Ahh, Beth my child, that is where you are wrong. The Prince has chosen you to be his bride."

"You mock me. This must be the babbling of a deranged mind."

Taking a step forward, the ancient messenger pulled a leather volume, like a jewel encrusted case from her cloak. She held the book out.

"From the castle walls he watched. These are letters he wrote of his love for you."

"He watched me?"

"He did. And gave instructions.

You must prepare to travel. He is expecting you to go to him."

It was too much to believe. Beth started to turn away but the beauty of the book pulled her back. What words had he written to her?

She looked hard at the wrinkled face in the shadows.

"Are you sure you are telling me the truth, old lady?"

So the journey began. On the road, Beth is transformed and tested beyond her limits as she is challenged to search for Him with her whole heart.

Love Letters

LOVE LETTERS

At the end of a broken journey,
you will find Him, if you search with all your heart.

By Joe Castillo

ArtStone Publishers
130 4th Street
Fayetteville GA 30214
ArtStone@me.com
LoveLetters@joecastillo.com

Praise for

Love Letters

"The many young women we minister to through Well-Spring Living and have the privilege of speaking to, need to hear that their journey is really a love story. This book is a wonderful reminder that when the journey is long and difficult they can always find encouragement and guidance in God's loving words."

Mary Frances Bowley
Founder and Director of WellSpring Living,
a ministry transforming the lives of women and youth.

"This rich story full of beautiful illustrations highlights the challenges, fears, and hardships young women face in the journey to find acceptance and true love. It is also the struggle we all face in seeking the transformative love found only in *Love Letters* written to us by God."

Jennifer Ceppo, M.Ed.
Director of Program Innovation and
Non-Traditional Learning.
The Kings Academy, Jupiter Florida

"*Love Letters* will remind you of all the best things you know to be true, like the stubborn love of God, what it means to fight battles that matter, and that the best stories are the ones that grow out of God's biggest story: His pursuit of your heart."

Kimberly Stuart,
Author, Speaker, Podcaster and Writing Coach

"As a constant overthinker, I often become weighed down by thoughts that overwhelm me. *Love Letters* encouraged me to be able to see my own life as a journey. It is a great relief to realize that my life can be a part of something beautiful, bigger and much more significant than I could even imagine!"

Lydia Grace Barbee,
Digital 3D Animator, Student and avid reader.

"All my books are about telling stories. 'Love Letters' is a romance woven into an adventure about ancient letters based on the love story that God told. That is the best story ever written. 'Love Letters' will change how you think about the story God wrote for you.

Bob Goff
Multiple New York Times best-selling author,
podcaster and recently turned farmer.

Love Letters is a work of fiction. The characters, Incidents, and dialogues are products of the authors imagination and are not to be construed as real. Any resemblance to actual events or persons, living or dead, is entirely coincidental.

LOVE LETTERS
Published by ArtStone Publishers, LLC

Print Edition
ISBN: 978-0-9840459-5-2

Library of Congress Number 2022905104:

Cover Design and all artwork: Joe Castillo
Photo Provided by: Alfredo, Dream Studio, Eugeny Lis

Printed in the United States

A significant portion of the revenues of this book
is being given to ministries who rescue
young women from human trafficking.

For information on special discounts, bulk purchases
And live programs contact:
ArtStone Publishers
LoveLetters@joecastillo.com

LOVE LETTERS

is dedicated to my three

special and unique granddaughters.

Cici, Olivia & Sophia.

May your journey be victorious.

You will find Him when seek with your whole heart.

Acknowledgements

THIS BOOK WOULD never have come into being if God had not prompted me, given me the story, the vision and the people that affirmed and encouraged me along the way.

The seed of this story was planted in the year 1998 as I struggled over the mysteries of dative, ablative and accusative prepositional particles of ancient Hebrew. Yikes! Thank you, Dr. Bill Arnold, for patiently coaxing me to learn a rich and fruitful language that in many ways provided the good soil for this story. It was nourished and watered by Dr. David Bauer who gave me a glimpse into the infinite value and beauty found in the Scriptures. Thanks also for Asbury Seminary where they both still teach.

In my head I believed it was a good story and worthy of being written. Twenty-two years of retelling the unwritten story in my head, dabbling, apologizing, and making excuses all exploded when author and motivator Bob Goff heard my story, rolled his eyes, looked me in the face and said, "Joe just write the damn book!" Thirty days later I finished the rough draft. Thank you, Bob!

The very successful author Kim Stuart, who agreed to become my mentor and writing coach, walked with me a paragraph at a time. She has become a solid friend while reminding me over and over again, "*Joe, listen to me. I know what I am talking about. This book needs to be a love story! You are writing for young women, and you are neither.*" God bless you Kim for your persistence.

"*Who needs an editor?*" I thought, after four revisions. I did. I needed one desperately. Professional editor Jamie Chavez became my "cranky older sister" and helped me tell a better story by chiseling my manuscript down to a readable length and helped it make sense. Kudos Sis.

Thanks to Taylor Hughes, magician and comedian extraordinaire for leading the way through the maze of self-publishing with his own book; 'Road to Wonder, and Brett Phillips for introducing me to the mystical 'shadows' of ancient Hebrew.

Special thanks to Tim Grable, my friend, agent and co problem solver. Together we know how to fix every problem in the world if they would just ask us.

In the end, I can't say enough about my "Glad Girl" Cindy. Wife, proof-reader, encourager, cheerleader, cozy peaceful partner and patient friend. She deserves more than half the credit and all the royalties. Thank you!

The Letters

WALKING HOMEWARD AS evening slid down the massive ancient stones at the base of the castle wall, Beth wondered, as she often did, what it would be like to be inside.

Along the castle wall were occasional metal-studded doorways banded with iron, hinting a way in.

Out of one of the doors, a wrinkled hand reached out and clutched Beth's wrist. Sudden fear brought a gasp to her lips and set her heart racing. She tried to pull away. The hand extended from a gray hooded figure blending with the early evening shadows. Beth tried to run into the fading light ahead but the grip held her fast. Her struggle was checked by a raspy, voice coming from the shadowy figure—an urgent whisper.

"Beth—wait, child!" It was an old woman that knew her name. "Fear not lady, I have an urgent missive from one who loves you."

Still trembling from the shock, Beth spoke. "Wh—who are you? And what do you want?"

The old woman pulled her close and whispered, "Come, step into the shadows. No one must see us together."

Beth resisted, speaking urgently. "I must go! My father has made it clear I should always be home before dark. He will worry at my tardiness."

"Your father, Baruch, will understand, child," the old woman said. "Listen now to what I must tell you. It is an order mandated from the Prince. It bears his seal and is written by his own hand."

At that word Beth hesitated irritably.

"I am Tzaddi, guardian and governess to the Prince. The King called upon me to nurse him, tutor him, and train him in justice and righteousness. I was the only mother he ever knew."

"Well, what do you want with me, old woman? I don't know you. I have never been in the castle nor even seen the Prince. What interest would he have in one who is lives at the foot of the castle, the refuse of his kingdom?" Even in the deepening gloom Beth could see a thoughtful smile crease the leathery face, a twinkle in the beady eyes.

"Ahh, that is where you are wrong, Beth, my child. There is much you must learn, for the Lord himself has chosen you to be his betrothed, his bride. Some day he will take your hand in marriage."

Irritation stirred in Beth's heart. "Oh, let go of me. I told you, I have never seen the Prince and he has never set eyes upon me." She tried to shake the strong grip.

The old woman held fast. "You are wrong again. Many hours, days and years the Prince spent on the battlements of the castle watching you. His eyes have been on you since he was a boy and you a mere slip of a child playing outside your father's house. Your cheerful spirit captured his heart many seasons ago."

"Now you are joking with me. This is just babbling of a confused mind . . . and also"—her voice a touch petulant—"I would appreciate it if you did not call me child."

Taking a slow step out of the now inky shadows, the ancient messenger pulled from beneath her cloak a richly bound leather volume. Even in the dim light its delicate craftsmanship gave the appearance of a jewel-encrusted case. Sparkling amethysts, emeralds, and sapphires decorated the cover. Beth's eyes widened at its beauty.

The smile formed again as the ancient voice spoke mischievously. "All of his love for you, and admonitions for his future bride, along with encouragements, exhortations, and promises he recorded patiently over the years. It was all written to you." She held the book out.

"He watched me?"

"Aye, he did," said the whispery voice.

"You really mean the future King, master of the realm, giver of laws wrote love letters . . . and he wants to marry me?"

"I already told you that. Tomorrow, you must meet me here at the same hour. You must be prepared to travel, I have instructions for you. He is expecting you to go to him."

"This is unbelievable. You are deceived, old woman. If

you think even for a minute that I am going to go wandering off to some unknown place, looking for some man I have never met, never spoken to, nor even seen. How can anyone love someone they have never seen?"

"What the eye cannot see the heart can perceive," the old woman said.

"You have taken leave of your senses." Beth was getting annoyed and anxious about getting home. She started to turn away, but the tantalizing beauty of the jeweled book pull held her back.

"Hush, none can promise safety if you go or if you stay, but the answers to your questions are all in his letters to you." The old woman lifted the volume into the nascent light of a full moon just risen above the castle wall. It glistened with a cool luminescence, as if glowing from within. Her eyes drawn to its beauty, Beth began to wonder what the Prince had written. Curiosity rooted and grew a small tendril into her imagination. *Could it really be he watched me from the wall of the castle? What would the Prince write to me?* The thought made her flush with embarrassment. She needed to know what this royal stranger had written in those letters.

"This man, the Prince, what has he written of me?"

"Calm yourself, child." The voice had become soothing, weighted with truth, a voice to trust. "He has written of his love for you and admonitions proper for a Princess."

Beth felt drawn to the book sparkling in the moonlight. She then looked hard at the face shrouded in shadow.

"Are you sure you are telling me the truth?"

"Of course—this is too fantastic a tale to be imagined. Now take the book and be here tomorrow." Without effort the book slid into the young woman's hands and the elderly apparition vanished into the night.

As the door closed, Beth imagined elegant people inside enjoying music, laughter and lavish parties, but knew she would never be a guest. Perhaps she could be a chambermaid or work in the castle kitchen. Her real dream was to be an artist like her father. *I would love to be a scribe illustrating parchments, writing calligraphy, or drawing colored plates for beautiful books,* she thought. *I could paint murals and design banners for royal events.* It was glamorous to imagine those things, but it was just a dream. Beth was always on the outside. At the front of the castle was a massive, gated portico opened exclusively for the special few. Only those with the right status were ever admitted. There was no advocate. No one she knew would help her in.

Her mother was gone, her father weak and saddened by loss. Beth felt alone, alienated, walled out. *I was just born in the wrong place and time,* she thought. Wanting to be loved and appreciated, she longed for a place inside the castle where perhaps she could find both. It would take a miracle.

Feeling torn by more questions than she could answer, Beth moved to follow the figure into the darkness, but the door was shut tight. She pulled back. Irritation surfaced for a moment, but her inquisitive nature turned her eyes to what was in her hand. The texture and weight of the book was real. Smooth tooled leather felt warm beneath fingers. She looked closer at the beautiful volume. Her mind suddenly filled with new hope, an amazing vision. Dreams of being allowed into the castle as a servant were replaced. The vision that now rose in her mind was enough to cause her breath to become shallow and her heart beat fast again.

What a dream! Could I ever be married . . . to the Prince? Trumpets would announce the opening of the main gates. Courtiers and castle guards dressed in their finest would step aside as I was ushered into the ballroom, honoring me, the soon-to-be bride! To be with the Prince is almost inconceivable. The future queen of the entire kingdom.

Clutching the volume to her chest, shaking with excitement and apprehension at the rebuke she was going to hear from her father, Beth raced for home.

I don't want to disturb my father with this strange story. He would not understand. Quiet but firm disbelief and prohibition would be the likely response. She was not the child, Tzaddi had called her, although the protective nature of her father often treated her that way. She slipped into her small room through the back door. With shaking hands, she lit an oil lamp at her bedside. Taking up the book, she settled into her narrow cot. Soft knocking caused her to jump and clutch the book to her breast.

"Beth, daughter," her father said, "I heard you enter. You must come and eat something before bed."

"Please father, not tonight," she called out, somewhat breathless. "I have no appetite." She spoke the truth, for thoughts of the book filled her mind.

Her father understood nothing of her moods, but in his strict way he still cared for her. Resigned, he spoke through the door. "Very well, there is bread and cheese in the larder. I will see you in the morning."

Silence and solitude returned. Beth leaned back against her pillow clutching the book of letters and pondering the weight of what she had been told.

‡ ‡ ‡

BETH HAD TAKEN on the responsibility of purchasing the daily foodstuffs and home goods as her mother's health had declined. She was often out in the market after a day of work in her father's studio, but her pleasant smile would hardly ever catch the eye of a young man. There were too few choose from, yet the rare suitor was most often too old or unattractive to be considered.

Things were different now. At the death of her mother, the smile had been replaced by a distant look of sorrow mingled with longing for something she could not describe.

"Beth," she would hear again and again working under her father's stern gaze, "this is soon to be your home, your studio. You must listen as I teach. Artistry might give you some small income but finding and caring for a husband is essential."

She tried to listen and learn. She wanted to fill their days with some of the joy her mother's memory left behind. But getting forced into an arranged, loveless marriage was hard for her to swallow. Every day was more difficult.

Nights occasionally told a different story, a significantly darker one.

Within her, Beth already carried a vulnerable and wounded soul. The sound of the bell ringer collecting the bodies taken by the cold hand of the plague was heard too often. It had struck with ruthless precision two of every five villagers. It had taken her mother and left Beth with a broken heart. Lying alone long after sunset in the cold silence, ice was congealing all her dreams. Her relationship with her mother had never been a perfect one. Disagreements and hard words had become more frequent as she approached and passed the age most young women left to make homes of their own. It had carved a distance between them. Now looming beyond the void was residual guilt from those angry words.

Lying in her cot at night, the darkness could invade her thoughts. *Father,* she wanted to say to him, *you truly do not understand the needs in my heart.* Now she thought, I am facing the intolerable reality of being alone under the same roof with this stern, inflexible man who has ruled our home all my life.

To add to it all, that week she had shared her woes with the butcher's wife, who responded in her nasal voice, "You know Beth, our kingdom has been in this bloody battle for decades. You should not complain. Good fortune has allowed you and your family to live secure at the foot of this great castle and inside these walls."

It was true the massive stones protected them from the constant attacks by the enemies of the king. Fighting was frequent and fierce, but other than the noise and commotion outside, Beth and her father were unaffected by the escalating conflict.

Then came the plague. No wall could protect them. All feared the plague. Every family was touched by it, leaving behind wounds in the body and the soul. And then death.

The butcher's wife had made a point of reminding her, "Our King, you know, has grown much white in his beard. He has handed most of the rule over to his only son, the Prince. We know that every day, discouraged soldiers come through the gate. I can see their lagging spirits. They need hope and encouragement to rout the enemy. Nobody has seen the Prince for many seasons. I heard from my daughter who works inside the castle that he was on a mission to find and crush Belial, the prince of darkness. She told me that hordes of our own soldiers have gathered to him and threatened the entire kingdom."

On her way home that day, spring rains added to the gloomy news. Fears and rumors spread of the old King and dwindling soldiers who might not hold till fall. And the butcher's wife had said they might not withstand the onslaught until the son returned. Defeat seemed right at the gates.

Arriving home Beth had been glad to see her white-haired father standing straight as a spear in his workroom. He did run the home like his time in the military: stern but more fierce than angry. *Don't complain,* the butcher's wife had said.

It was true, there had been many good times together. Good memories of working in my father's studio will always be a part of my life, she thought.

The modest wood-beamed, high-ceilinged room had windows open to outdoor views. Mountains, hillsides, meadows could be seen over and beyond the wall. She had smelled the linseed oil mixed with brightly colored flower petals, intensely hued powdered minerals, and metallic liquids. It permeated Baruch's studio with a special fragrance. And Beth loved the pots of paints, brushes, quills, rolls of parchment, canvas squares and frames that filled every nook and cranny. Under her father's precise tutelage, Beth was learning the joy of scribing beautiful arabesques, letters, and alphabets in as many languages as were spoken and written in the kingdom—even some strange, mysterious ones she did not understand. She had heard Baruch say many times, "My great desire for you has always been to create art and beauty. I am passing my skill on to you."

Baruch had made a modest living as a scribe. His skill at forming the ancient runes and glyphs on parchment and illustrating them was legendary, but without a patron his lot was to teach Beth to paint signs for taverns, scribe letters for the illiterate, and complete legal forms. The pay was a pittance, yet it put food on the table. On a few occasions special scrolls had been prepared for the King, which had given Baruch some renown long ago. Too long ago. As the King declined in the kingdom, Baruch's loyalty had shifted to the young Prince, hoping one day to create something beautiful for him.

Beth also longed for the day she could receive some recognition from within the castle.

Yet the war and the plague had changed everything.

Baruch was quiet and intense. He rarely exhibited his passions, but there were a few things that stirred those passions—like discussions of his daughter's future. She was intended to be his magnum opus, his vicarious masterpiece, a creative work filled with art, beauty, and, he hoped, children. He had passed much of his creativity and ability on to his daughter, along with a steel-willed sense of resolve, which often got her into trouble.

Her mother, on the other hand, had been much at home—quiet, musical, often spilling over into song. She had tried to give her daughter joy, laughter, and hope. What was seldom spoken of, coming now with greater frequency in the growing girl, was the dark moods. When they came, Beth's fears would sink her into days of depression and nights full of terrors. When she would succumb to these fits it brought great anxiety to her poor mother and created a growing distance from her father.

Yet he worried about her.

"Listen to me Beth," Baruch would say. "Stop dreaming. If you honor the Prince and apply yourself to your skill, you might find a source of income to provide for yourself after I am gone. But it is a fantasy that some knight in shining armor will come and rescue you! Young men are scarce from the plague and the wars. Work is scarce even within the castle. You must take the man willing to have you or fend for yourself."

"Oh, Father," Beth had argued, throwing down her quill. "I cannot even think of being chained to the callous, immature boys you have suggested—or even worse the old, wrinkled fossils you have dragged to the house to look me over like a prize horse. I would be mortified."

Raising his military voice, Baruch would remind her: "You know there is no dowry, I have no land, no title, and very little work. You will marry whom you must—or starve."

And then Beth would lower her head and weep silently. For years she had hungered, dreamed, and hoped to find one to woo her and take her away to fulfill her daydreams and satisfy her night fantasies. Infatuations had come and gone, but each had evaporated like the droplets on spiderwebs left by the morning dew. Each morning she woke disappointed, and each night dreamed in vain.

In the bleak face of all of this, Beth longed for day when a

Prince, a hero, a handsome and kind young man would love her completely, just like the stories her mother told her as a child. With the loss of her mother, hope was fading away. The will of her father would be imposed. Somehow, she had to find a way out.

‡ ‡ ‡

AS SILENCE DESCENDED on this night, Beth caressed the bright jewels and dainty filigree on each corner of the beautiful book given to her by the ancient Tzaddi. She wondered if in these pages lay hope for her future, perhaps a fulfillment of a dream. Her fingers traced the vines, caressed the jewels on the cover. With a click she opened the latch. The soft sound of skin against parchment she turned the first page and began to read.

Chapter One

Aleph

HIS STORY, THE words of the Prince penned in his own hand, began to pour off each page.

Peering over the crenelated walls of his castle home, the boy Prince wrote of catching sight of young Beth the very first time, playing girl games in the outdoor courtyard of her humble home. Longing for friends his own age, his young heart ached for that companionship. He wrote of having no brothers, sisters, or other children included in training for royalty. Always wanting to shout down to the girl he watched, shyness kept him wistfully hoping for her friendship. He wrote almost daily as he watched from the battlements and tower windows. Long years passed and the Prince grew to love the girl transforming into a young woman. Many times, he observed her sitting in the sunshine, dabbing brushstrokes he envisioned as masterpieces on her father's easel. Close enough to see the tilt of her head, the gesture of her hand, too far away to tell her he loved her work—yet he wrote of how he longed to be at her side. At last, the growing love gave him courage to request her name from his nurse and tutor, Tzaddi. A personal tone and warmth became the deepest part of the letters.

Beth's mind was captivated by the profound and sincere words, penned by her unseen lover. With her imagination set free, and a heart burning with words of selfless devotion and single-minded love, Beth read long into the early morning hours. Eventually she drifted into a soaring, dream-filled sleep.

Uncharacteristically, Baruch sensed his daughter had struggled with one of her dark episodes and allowed her to sleep late. He knew she had been awake in the night and decided to not disturb her. After sleeping most of the day, Beth with disheveled hair and dark circles around her eyes, shuffled into her father's studio. She had to tell him.

Hesitant and timid, but standing as straight as he always stood, Beth spoke with a quaver in her voice. "Father, I know there is nothing about this you will believe, but I have been summoned to the castle. The nursemaid of the Prince has requested . . . I am supposed to go see her . . . be with, no, I am to find, well, I must go to the castle tonight."

Slowly, with concern on his face, Baruch lowered his brush to the easel, wiped his hands on his smock, and gazed at his daughter for a long time. Windows fully open, with light streaming around her from the afternoon sun, he noticed as if for the first time, Beth was no longer a child but a stately young woman. Her maturity was evident in her stance, the intense look in her eyes, and the set of her jaw. He could see her mother in her, and it deepened his love for his only child. Moisture formed at the corners of his eyes as he thought of the years they had enjoyed together as a family. Also brought to mind was the reality that the time might have come when he would have to let her go.

Always a man of few words, he asked, "This nursemaid, is she making provision for you? Will someone watch over you?"

Her thoughts racing, Beth spoke in a rush, "Yes, her name is Tzaddi. She has word from the Prince that I am to meet with him." At first, she wanted to explain and show her father the amazing love letters she held behind her back, then thinking how preposterous the entire story was, she decided to say no more.

"Hmmm." Her father looked down at his hands. "I have heard of this faithful and truthful woman, Tzaddi. If she says you have been summoned by the Prince, then . . . you must go."

Great ambivalence descended on Baruch. Grief swelled up, knowing his child was maturing and needed to go on a path of her own choosing. And yet excitement to hear she had been summoned by the Prince was there too. *Perhaps* he thought, *she will be given a position within the castle: painting portraits of royalty, large murals, designing fabrics or furniture for the King and his family.* She would be cared for and paid although sparingly because of the plague, if there was anything left in the royal coffers. Yes, it could be a good thing. "To stay here," he continued thoughtfully, "if your dreams are in another place, will divide your heart." With a great sigh, he spoke again. "Yes, my child, you must go."

‡ ‡ ‡

DUSK WAS STRETCHING long indigo-shadowed fingers, from the castle turrets across the village streets as Beth returned to the hidden doorway. Her meager possessions held in a small bundle in one hand, and the newly acquired book of letters, wrapped carefully in a shawl, in the other. Tzaddi, the wizened governess to the King's son, stood impatiently in the lavender darkness. As soon as Beth approached, she grabbed her arm, yanked open the door behind her, and pulled her through.

The smell of damp mold and darkness enveloped her.

"My father gave me his blessing, but will be frantic if he does not get messages from me occasionally," said Beth breathlessly. "I told him nothing of a journey. There is no way he would approve. He cannot understand what this is all about and why I must leave. Whether the Prince cares a fig for me or not, there is nothing left for me here. Will you explain this to him?"

"Not today, my child. You will return to him in due time,

but for now, haste is essential. The enemies of my Lord are around every corner, and you have a vital mission to fulfill. Do you have the Book?"

Beth nodded quickly.

"Then we must go! There is danger everywhere. Speak no more, only follow."

With that stern admonition ringing in her ears, Beth followed the hunched figure into the darkness of a long corridor ahead of them. Spaced evenly along the mossy stone walls were torches casting grotesque shadows ahead, beside and finally behind their hustling shapes. After what seemed like a long time, the descending tunnel opened into an underground courtyard where the smell of horses and hay indicated their entrance to a stable. Tzaddi turned toward a spacious chamber and motioned Beth forward.

"First, you must meet your traveling companion," she said, still speaking in a hushed voice. "Squire, come forth," she called into the darkness. With the rustling of a small animal, a hesitant form appeared at the doorway to the chamber. Head down, hands clasped meekly behind him, a strapping young man with his face almost completely shadowed by a beaked cap shuffled forward.

"This is Aleph," said Tzaddi, pointing. "Aleph, you must care for Beth as the chosen one. Care for her steed and guide her on her journey." Then turning to Beth. "He is properly submissive and prepared to do for you as my Lord, the Prince would do. He was trained by his father before him."

Unsure of Aleph's part in this journey, Beth spoke up.

"If he is just a stable hand, does he know where the Prince is? Can he properly care for a horse? Has he even been outside the castle?"

"I have been sent to serve, milady," Aleph said in a quiet, firm voice. "My life has been spent caring for the animals in the stables. I also know the way we must travel if you are willing to follow."

‡ ‡ ‡

FOR ALEPH IT all seemed strange, yet so familiar. From the beginning they had known what his life was to be. My father knew this was for the best, he thought. Working for most of his life as a stable boy, he had learned the role of a servant. He knew when to bow, lower his eyes, take orders, commands, even abuse. He learned to anticipate the needs of those he served. It was his destiny. Servanthood was so daily, yet he had agreed willingly to be indentured to the future bride. It was to be his most difficult assignment. *Yes,* Aleph thought, *my father always knew this was for the best.* The servant Aleph then doffed his cap, tugged his forelock, bowed meekly to the young woman, and then slipped back into the shadows. His journey had been set.

"Come now, child, I must give you explicit instructions," Tzaddi said as she led Beth into a small triangular alcove connected to the chamber. Barren except for a cot, a chair, and a crude desk, it had all the appearances of a prison cell, even to the ironclad door. Three candles set in niches recessed on each of the three walls lit the room dimly. Tzaddi turned and scrutinized Beth carefully. Resistance was written on her young features. She was still wrapped up in herself, probably arrogant and willful. She could be, Tzaddi knew, at times selfish, unkind, and even petulant. Yet because of the Prince, she loved her. Beth was not worthy. But then, Tzaddi knew, that was the point.

"Sit now, and listen well," Tzaddi said, her voice still in a whisper. With the heavy door shut behind them, Beth wondered if even a loud cry could have been heard outside the room. Obediently she sat on the foot of the bed, lay her bundle beside her, and turned toward her mysterious guide.

"Beth, remember this daily. Long ago you were chosen, you and no other. You were loved and selected to be the betrothed of my Lord. It is an unimaginable and unique privilege to be loved and lifted to such an exalted place. He who loves you is destined to sit on the throne. Dominion of all things will be given into his hand. He is the Lord and will soon rule over the entire kingdom. All glory belongs to him, and all power is to be his alone. When his enemies are vanquished, and mark my words well, they will be defeated, he will rise with power to take you as his bride. He instructed me to give you his written messages—the inspired book you now hold in your hand—and direct you on your way. Also remember, child"—her words becoming even more stern and intense—"the words he has written to you are clear and to be followed. He expects you to be true. You must keep yourself for him alone, that when you meet him, you need not be ashamed."

"I wish you would stop calling me a child," Beth mumbled. "I am of marrying age and left childhood many years ago."

Tzaddi pushed her face close to hers and said with gentle sorrow, "Beth, you are yet a child, but you are soon to enter a furnace that will burn away all traces of your childhood. Then I will bow and call you my sister and my lady and"—after a long pause—"my queen." She held Beth's gaze.

"Show me now the book," the old woman said, returning to her serious, austere tone. Taking the book from Beth's hand, she opened it to the back, revealing a number of gilt-edged pages that were blank. Then reaching into a small cavity exposed at the spine when the book was open, she withdrew with gnarled fingers a delicate black and gold writing quill.

"My Lord also wanted you to record any thoughts you may have for him. On these blank pages"—she nodded toward the book—"you can write your thoughts to him."

"How can I have any thoughts?" Beth asked. "I don't even know what he looks like. I have never talked to him, much less have any kind of feelings for him. The longer I sit in this dungeon, the more I wonder why I agreed to go on this strange journey anyhow. Maybe I just need to forget all this and go back to my boring life, being lonesome, and putting up with my stubborn father." The girl stood and, turning her back on her ancient guide, started toward the door. As she reached for the massive handle, Tzaddi's voice came mocking to her ears.

"This night, why did you come, child?"

Beth turned and with anger in her voice responded. "You know it had nothing to do with you. It was the words in the book that brought me and nothing else. If they are true, and written to me by the Prince, then I will follow him. If they are not, then this is the cruelest trick, ever played on anyone"

Motioning her back into the room, Tzaddi closed her eyes, lowered her head, and shook it slowly from side to side. "It is no trick. The words he wrote are true, sincere and from his very heart. Only the road to find him will be long and perilous. The dangers will be great, and temptations many. You must have great determination if you are ever to find and be favored by him who you seek."

Lifting her head and looking directly into the girl's dark eyes, she continued. "You may also have confidence in this: my thoughts and those of your father will be with you every moment until you are united with your beloved."

Tzaddi rose, handed Beth the precious book, stepped past the confused girl, and pulled the heavy door open. "Aleph will wake you when it is time to leave," she said wearily stepping out of the room. "You will not see my face on the morrow."

"Wait!" said Beth, a frantic note in her voice. "How will I

know when I find him? The Prince, I mean." As the door closed slowly behind her, the thin quavering voice spoke words that returned to her many, many times in the dark days ahead. "You will find him when you seek him with your whole heart."

Dropping into the small wooden chair with an exhausted sigh, she opened the gracious volume on the desk and by the flickering candlelight, began to read again passionate words that had lured her into this strange and fearful adventure.

Reading the stories of his solitary life as a royal child, in the dark rooms of this very castle where he grew and was tutored, pierced her. Wandering lonely halls thinking of her and then being lifted from his gloom by those very thoughts, he wrote of some imagined future. Perhaps gazing at her intense face as she painted or running hand-in-hand with her across a meadow. The delights he described were euphoric, heady.

The silence grew long. The candles short. Hope in the reality of the love expressed in the words of this amazing book captured her imagination again. Finally, when one of the candles on the far wall began to gutter, she reached into the hidden compartment in the book's spine and withdrew the delicate writing quill.

Am I really going to go on this bizarre expedition? she wondered. I am going to leave behind my grieving father and frustrating lonely life. But it is what I know. It is what I am used to. Now I am headed who knows where into all kinds of dangers with a half-wit stable hand for a companion, all because of the words in some book. I am supposed to be looking for a man I have never met. Someone who claims to have seen me and fallen in love with me from the castle wall. Then he wrote it all down in love letters for me to read. Does this make any sense?

That the Prince existed she did not doubt. Yearly, the entire kingdom celebrated his birth as the only son of his father. Banners, decorations, and music surrounded the celebrations that filled an entire month before that day. The sounds of celebration floated tantalizingly over the castle walls. His exploits were legendary, and almost everyone in the castle knew him as the future King. Beyond the walls many did not. Whether or not she had been hand-picked to be his bride was much more difficult to accept. She didn't think she was ugly, but she was not a beauty, and she knew it. *Why would the unchallenged ruler of the entire kingdom want me? He could have anyone he wants. Has he really picked me to be his beloved?*

If this was a deception—if she spent her days traveling, looking for one who would spurn her in the end, or one who would merely use her, and then leave her forsaken—it would be better if she never sought him at all.

One thought did amaze her. For the first time ever—even if only in the underground stable—in a small way, a dream had come true. She was inside the castle.

‡ ‡ ‡

WHEN BETH TRIED to reason it out, it became too incredible to believe, but as her mind drifted back to the searing words penned by his own hand, her doubts dimmed into the background. Then her imagination again took root. With those words echoing in her mind, she saw herself in the great hall, standing beside the Prince, the Lord of all the kingdom. Her ragged old hand-sewn clothes gone. Draped in a gown of radiant white, just like the fables her mother had read her as a child, she would live happily ever after with him. As her imagination flowed unhindered, words the Prince might want to hear floated to the surface. Before logical arguments could intervene, she lifted the gold quill and began to write.

Yes, my Prince, I think it would make me happy
to follow you and live in the way you want me to.
I love your letters to me, and I am willing to look
for you,
perhaps with my whole heart.
I'll try not to do anything to shame you:
It would be nice to please you.
You want me to follow your guidance faithfully.
I think I might want to do that, to listen to
your advice.
Then, I don't think I would be ashamed,
as I read your letters.

I would like to offer you a clean heart,
as I learn your true message.
If I follow your lead: I really hope
my search for you won't be a failure!

Chapter Two

Beth

SOMETHING WAS CHASING her. In full darkness she could not move. Panic surged. Held as if by leather cords, she strained to pull free. Way off in the blackness, voices were talking and laughing. A scream welled up within her chest only to die away to a whimper by the time it reached her lips. Faint light pushed at her from the hard blackness. Anger, followed by a burst of energy flooded in, giving her strength to push away the grasping dark. Sitting up suddenly out of a heart-pounding nightmare, Beth found Aleph, servant, keeper of animals, bending over her with a stubby candle in his hand. She pushed him away.

"What are you doing sneaking in here in the dark? Were you going to try something while I was sleeping?" Beth snapped at the quiet, impassive face dimly lit by the flickering candle.

"Nay, Mistress, I was merely trying to wake you."

"Well, what are you doing that for? It's still the middle of the night."

"We must leave before light for your safety, Mistress; enemies are everywhere. Your horse is already saddled. The Prince longs for you to be with him. To find him the journey must begin."

"Look, stable boy, I am not even sure I am going yet. Just light one of my candles and go away. I need to think about this." As he hesitated, she commanded, "Go on, give me some privacy!"

Quietly he nodded. "I will stand waiting, Mistress. It is the will of the Prince that I serve you." Turning to one of the sconces in the stone wall, he lit first one, then another of the candles, slipped out, and closed the door behind him.

Beth felt as if she had not slept at all. Her still pounding heart, shallow breath, aching joints, grainy eyes, and sore muscles all made her wonder what she was doing in the bowels of the castle preparing to venture out on an insane journey. *I am not going to do it*, she thought. *This is ridiculous!* Then as she stood to stretch, her gaze fell on the open book and what she had written the night before. Some of the words the Prince had written filtered back into her mind; incredible words of love, commitment, and willingness to sacrifice for her. For long moments she stood staring at the open pages caught up again in the meaning behind those words.

Maybe I can go a little farther, she thought, just a couple of days. It would be nice to at least see this man with the fervent words and eloquent pen.

Like her father, never one to dawdle when her mind was made up, it was quick work to repack her few belongings and stride out into the underground barn. In the middle of the enclosure a massive black horse stood switching a long tail that reached to the ground. A thrill rushed to her cheeks at the thought of riding such an elegant steed. Liveried in burnished, hand-tooled leather, covered with shining solid-silver studs, it looked like a thoroughbred prepared for royalty. As her eyes ran over the sleek black hide glimmering in torchlight, they finally rested on the patient servant holding the reins.

"Aleph, is this what I get to ride? Why didn't you tell me I got to ride a stallion like this? He is magnificent! Don't just stand there, grab my bag, and help me up!"

"It is a mare, Mistress. She is the best in the King's stable."

Taking her bag, he turned to a small pack donkey standing in the shadows and began to tie it beside other bundles.

"Wait, I need something from my bag," Beth ordered. Taking it back, she removed the item that had touched her heart and triggered this mysterious quest. In the dim light of the underground stable, the book glowed with an inner light. It was a very short time since she had begun reading it, yet possessive feelings had already formed around *her* book.

Trying to keep it hidden, she slipped it quickly out of her bag and into the deep pocket of her traveling cloak. Striding to the side of the huge mare, taking the reins in one hand and reaching up to grasp the pommel with the other, she turned.

"Well, are you going to help me up or not, boy?"

Aleph set the bag down and walked calmly to her side. "Of course, Mistress. If you will place your—"

"I know how to mount," she said tartly as she bent her left knee for him. Then with strength and gentleness that surprised her enough to cock one eyebrow, Aleph cradled her knee and hoisted her quite high enough to swing her right leg across the saddle. He set about adjusting the stirrups, patting the giant mare who seemed to know and trust his gentle hand. After tying her bag to the donkey's pack, he took its halter. Putting a finger to his lips, he grabbed the mare's chinstrap and led off into the darkness of the gray stone cavern.

For long moments, echoes of giant hooves and *trip-trip* of smaller ones were all Beth could hear. Then eyes widened by the darkness, she perceived the gray light of early dawn a long way ahead in the upward sloping tunnel.

"You must stoop low for the next distance, Mistress," echoed his bodiless voice drifting back from the darkness. She stooped as low as she could, even sliding a little to one side in the saddle, but still felt the damp roof scrape the back of her head briefly. Then they were outside. Mist shrouded the long valley sloping away from the massive stone keep behind them. Ghostly trees loomed to the left, marking the near edge of the King's hunting preserve.

Shifting forward in the saddle, Beth called forward to the gray form leading the pack animal ahead. "Are you not riding, boy? How are you going to keep up?"

Slowing till the mare came up beside him, then pausing, the young man responded in a low voice. "Mistress, I remind you to keep your voice low. The sound of animals will not attract attention but if our speech is detected, our lives could be in danger. Do not trouble yourself. It is not the speed but the constancy that will mark our progress."

She stifled an urge to rebuke this stable hand for telling her what to do. Somehow his quiet but firm commands nettled her. She would have to learn to endure or ignore them to keep from being miserable.

"How long," she asked, "is this journey going to take, and do you know where the Prince is?"

Moving back to the lead, Aleph spoke over his shoulder. "Direction and destination can be planned before setting out, but the days of the journey are measured by how often the traveler strays from the path."

What does that mean? thought Beth. I am not sure that is even an answer.

As they began to move forward again, the mare turned her beautiful head back toward the castle. Dainty ears perked, she made a move to return. Aleph pulled on her lead to no effect. Finally with a click of his tongue and a practiced murmur, the horse faced forward and began to follow again. Soft misty dawn-light shimmered off the mare's black coat and Beth, amazed at her beauty, leaned forward and patted her silky neck.

Willing her puzzled thoughts outward, Beth began to notice the lush greenery of her surroundings. Dark evergreens draped long, curved branches toward a mint sward of grass ahead. After dropping down between plowed lands and meadows scattered with wide fields of mint, sage, and puffed dandelions, the trail led into shadowy woods where she had never gone. One last look over her shoulder revealed the massive towers of the King's castle almost blotting out the entire sky then the forest hid all from view.

Jade-leafed ivy festooned the trees overhead and dripped moisture collected from the drifting mist. Everything seemed to be coated with emerald-green moss, even the trail beneath their feet. Carpet-soft, it silenced the horse's hooves. Overhead, vaulted trellises filtered the early morning light through translucent leaves and flower petals, patterning the mossy carpet with stained glass light and cathedral silence. The spiritual hush lifted her thoughts to meditations on the precepts and statutes found in the pages of the love-book in the pocket against her heart. Commanded to silence and forced to inactivity, the words came sweetly to her mind. A great peace seemed to steal into her soul. The beauty and silence of her surroundings heightened the words of her unseen lover and lifted her spirit to a level she had never experienced. Often, she found herself opening the volume to those first pages and going over one special phrase or another, allowing them to anchor themselves firmly in her memory. This blissful reverie lasted long into the day, until finally Aleph halted the steed and walked back to her.

"Mistress" he spoke in a low voice. "If you are hungry, I can prepare some food."

"Well," she responded stiffly, "I was having a wonderful time reading and I don't really appreciate being interrupted, but since you have already done that, I guess we can eat. Can you fix something edible?"

"We have meager fare, but I will do my best, Milady."

The massive steed came to a standstill and Beth dismounted with the help of her servant. An awareness crept in that for the first time in her life she was completely alone with a man. Menial and servile as he was, she still was alone with him. Warnings in her mother's voice echoed in her head. *Don't ever trust a man alone! It is not seemly for a young girl to place herself in solitude with a man! Guard your heart from temptation!*

Much as she disliked admitting it, her mother's admonitions sounded somewhat like the desire for purity the Prince had recorded in his love letters to her. There was a big difference. Guarding herself from defilement because her mother had said so seemed old fashioned and restrictive. Keeping herself for her lover alone was noble and worthy. She liked the thought of presenting herself unblemished and innocent to the Prince. If he loved her, as his words said, she could withstand temptation for him, or so she thought.

Glancing over her shoulder at Aleph as he meekly bent over a small fire preparing their afternoon meal, she thought, *No problem there. I could never be attracted to someone like him.* Even though her family status put her above him, a stable boy, he just was too quiet, too dull and mousy, to attract her attention. For sure, he was too timid to ever try any advances on her.

After a small meal, Beth waited while Aleph brought water from a nearby stream for the animals. A small dollop of water splashed on to her cloak as he passed by.

"You clumsy oaf!" she snapped, then immediately regretted it. "Try to be more careful, squire."

Not even lifting his eyes to hers, he murmured, "Great apologies, Mistress. Would you like me to sponge it dry for you?"

"No. It can dry by itself. Just be more mindful when you are sloshing stuff around. And by the way, why all the Milady, and Mistress stuff? Can't you talk to me like a normal person?"

"No, I cannot, Milady. For it is known you are the bride of choice of the Prince. You have been selected from all the young women in the kingdom. You alone were given the inspired words. I am duty bound to respect and speak to you as royalty."

"So, you talk to me that way because you were instructed to?"

"Servanthood can be commanded, Milady, but respect must be given willingly." With that pronouncement he looked about, laid his finger to his lips, and whispered, "Again, Milady, silence is imperative."

The pace to this point had been stately and slow. Beth wanted to urge the horse faster. The Prince was somewhere up ahead and finding him was urgent in her mind—but she did not feel the same urgency in her stable boy.

Aleph helped her mount with smooth and careful movements, tied up the remainder of the food on the donkey's back, and set off at a steady pace into the green tunnel.

She was so full of questions, but his amazing pronouncement kept her silent. *Am I chosen? Should I be treated as one of the royal family?* These thoughts were all new to her. It was heady and sobering at the same time. Words, dreams, and hopes spun around in her mind. Phrases from the book surfaced in her swirling thoughts. Reading a few of the lines out loud seemed appropriate, softly, so Aleph could not hear and make fun of her.

Promised to one husband . . . presented as one pristine for him. Prepared as a bride, beautifully dressed for her husband. Visions and images flashed before her. The stained-glass–like cathedral light drifting down from overhead washed across her as she passed. It was very much like a bride adorned, pacing stately down the center aisle of a silent church.

Finally, with nothing to do but be led along, Beth began to look around her. The pale, mint-colored leaves within her reach hung from some tree she had never seen before. Soft and velvety on one side. Smooth like leather on the other, they were the size and shape of her unusual book. Plucking them one at a time, she collected more than just a handful, and without any thought about what she would do with them, she opened her book and pressed them behind the back page.

Suddenly, there was a shout. Off in the shadows to her right, there was the swell and murmur of many voices. Yanked from her dreams and a sudden jerk at the lead she found Aleph had left the path and was rushing down a steep slope, towing the animals behind. Over his shoulder he hissed through clenched teeth.

"Hold on well, Mistress, our passage will be rough!"

With amazing swiftness and silence, the lackey on foot and the two animals at almost a full canter rushed down the darkening steepness. Holding the pommel with both hands, Beth had to duck low to keep the vines and branches from slashing at her face. Light faded. Moss gave way to rocks. Graceful tendrils became harsh thorny cables, the slapping leaves roughened. What seemed to be bodies of fallen soldiers lay to either side. Weapons were scattered across the path. The clang of steel against steel and roar of battle could be heard in the forest beside them. Grunts of effort, screams of pain, and a chorus of moans from the wounded howled from the woods. The sounds began fading to their rear.

Their headlong rush seemed to last forever. Clutching the

mare's long mane with all her strength, Beth ducked and jounced down the steep slope. Hands and fingers began to cramp as she held on for her life. Fear akin to panic attacked her with the possibility she could be thrown from the saddle and dragged down the winding trail to her death. *How long can I hold on?* reverberated in her thoughts.

The pace finally slowed and in the deepening gloom the sure-footed mounts and their agile leader trotted into a small opening in the thick forest. Old stones, massive, un-hewn, set one upon another, ringed a small clearing. For a long time, Aleph stood with his head cocked, listening for any pursuit.

"We will rest here." His soft voice came out of the gloom. Aleph, Beth noticed, was barely breathing heavily.

"Wh-who was that and where are we?" Beth whimpered as she slumped against the strong neck of her sweating horse.

"The battle has begun. We have descended into a secret keep of the Prince. Here we are safe for a time."

With gentle hands, he assisted her to the ground and led her to collapse onto one of the smaller stones. As he busied himself unpacking and working to light a fire, she sat nervously watching him go calmly about his work. The day had been long. Closing her eyes, the warmth of her morning meditations flooded back into her soul and calmed her fearful heart. As the fire grew large, delicious smells reminded Beth of her growing hunger, but questions were still flying around in her head.

How much does Aleph know about the letters? Who else

knows about my quest? What would the Prince say to calm my fears? The book of letters opened to where she had left off reading and the words written for her did begin to quiet her mind and soothe her soul. As tantalizing as the aroma of the food on the fire, they drew her in and fed her as no meal ever had. Then wondering what words would please the Prince, she pulled the quill from within the book, turned to the next blank page and began to write.

Why should I keep my way pure?
You say you want me to live according to your words.
I am going on this search with all my heart;
I sincerely hope I will not get lost!
I am hiding your words in my heart,
meditating on them so I won't disappoint you;
Please, don't let me stray away from your
loving words!
I have heard that you are good, O Prince!
Help me memorize your proverbs.
I would like to announce out loud
and tell others about what you have written to me.
I will rejoice in the things you shared with me,
they are good and comforting.
I will think about your suggestions,
and meditate on your ways.
I love what you have written to me;
I don't want to lose your words.

Chapter Three

Gimmel

BATHED IN A pool of golden firelight, the two travelers ate their meal in silence. Although quite tasty, Beth almost complained about the small amount Aleph had dished out, but she had a far more pressing question forming in her mind. He had stepped away from the firelight to care for the animals before she had a chance to speak. Resting her weary head on the sandy bank behind her awaiting his return, she fell off the edge of wakefulness into a slumber.

The world was a cold, leaden haze when Beth finally opened her eyes. Every edge was blurred by a foggy blanket that settled during the night. Charred ashes of the burned-out fire lay on the gray soil extending to the drooping leaves and trunks of gnarled trees beyond. A shadowy form loomed above the bushes. Then several more appeared out of the dark shrubbery. Sitting up with a jerk, panic shot down her spine. She was alone! Jumping to her feet, his name burst from her lips. "Aleph, Aleph!"

With a suddenness that alarmed her, silent figures detached themselves from the forest shadows and strode forward. Hulking forms with faces as impassive as the leaden surroundings took shape. Weighed down with massive tools of war, they looked even more fearsome. Axes, spiked maces, swords, bladed daggers all hung from their shoulders and sides. Spears and hooked lances were gripped in massive fists. Dread clamped the young girl's throat as her heart began to race.

Twelve intimidating warriors moved into the clearing. The largest of the warriors strode up to her in long bold steps. Helmet, breastplate, belt, boots, sword, and shield came into focus with a glint of steel.

"ALEEEEEPH!" she screamed with terror in her voice. Then stooping, her hand scrabbling for a brand from the dead fire, Beth prepared to defend herself. Halfway through a panicky back swing a voice so deep it seemed to vibrate up from the earth, came from the warrior's lips.

"Melech."

The futile blow from the charred stick bounced off the huge man's thigh. His sword leaped into his raised hand. Suddenly Aleph was at her side. Flinging herself against him, she grabbed at his tunic, shrinking from the terrifying figure. With both hands on the hilt, sword raised high, the giant warrior swiftly plunged the blade into the sand at Beth's feet.

The massive form then fell to one knee, forehead placed against his closed fists.

"We bow to serve," rumbled from beneath the lowered helmet. As one, the entire band of shadowy forms kneeled, bowed, and murmured the same.

"Gimmel!" Aleph said in a jovial voice. "Arise, brothers, but hold your tongue, you are in the presence of royalty."

Beth's head whipped wide-eyed toward the kneeling company now rising to their feet, then back at Aleph only inches from her own. Narrowing to slits, her eyes skewered into Aleph's face. He had steadied her with his left arm, his hand still resting lightly at her waist.

"Brother?" She pushed herself away from him. "You called him brother! He almost scared me to death. You horrid person! I thought I would have to fight for my life while you were off hiding in the trees. I just knew you had dragged me out into the wilderness where I am a total stranger just to leave me to be killed. OOOO, I hate you!" Raising the charred stick as if to strike, her eyes for the briefest of seconds met his. They were filled with tenderness and calm. It was an unsettling feeling looking into the eyes of her servant who, it seemed, was not going to humbly bow his head and look away. Seconds seemed long holding his gaze until with a shiver she broke away.

Then throwing the branch forcefully into the trees, she spun away from him, almost bumping into the massive form of Gimmel the warrior still kneeling before her. He was tall as she was, even on one knee. As she passed him, it was impossible to ignore the dirt and sweat on his brow, cuts on his muscled forearm, and shoulder still oozing blood. Fear and anger began to dissipate. Stomping over to the horse standing patiently behind Aleph, she grabbed the halter.

Returning to his quiet servant voice, Aleph spoke to her stiffened back. "These are good men, Milady. They are brothers and warriors loyal to the Prince. Gimmel, their leader, gives as much as he receives. He is truly gentleness and strength, completely trustworthy, and will defend you with his life. I am grieved that he frightened you."

Another scathing rebuke on her lips, Beth turned to see Aleph face the group of soldiers.

"Tell me, Gimmel, you bring news?" Leaning closer he spoke a few words, either in a foreign tongue or too low for Beth to understand. As they conversed, Gimmel occasionally glanced in her direction. It was a brief glance repeated, becoming gradually wide-eyed with unbelief, finally lowering in respect.

Annoyance on Beth's face shamed him for isolating her from the conversation, causing him to pull back his massive shoulders, raise his head, and speak clearly with rumbling undertones.

"Yes, the main battle has not yet begun but Belial is amassing his forces. He has gotten word of the coming bride."

"And what has he spoken about her, brother?"

Stepping closer, with anger tempered by curiosity, she wondered, *Is Gimmel is talking about me?*

"Belial has spoken against her with scorn and contempt. He has vowed she will be defiled."

Standing slightly behind him, Beth could not see Aleph's face, but she saw him visibly stiffen. Whether in anger or in fear, she could not tell.

"It is no surprise to hear of his vile plans. Come brothers, we must hurry, but leave no trace of our passing."

"Wait, wait!" Beth demanded, pulling at Aleph's shoulder. "Who is Belial, and why has he decided to come after me?"

Stooping to obliterate the traces of the dead fire at his feet, Aleph spoke but tightness could be heard in his voice. "Belial, pride of darkness, covetous ruler of this age, has singled you out for defilement because you are the beloved. The bride chosen for the King's son." Then he continued as if to explain, "A cruel enemy attacks the strong by targeting the defenseless."

That last statement brought to mind the question she had wanted to ask the night before—but Aleph made it clear the conversation was over and it was time to depart. Helping Beth onto her horse with unnecessary gentleness, he handed her a leather bag with bread, cheese, and a gourd of water. Nodding silently to the already assembled men, he followed them out of the clearing into the forest.

No sunlight pierced the foliage overhead. There was no

way to determine what direction they were headed, and the constant gray surroundings made the time monotonous. The band of soldiers moved easily through the trees around her. Most of them disappeared for long periods of time. Only Gimmel, their leader, remained constantly in view, often conferring with Aleph in hushed tones. It seemed odd to Beth: this great and mighty warrior appeared to treat her servant with the respect of an equal, perhaps almost with a touch of deference. Munching on pieces torn from the loaf and sipping from the gourd of sweet spring water, Beth, feeling a little refreshed, pulled the sole book in her library from her cloak, and began reading.

Each page held more revelations. The Prince wrote of the emptiness he felt having never known his mother. He described struggles with dictates from his stern father, the King. His feelings mirrored hers. Then an announcement was given that he was required to be trained and serve with the soldiers of the realm, a requirement of all young men his age.

Beth was astounded that the Prince would have to trade his royal robes for the rough leather and canvas of men-at-arms. Yet his narration was filled with courage, never complaint, only a sharing of the emptiness he felt when he could not watch her from the window of the north tower or think of her in the quietness of his room where he penned his feelings of growing love. As in each of the previous times, his words cleaved her heart, a tender rapier, discerning every thought and intention dividing her very soul and spirit.

Closing the book and storing it in the pocket close to her heart sent her thoughts soaring. For long hours her meditations flowed around the Prince and his love penned sweetly in ink on parchment. It was soul lifting and heady musing.

Now the pace was a faster, a steady march but caught up in the flow of good words she lost track of the day slipping by. With very few stops, the two and their fearsome guards continued through the woods, ever climbing upward. Then, as an uninvited guest, Aleph came to mind. Being angry with him was pointless. Lifting the stick to strike that humble servant shamed her. *I must apologize to him*, she mused, shaking her head. *He cannot be at my side every minute.*

Finally in a moment of brief respite as he cared for her horse, she had an opportunity to speak to the stable hand.

"Aleph, I am sorry for being angry and almost hitting you with that stick. I can't expect you to be hand and foot day and night."

"It was a small thing, Milady," he answered while checking the mare's hooves. "But you may rest assured that I am available at your call at any time." Then, looking up from his menial task, he continued, looking intently into her face. "It is my duty to not leave you, nor would I ever forsake you."

Beth, still locked into his earnest gaze, tried to shake it off by quickly asking the question waiting in her head. "By the way, Aleph, how did you know I had been given the words of the Prince? Did Tzaddi tell you?"

The awkward moment now passed; Aleph stood in preparation to help her mount.

"Tzaddi, the wise and just governess to the Prince, did speak of the letters guardedly, but it was well known in the castle that the Prince was writing of his thoughts toward you. All believed they were words that would open your eyes to the wonderful things he longed for."

"Tell me, Aleph, did you see the Prince? What did he look like? Did he ever speak to you?" Those last were never answered as Gimmel interrupted.

"Forgive me, your royal exalted highness," he rumbled, bowing low. "Pressing issues have become known. We must alter our plans." Beth felt sure he was somehow teasing her but would never say it to his face or even to Aleph. The two walked forward discussing the pressing issues, leaving her with too many questions and not enough answers. When they returned to her, everyone hastily moved on.

Signs of civilization began to appear, as the path became broader, and the trees thinned. Barking dogs and shouts of children could be heard ahead. Soon a few hastily built hovels began to show among the tree trunks. They were entering the fringes of a small village. Beth called out to Aleph, only to discover Gimmel leading her horse and donkey.

"Where are we, and where is my squire?" she asked Gimmel brusquely.

"Aleph had other matters to attend, your royal eminence," he said. "We have arrived at the village of Daleth. This town is the doorway we must pass through for the rest of our journey. The people are poor but kind. They are loyal to the Prince. We shall rest here for the night, if it is pleasing and acceptable to your exalted standards."

Beth looked at him, squinting one eye. *Is he making fun of me?* she wondered.

A glad cry from one of the children announced their arrival. Soon Beth was surrounded by cheerful people calling out a welcome. She was obviously the center of attention. Bone weary from being in the saddle all day long, she slid to the ground by herself, wishing silently that her servant was there to make her life a little easier. The villagers thronged around, and little children picked at her skirt looking up at her with shy wistful eyes. She pushed their hands away brusquely. With a veiled look, Beth scanned the crowd, avoiding contact with the smiling eyes. The village was obviously poor, and the people were simple but cheerful in their colorful garb.

A tall spokesman wearing a bleached white robe almost the color of his hair stepped forward. His young-looking but weathered face was festooned with a cheerful smile.

"Welcome to Daleth, your highness—all we have is yours. What can we do to serve you?" He then bowed deeply, gesturing toward a strange yellow portal, a trilith of hewn logs that opened the way through a wall of woven branches and thorns. Decorations were carved in the posts and lintel, with a narrow box affixed to the post on the right.

With a heavy sigh Beth closed her eyes momentarily and then muttered, "I really am tired, I am dirty, I am hungry, I am thirsty, and I am upset that my servant has disappeared. What I really need is some food, some water to bathe, and I just need some peace and quiet." A small look of hurt and confusion crossed the man's tanned face, but with a clap of his hands people scurried to meet her demands.

Then turning to Gimmel, Beth spoke with just a little petulance. "And tell that no-good Aleph boy that I am really displeased that he has run off again."

"As you wish, your highness," rumbled Gimmel. "Although Aleph, your squire, must on occasion scout ahead for safe passage. But fear not. He will always return at your call. And I, your very humble servant, am instructed to care for your every whim and desire as well. As long as I live, nothing shall harm you." Then with a deep chuckle, he added, "Not even charred sticks."

She didn't think it was funny.

Led through the carved portal, Beth and her horse were guided to the largest hut in the village. Within, rustic furniture included a couple of chairs, a table with a generous helping of food, and a copper-lined wooden tub many hands began filling with hot water. Then even the small, chattering children, eager to touch her hand or skirt, were whisked away, and she was alone. Some of the weariness of the long day seeped out into the hot bath as she soaked. Later with a full stomach, she snuggled into a pile of warm furs and by the light of two smoldering lamps, casting long shadows in the simple one room hut, she pulled out her book.

For the first time, before putting quill to paper, she paused and thought through her day. She shuddered at the memory of the fierce battle, the wounded and dead soldiers, the threat of being hunted, and marveled at the brave men fighting the enemy risking their lives to protect her. She did remember and chuckle at Gimmel's wry comments. Then the faces of the good people and children of Daleth filled her mind. She felt ashamed at how she had treated them. The letters from her Lord, the Prince, inspired her to be better. With regret for her actions, she took the quill and began to write.

Your good thoughts about me my Prince, will help me
do better,
I will try to follow your words.
Open my eyes, yes, I long to see
the wonderful things you are writing to me in
your letters.
I am a stranger in this land,
thank you for not hiding your love from me.
My soul is consumed with longing
for your sweet thoughts all the time.
You will rebuke the subjects
who stray from your commands!

Protect me from me from scorn and criticism,
because I really want to keep your statutes.
Even though princes and rulers
will sit and speak against me,
I am concentrating on your instructions.
Your sweet words are my delight and my counselors.

Chapter Four

Daleth

BETH LAY WITH her eyes closed, enjoying the luxurious pile of furs, hanging onto the last remnants of sleep. A small scratching sound finally pried her eyes open. She jumped at the sight of two large black pupils inches from her own. They belonged to a tiny little girl not more than three or four years old. Her unblinking eyes, surrounded by long black, thick lashes, widened even more as her lips parted in a coy smile.

"You little gamin!" Beth laughed, glancing at the entrance. "How did you get in here? I double latched the door last night."

In a sweet lispy voice, the girl answered. "Thoo du win-do."

Beth laughed out loud at her cuteness. She was sitting on her heels beside the mounded furs that made up Beth's bed. Chin on her knees, arms wrapped around her legs, and one hand scratched occasionally at what looked like a mosquito bite on her elbow. "Why did you climb in here?" Beth asked.

"I wath athleep when you came latht night, an I wan-ned to thee the printheth. You're preety!" Her reply was cheerful.

"Well . . ." Laughing louder this time, Beth replied, "I am not a princess yet, but maybe someday I might be." She reached out from under the furs to stroke the girl's dark head, but somehow it came across as an invitation, and two thin arms shot out and circled Beth's neck in a spontaneous hug.

"My goodness, child!" Beth exclaimed. "You are freezing! How come you are so cold, little girl?" She pulled the girl to her.

"We had no blanketth latht night."

"No blankets? Where were your blankets, dear?"

"Dey was all in heo."

"You mean I have all your blankets? Not the whole town?" She backed her face away from her chilly bedmate, who was nodding vigorously.

"Yeth, Mommy said the printheth should always get the betht of evething."

"Oh gosh," Beth muttered, pulling the cold child under the furs, and hugging her tight with both arms. With a giggle, the shivering child squirmed to snuggle into the warmth.

Beth was puzzled. *Why would the entire town be so sacrificial as to give up the warmth of their blankets and furs for me?* As an only child, Beth was never forced to share.

Generosity was not a part of her makeup and now this frail, big-eyed little girl had climbed in her window to tell her the entire town had given up something essential for her comfort. The memory of how coldly she had treated them on her arrival stung her conscience. As soon as the little interloper had stopped shivering, Beth popped her out from under the blankets and pronounced;

"OK, little one. From the angle of the sun, it looks like I have slept half the day away. We need to get up and get all these furs back to their rightful owners. Can you help me with that?"

The dark head nodded, then with the speed and agility of a field mouse, she hopped onto the table and disappeared out the window.

As Beth proceeded to dress and organize her things, there was a knock on the door. Two young women, probably close to her own age, came in, smiling shyly and bringing food and fresh water for washing. Still wondering what had happened to Aleph and why her servant guide had disappeared, Beth cleaned up and sat down to eat. Feeling more than a little embarrassed because of yesterday's behavior, she sat silently trying to think of something kind to say to the two girls. They were both standing with quiet dignity against the wall by the door.

"Will you eat some food with me?" Beth finally asked with a strained smile. They smiled back and the tallest of the two answered.

"We have already eaten, Milady, but you must go ahead. And we have seen to the care and feeding of your horse. She is a magnificent steed. Have you owned her since she was foaled?"

"Yes," Beth lied. Shame immediately swept over her for misleading the girls. She realized trying to impress them made her feel more important, a reality that unnerved Beth even further. She had gotten used to Aleph treating her like royalty, but it was heady being looked up to by those her own age.

"Also, we are to tell you our shepherd would request if you would be willing to be at the gathering this evening and share your words." The tall girl leaned forward and sounded excited as she spoke the last phrase.

"Do what?" Beth asked.

"Share . . . tonight . . . at the gathering," the girl said a little more reservedly.

"What is this gathering and what kind of word does your shepherd want me to share?"

"Our shepherd, Milady, he is our leader. And the gathering is our weekly time of sharing for growth and encouragement."

Beth put down the food she was eating and looked at the girls. Her spicy temperament was beginning to rise. "Well, I don't know who this shepherd person is or what he wants me to talk about, but I really don't think I am going to do any sharing anywhere, thank you very much."

The girls looked startled. "But Mistress . . ." A faint tone of anguish came into her voice. "We are loyal servants of the Prince. We have honored him and obeyed him. Our whole lives we have longed to hear from him. We have never had even so much as a note or a scrap of his words. And now you are here, his betrothed, his messenger."

"Look, this is ridiculous! I don't have anything to say. I have never even seen the Prince either. What kind of word am I going to bring?"

"But the book! Don't you have the book—the very words of the Prince? Does that mean nothing? People in our village have died for a few words from the Prince, and you are carrying . . ." Her voice trailed off. Then with a look of genuine pain on her young face she whispered, "You do have the book, do you not?" The two girls stared at her with anxious faces.

Beth paused to think. The book . . . I have the book, all right. How do they know I have the book? Did Aleph tell them? If he did, I am going to really reprimand him. Maybe it was Tzaddi, the old nursemaid that told them.

Annoyance frothed in her chest. She did in fact have the book. It was the power in the words of the book that had led her into this predicament. Somehow though, she had become quite protective of it. *It is mine! It was given to me. The letters were written for me. To me! Why do I have to share them with anyone?* Perhaps the girls could see the hardness cross her face. One of them took a step forward, reaching out as if to plead with her.

"Yes," Beth said through tight lips "I have the book." A look of relief lifted the two faces. "But I really don't see why I must share it with anyone else. You tell your shepherd; he can get someone else to do the sharing tonight. I must be getting on with my search anyway. Oh, and thank you for the food."

The girl that had stepped forward turned with a jerk, grabbed her friend who looked on the verge of tears, and ran out the door.

This whole experience was getting stranger and stranger for Beth. Her emotions seemed to be getting tossed around daily. Her irritation rose again to the surface. The Prince could not have any idea of the indignities she was suffering on her journey to be with him. He would not have expected this of her, Beth was sure of it. Having lost her appetite, she folded the remaining food up in a napkin and placed it into her travel bag.

She had to go find out where Aleph was and continue her journey to locate this Prince. A mental list of questions she planned to ask Aleph was forming. Not the least of which was why in the world she was on this chase across the country to find the Prince. This quest was getting way more complicated than she had originally thought it would be. As she gathered her things in preparation to go find her stable hand, a shadow fell across the floor at her feet.

The man standing there was the tall spokesman who had

greeted her the night before. Strong features and a kind expression on his face characterized him. For the briefest of moments, Beth paused. It was a face that carried within it some of the dignity and beauty she read of in her book. *No, he can't be the Prince. Kindness and compassion does shine from his face. It could almost be him, but I know better. When I meet the Prince, he will command such respect and awe, I am going to melt at his feet. When I see him, I will know immediately* A hint of disappointment leaked into her voice as she spoke.

"Are you here to get one of your blankets? I didn't ask for all these things, you know."

"No, your highness, but if I may be so bold, I have a small request. Not for myself but for the benefit of my flock."

"You must be the shepherd the girls were talking about this morning."

"True, I am the shepherd for this village. I am Hei, a whisper, a mere breath, a helper. With your gracious permission I would ask if you would grant us a great blessing."

"Oh yes, the girls said something about speaking at a meeting you are having tonight. Is that what this is about? If it is, I really don't want to do it. I have better things to do than to go around talking to people I don't know about something private and personal. This was not part of the agreement. I am on a journey to find the Prince, and he has not written anything about sharing his words."

The shepherd's gentle eyes caught hers. A soft sigh escaped his lips. She knew all of this was very important to him.

"This book you possess is too wonderful to be nourishment and sustenance for you alone. It is words from the Prince. We, his loyal subjects, have toiled for years without even so much as one syllable. My flock often grows faint for needing to hear from him. Doubting his interest in us becomes real. You are the bearer of an infinite treasure. You must come and share with those in need."

Beth felt her resolve beginning to slip at his impassioned plea. "Wait, I am not a minstrel, not a teller of tales. I don't have the gift to speak. I would be too terrified to even open my mouth!"

"None of that is of importance, your highness. If you would merely read the words aloud, and any understanding you might share. You know of his love; you have his words and been called on this great quest. You must share what is already yours. No one can take it from you . . . but you can share . . . if only a morsel." That last phrase drifted plaintively into silence.

With one last look of genuine longing, the shepherd turned and disappeared from her sight. Taking a step back and collapsing into one of the chairs, Beth shook her head. *This isn't fair,* she thought. *I am not in control over my own life anymore. Somehow, I keep getting farther and farther into situations that are beyond me. I don't know what I am going to do.*

All she could do was to pull the book from her cloak and begin looking for a passage that might apply to these kind, generous, and hungry people. As she read, the words, as always, seemed to burn from the page. But it was clear now, almost all of what she read could be shared—words of hope for the hopeless; words of encouragement for the downtrodden; words of cheer for the sorrowful; words of instruction for the ignorant. It shamed her for being selfish. Her lie also added to the remorse.

Her meditations were interrupted by a flock of chattering children, led by her early morning friend. They barged in the still-open door and at the direction of their diminutive leader began rummaging through the pile of skins and furs on the floor. Within a few minutes the huge pile was gone, as each child gleefully ran out the door with an armful. Only her little friend remained.

"Ith time for the meeting, do you wan me to tho you where it ith?"

With a long heavy sigh, Beth closed the book, rose to her feet slowly and, taking the tiny hand, followed her out into the late afternoon sun.

The moon had fully risen by the time Beth wearily closed the door behind her. She lit a lamp on the table, glancing at the dusty spot on the floor where her luxurious bed had once been. A small, thin blanket remained folded in the dust. How could she describe what she had just experienced? Beyond the village, in a covered area the crowd of cheerful, eager villagers had gathered, waiting for her. They were singing as she approached and joining them she found herself lifted by the simple melodies. Words she had never sung came easily to her lips. Words describing the coronation of the Prince and the coming of his glorious kingdom were a sweet fragrance to the ear. The shepherd then stood at the front and spoke briefly about the joys they had being servants of the Prince and with longing, mentioned the hope of his return.

Ending his comments, he emphasized, "In this life, only two things are eternal, those souls you see around you, and the everlasting words of the Prince." Then reaching out, palm up, he nodded toward Beth and stepped aside. All eyes of those gathered fixed themselves upon her. There was a collective intake of breath as if in anticipation. A flush bloomed on her face. The strong urge to run grasped at her but she found herself taking courage from the words and walked slowly to the side of the waiting shepherd.

What happened next was hard to describe. As she opened the book, every person in the room stood. An expectant hush swept across the entire company. For a long time she read, and the good words dripped from her mouth like honey. How the people responded she could not explain. Many wept openly. Even young men stood enraptured, with tears streaming down their faces. Some came forward and kneeled at the front as if in devotion to a Prince they had never seen. All stood silently with an overpowering sense of awe for as long as she continued to speak.

It was all a great mystery and wonder for Beth. When she could read no more, a quiet hymn of praise was hummed with upturned faces and then in total silence, one by one they all slipped into the night.

Back in her room, with no sign of Gimmel and his men, her first thought was penitence for her callous treatment and dishonesty toward these gentle and kind people. In her letters the Prince had written openly of curbing his tongue when speaking to lessers, of going to those he had insulted with words of apology, admitting his failures. This man opened his heart in a way so vulnerable she had never seen or heard of before.

Tears filled her eyes, spilling on to the table at the convicting thoughts. From the very words she had shared, the calling to encourage others was connected to the calling to go be with her Prince. Those same words assured her that own selfish behavior was forgiven and moved her into the freedom of a forgotten past. In that freedom she pulled out the golden quill and turned to a blank page in the book.

I have to sleep in the dust tonight;
but your letters encouraged me the way you said they would.
I shared my plans with you, and you answered me;
Please keep teaching me Your wisdom.
Help me understand the meaning of your insights;

I am thinking very deeply about your
wonderful sayings.
I wept with grief; but your words encouraged me.
Keep me from lying and give me the privilege of
knowing your truth.
I want to be honest; I am determined to live by
your teachings.
I want to cling to your instructions, my Prince,
don't let me be put to shame!
If you will help me, I will run to follow your guidance,
for you have set my heart free.

Just then the door opened, and a tiny figure appeared carrying a large woolly blanket. With a silent breath of thanks to the Prince for his people, Beth snuffed out the lamp, snuggled under the fleecy warmth with her little friend in her arms, and went immediately to sleep.

Chapter Five

Hei

GIMMEL FILLED THE doorway. "It is still early, Milady but we must go. He has decreed it." Never would Beth get used to his rumbling voice.

Startled by his early and sudden intrusion into her sleep, Beth sat upright and snapped, "What is the hurry Gimmel? And why are you waking me instead of Aleph?" She groaned, flopped back under the single blanket, and felt the hard ground beneath her.

"I gently remind your exalted royal highness, the enemies of the Prince are also after your soul. Belial's henchmen are pressing hard on our heels. We must go before daylight, lest we are caught unprepared."

Beth could not ignore the deep intensity and solemn warning of the giant warrior, and his words, as always, seemed to vibrate in her bones. "Well, all right, Gimmel, I will get up, but can you tell me where Aleph, my runaway squire, is? I will need help with my horse."

"He has not run away, your highness. His thoughts and his presence, though not seen, are always with you. If it is urgent, you can always call out to him. But your steed is ready and waiting. Fear not, Aleph will meet us farther along the road."

"I thought he was supposed to be taking care of all my needs. Some servant he has been. I am going to tell Tzaddi what a worthless slacker he has become."

Gimmel turned his head slightly and lowered his eyes to the ground. She could tell a broad smile creased his face, squinting his eyes. "I am aware, your highness, your needs and wants are many." His quiet rumble was followed by a chuckle. Beth could not help laughing at this gentle rebuke.

Grabbing her sandal and tossing it in his direction, she said, "Oh, go on Gimmel! I'll be out shortly." Then either ducking to avoid her flying shoe or stooping to avoid hitting his massive head on the lintel, he stepped back and shut the door.

Climbing to her feet, Beth covered the small form still snuggled in the blanket and made preparations to leave. Within a few moments she was ready and bending over the sleeping girl she gave her a kiss on the tousled forehead.

Stepping into the cool silver moon light of pre-morning was instant refreshment. The two young girls she spoke to the night before were standing in quiet humility to hand her some food and water for the journey. At a distance, looking like a massive black statue, stood her magnificent horse. No movement did she notice except plumes of misty breath coming from the mare's nostrils. Fully saddled and bridled in the magnificent tack from the castle stables, it was still a thrill to see and be seen on this powerful horse. She sensed envy in the two girls at her back. With a jaunty toss of her head, she strode over to the giant horse and turned to Gimmel for a hand up. As she reached for the reigns with one hand, the pommel with the other, one of the young girls touched her shoulder.

"Your majesty." She spoke with a mix of reverence and awe combined. "I—we merely wanted to thank you for—for sharing the words of the Prince with us." Dropping the hand holding the reins, Beth sighed and then with kindness reached out to the girls, so close to her own age, and gave them both an appreciative hug.

"Oh, this has been much better for me than you." Then chiding Gimmel with a smile, she said, "Come on, big oaf, we don't have all day." Although Aleph seemed to lift her with the same ease Gimmel did, she knew the stable hand would be no match for the massive warrior with the rumbling voice and cheerful manner.

"We go now, your highness. Have all your many needs been met?" His droll bass notes brought Beth a chuckle, and they set off into the dim light. Other warriors seemed to materialize out of various houses and by the time they had reached the edge of the small town, the entire force was striding alongside. Parting the cortège like a boulder in a stream was a small group of townspeople holding torches for light, led by Hei the shepherd. As they passed around them, radiance on their upturned faces reminded Beth of the spirit of deep joy she had kindled by reading the words of the Prince. The mare paused mid stride.

"With sincere gratitude," Hei said humbly, stepping forward, "we would like to express our appreciation to your highness for sharing with us the words of the book. We bestow this small gift."

He stretched out both hands, lifting a velvety purple leaf. At its center lay a pool of shimmering moonlight. "It is *Yohd.* We present it to you as a remembrance of the spirit you have within. Through the spirit you will be given truth, knowledge, wisdom, and joy." A silver necklace with a curiously carved charm reflected the torches and moonlight. Lifting it from the leaf, the pendant glowing fire and ice, appeared to be two delicately crafted hands raised in praise. As Beth lifted the ornament by its finely wrought chain, it turned, and she noticed the two hands transformed in a miraculous way to form a graceful dove flying upward and then became a strange shape in which she could find no meaning. The beauty of the pendant and the graceful gesture, combined to tighten her throat briefly in appreciation.

Glancing over the crowd, her eyes caught the look of silent adoration of the two young girls. Between them, holding each hand was her tiny midnight companion, wearing a smile that seemed to add light to the darkness. The little girl blew a spontaneous two-handed kiss. Beth mouthed a silent *thank you* and blew a kiss back to her little friend. Then at Gimmel's urging the regiment moved forward into the forest.

With great care Beth separated the silver chain, found the clasp and attached it around her neck. A gentle tug assured it was fastened well and she tucked it beneath her cloak. Cool silver almost instantly became warm.

‡ ‡ ‡

AFTER MANY HOURS Beth noticed the earth under the feet of the warriors and the hoofs of her mount began to become wet and marshy. Slowing to a much more sedate pace, the men fell back behind her in single file and Gimmel, with a few others ahead, scrutinized their path carefully. Pools of brown water with floating carpets of sepia colored scum were visible intermittently through the trees. The air also changed. Damp, fetid smells drifted through the branches.

"Gimmel," Beth called to the warrior leading her horse, "are we going into a swamp, and where is the boy, Aleph"?

Without turning his eyes from his now careful steps, he responded. "This, Milady, is the Gypsy Marsh; its crossing and waters are treacherous. Few that I know of have crossed alive on foot. The marsh has been known to suck down both man, woman, and beast."

"Well, how, then, are we going to make it across?" Beth was alarmed.

With the same deep rumble he answered, "Aleph has gone ahead marking the trail. We follow the path he has set forth and will be safe."

Not at all satisfied, Beth remarked in a tight voice, "What does he know about marshes, and how can we trust him anyway?"

"He has written with his finger in the sand, Milady. He knows the way. We trust his guidance, that is more than enough." Gimmel spoke casually.

The slow trek through the marsh continued. Fetid water spread over all the ground and lonely hummocks appeared from beneath the brown, evil-smelling water. Moss hung in long ropes from pale, bony trees. Each step of her mount now made sucking sounds as it was lifted pulled from the quivering ground. Clinging to her saddle, Beth became interested in the markings drawn by Aleph's finger. They were the signs directing them to safe passage. Sometimes at the base of a tree or stump, sometimes in the sand at the side of the trail, a shape or rune, leaving directions for the next few paces.

Apprenticed to her father, Beth already an accomplished scribe, knew the importance of symbols, letters, and the messages they conveyed. Trying to remember if the shapes taught by her father were the same as those scribed by Aleph, she tried to understand what they meant. Gimmel made it clear following every detail of the instructions was critical, but the meanings eluded her. After a time, her mind tired of trying to interpret the shapes, her thoughts wandered.

Suddenly a hoof slipped! In an instant her charger's hindquarters slid from the path and the mare was up to her haunches, flailing with her front hooves for traction on the slippery ground. Swampy water sucked her down and frothed thickly around at her frantic efforts! Wetness clutched at Beth's ankles, and the lurching horse almost threw her from the saddle in her efforts to regain her footing. A scream broke from Beth's lips. Gimmel turned to see the mare sliding toward deep water and Beth's terrified face pleading for help. He leapt to the water's edge. Braced as well as he could on the quaking path, Gimmel grabbed the chest strap of the terrified beast and with a mighty heave, combined with the mare's effort, restored all four muddy hooves onto safer ground. For long moments the panting horse labored to catch her breath. Her mud-streaked legs and rump testified to the close call and danger on either side.

"Oh, thank you, Gimmel, I think you saved both our lives!" Beth exclaimed.

With nonchalance, Gimmel casually wiped his hands on his leggings. "It is my pleasure to meet all your needs, your highness."

His gentle mockery not lost on her, she replied. "Well, I don't think my missing squire would have been able to rescue me, as you did."

"Perhaps not, but he undoubtedly would have guided more carefully." There it was again, thought Beth. That deference . . . no, respect. All these soldiers showed it for her stable boy. *I am sure that he is more than just a servant. He must be an advisor or counselor to the Prince,* she thought.

After what seemed days of treading the quivering path, solid ground formed into a clay walkway between two canals. A dingy sky began to recede with the swamp stench and a warm sun peeked out of the clouds. Breathing a long sigh of relief, Beth looked ahead toward the open water canals. Clustered alongside the narrow dike were strange-looking watercraft: low, narrow skiffs made of bent planks that skimmed across the water with the ease of fish.

Soon a crowd of boats appeared, paddled by cheerful gypsies, shouting and holding up crafts and fabrics. As they approached, the laughing boat people all began offering wares for sale to the warrior band.

The soldiers took no notice of the noisy throng and made no eye contact whatsoever. But Beth watched one young recruit glance at a lovely trinket. In an instant he was surrounded by shouting merchants thrusting baubles under his nose. As she examined the various items held high, the beauty of rainbow fabrics and splendid apparel began to spark her interest. Hair combs and jewelry of filigreed gold, colored powders and face paints, gowns and cloaks woven and embroidered with bright needlepoint flashed lively colors before her eyes.

The travel gown and cloak she wore were hand-made and humble to begin with, but as she looked at them, brown and mud-stained, they looked drab and ragged. In a rush she was embarrassed. For some reason, thoughts of being seen by the Prince in her sad condition brought dread to her heart. After all this effort, charging around the country sneaking, hiding while reading these promises of royalty, it would be a disgrace to appear in this wretched condition before her love. Aleph was gone. She had still not seen or received any new message from the Prince and it looked as if she was going to have to take care of herself. *All these soldiers are quite willing to lead me around the wilderness and treat me like royalty, but I sure don't have anything royal show to for it*, she thought.

Reigning the horse to one side brought a whole school of watercraft flocking. One bold merchant, probably noticing her travel-worn appearance, held up a new cloak that shone in the sunlight. Twining delicate embroidery traced the collar and sleeves. As always for those from families of limited economic means, the question of how much it cost was primary. The few copper coins in her travel bag would probably not even pay for the buttons on the lovely cloak. The merchant lifted it higher and asked for an offer.

Smiling weakly at the gypsy merchant she mumbled, "I am sorry, I am certain the price is too dear."

With a big grin, sensing the beginnings of a dickering session, he popped back, "Oh miss, I can give you a special price. What would you be willing to offer to make this lovely garment your very own? You would look most beautiful wearing it."

"No, you don't understand," she answered glumly. "All I have is this." She held out her hand with six small coppers in it.

Looking into her open palm with skeptical eyes, the merchant frowned and shook his head firmly. "This is fine fabric and workmanship. I cannot just give it away."

Leaning down to run her fingers lightly across the shimmering cloak, the silver pendant given to her that morning spilled out, dangling down at eye level. The merchant's eyes widened and focused on the polished pendant. His face lit up as if reflecting its brightness.

"Ah ha, perhaps a trade? You could give that bauble as an exchange. I might even throw in a ring or two. And some other gift."

The thought startled her. To get the cloak and have something left over for perhaps some jewelry would be grand! She could even purchase a gift for her father. An impulsive rush caused her to reach for the clasp at the back of her neck. The moment her fingers touched the clasp, the pendant became hot, almost burning her skin.

The noisy crowd around her stilled suddenly. Turning toward an oncoming figure, many who were standing on the causeway began parting to allow passage to a very determined and purposeful young man. He directed his strides straight toward Beth. She released the clasp and felt the charm cool as it fell to her neck. It was Aleph! Aleph her missing squire, the stable hand, approached wearing a stern look on his face. The gypsy merchant lowered his head, doffing his hat. The rest backed away as if in fear or reverence.

Stepping between the gypsy and Beth's mount, he spoke. "Milady, there is no time for purchases, we must not be distracted from the journey. Also, your pendant was given to you for a great purpose. To relinquish it would be trading your birthright for a cup of soup."

"Wait just a minute," Beth said. "You wander off who knows where for days and then pop back into my life as if you owned me and start telling me what I can and can't do? I think you are getting above your station!"

Aleph's face turned up to look into her eyes. His voice softened. With the tenderness of one explaining to a beloved, he gently remarked, "My apologies, your highness. What you do not know is that your life is truly in danger. The enemy is at our very heels. If you truly seek the Prince and his kingdom, he will see that all these worthless things and much more will be yours."

Beth, still slightly flushed by his interruption, noticed the intensity of his look, which stayed briefly then transformed into sincere compassion. The warmth lingered just a bit longer than seemed appropriate. Turning briskly away, he took her horse's halter in his hand and hurried to follow the soldiers some distance ahead.

He this, He that! It just seems this Prince has taken over my whole life! I can't even buy anything without knowing if he approves! Does he own me?

"And you! You, Aleph, are so, so—infuriating!"

Neither turning back nor slowing his pace, Aleph joined the others and set off down the path leading away from the floating market.

Fuming inside, Beth yanked at her ragged cloak as if to rip it. Her thoughts ranged from wanting to jerk the bridle into her own hands and charge back to the vendors, to bitter resignation at her lot. Glancing over her shoulder she thought how lovely she would have looked in the shimmering cloak and bright jewels.

She stared at the back of Aleph's head, folding her arms. As her arms crossed, she felt the nudge of the book in her cloak pocket. Almost for spite she pulled it out and rather than just stare at Aleph's purposeful stride, she found where she had left reading. In her mood, at first she read with little interest and comprehension, but slowly meaning surfaced into the words and seeped into her thoughts. How could one whom I have never seen love me so much, and be so interested in my welfare? Truly, if it were not for the love he has written of, this journey would be over in an instant, and I would demand that this insolent stable hand take me directly home.

Describing humility learned by suffering the insults of his

military commanders, the Prince wrote about how he wanted to be as good a soldier he could be, *for her*. His desire was to have no shame when he met her face-to-face. Nobility, honor, and courage were listed as traits he was striving for in preparation to be a good husband. Yet included was the story of tending to the wounds of fallen enemy soldiers, which impressed her even more.

Again, as before, the words worked a very curious alchemy, easing the tight muscles in her neck and shoulders, relaxing the rigid look on her face. She brought up the image that had captured her imagination back at the gypsy venders—of her returning home in triumph. So the Prince had promised. Wearing the shimmering scarlet cloak of royalty with the Prince at her side, she visualized cheering throngs welcoming them back. What immediately took over that image was the dread of returning home with nothing. Nothing but shame. What would her father and friends and people from her village think of her great folly? To be ridiculed by those who would only know her as a silly girl who ran off on a pointless venture, chasing some imaginary Prince. That would be the greatest humiliation of all.

Darkness had fallen. The soldiers and Aleph were again talking in muffled voices as they prepared camp for the night on what seemed a small shrinking island in the middle of a vast swamp. Aleph first saw to her needs, providing bedding and food. He then set an interesting bronze and silver lamp with neither wick nor candle on a high stump beside her. In the flickering light, she withdrew her book of letters and laid it open on her lap. Thinking back on the day, she wondered how Aleph could be so much more patient with her than any of her teachers or even her parents had been.

"Aleph, you said today that the Prince could give me all those things that I long for. He does write about providing for me in his letters, but . . . do you know that to be true?"

Pausing in his preparations, Aleph looked at her in the light of the flickering lamp. "The Prince, Milady, will someday be king of the entire realm. Everything will be given into his hand. As he has written, everything he has will be yours. It is more than you could ever ask for. More even than you can imagine." He paused, eyes shining from the lamp. "For that reason, you must forsake all distractions in your journey to be with him. As his bride it will all become yours."

The words Aleph was speaking sounded as if he had read the letters.

"What service did you perform for the Prince? Your words reveal that you are more than just a feeder and caretaker for horses. Is that something you don't want me to know?"

Aleph lowered his head in humility. "As a child my father arranged my work in the castle. Whatever he wanted me to do, I obeyed. When I became of age my path was set. I served in whatever was placed before me." Some warmth entered his words as he looked up at Beth and continued. "It did please me when the privilege of serving you and guiding you on this journey was revealed to be my lot."

He never answers my questions, Beth thought. But there was no denying that Aleph was willing and pleased to care for her. As he slipped off into the darkness it occurred to her that having a young man treat her with kindness and respect was new. It was so different than what she had experienced at home. She liked it. And when he spoke, the dove hanging over her heart warmed, reminding her of the burn she'd felt early that day.

By the light of the flickering lamp, she pulled the silver charm from under her cloak. It was as beautiful and mysterious as before. The memory of the merchant's offer came back to her. Particularly the wonder that had appeared instantly in his eyes. Surely it must have a value she knew nothing of. As it swung, the shadow fell on her open book. It began to take the shape of a rune, a mystical letter. Then it changed to another and another, as if the charm hanging from its delicate chain contained hidden messages. Not able to understand it, Beth lowered it to her throat, smoothed the book open, and was transported by the words that almost every time she read brought a lump to her throat and tears to her eyes.

The lamp began to dim as she meditated deeply about what she could say to her Prince. *I wonder if he will ever read these words,* she thought. *Can I write anything that will make him feel as his words make me feel?* Withdrawing the quill, she brought it to her lips in thought, then yanked it away, appalled that she had started to chew on the end like she had her father's brushes. Concentrating, hoping to write something worthy, she forced her thoughts to the blank page.

Teach me, my Prince, to follow your decrees;
then I will keep them until we are together.
Help me understand, and I will keep your words
and obey them with all my heart.
Show me the safe pathway, I am amazed when you do.
Draw my heart toward you and what you
have written,
not toward selfishness.
Help me turn my eyes away from trinkets
and worthless bangles.
Your words tell me that you will provide me with all
those things.
Please, fulfill your promise to me,
so everyone who sees me will be amazed.
Thank you for taking away the disgrace that weighs
me down,
I know your words are good.
Each day I am hungry for more of them!
I know you will protect my life because you are kind.

Chapter Six

Vau

IN THE PREDAWN darkness, the warriors again stirred early, and the noise of their preparations wakened Beth. She was not rested. The ground under her had oozed cold moisture that soaked into her bones during the night. Another cold meal was passed to her as she rode into the black. Aleph was a shadowy figure in the lead, with his little donkey and the warriors strung out behind. Splashing from her horse's hooves confirmed they were still in the swamp. Wet floral trellises dragged across her face continually, forcing Beth to bend low in the saddle to avoid being torn from her mount.

As the sun began to rise, heat stifled each breath and the stench of rotting vegetation rose from the wet ground. Fleshy orchidlike flowers with fantastic plum-colored blossoms clung to the trees, exuding cloying fragrances that made her cough. Strange gossamer-winged insects began buzzing around her face, leaving painful welts where they landed. Perspiration dribbled down, staining her bodice, stinging her eyes, and wilting her hair into lank strands. The saddle chafed. Hunger pangs clenched her insides. *This is as miserable as I have ever been*, she thought.

Beth knew better than to call out. She had begun to realize the gentle admonitions from her guide were intended for her safety. Even so, she was not going to allow him the satisfaction of having to silence her again. As miserable as she was, whining was not the solution. The words of the Prince admonished her to be strong, courageous, and gentle. She could do that for Him.

As soon as that thought fortified her will, the hot, muddy caravan came to a halt. Blinking sweat from her eyes, she could see paving stones through the jungle vegetation. Aleph slipped past her for a brief consultation with Gimmel and his men. Then without speaking, the stable boy led her up a slope, out of the jungle gloom, onto a wide, smooth road. Beth looked back in time to see Gimmel give a wink, a cheerful wave, and the last few soldiers drifting back into the swamp.

She, Aleph, and their steeds were alone. A cool breeze whispered the leaves of mottled sycamores arching over the stone highway. Just as she was getting ready to ask where they were, with the breeze came the distant sound of trumpets, drums, and heavy metal wagon wheels rolling on stone. Someone was coming! A band, an entourage, a parade was headed their way. Far off in the distance, colorful pink banners and pennants waved.

Beth looked at Aleph. "Who is coming? Is it friend or enemy?" Looking back at the swamp, she shivered, not wanting to delve back into the fetid, insect-ridden marsh. "Why have our soldier friends abandoned us? Are we left alone?" A touch of panic edged into her voice.

With a heaviness Beth had not heard before, Aleph spoke. "It is one of the many rulers of Vau approaching, Milady. Vau is the valley of the presumptuous. Many insignificant fiefdoms, each with its own ruler, fill this valley. They all claim to be a king. At times they speak of loyalty to the Prince, and at times of dissent. Like a flock of crows they fly complaining loudly of woe. This road leads to the palace they quarrel and fight over."

Turning and making direct eye contact, Aleph spoke with greater weight. "Milady, it is imperative that I keep you safe. We must continue the narrow path." He pointed to the trail leading down into the jungle on the other side of the broad, paved stones. "We must continue until we cross to the other side of this valley."

Beth stared at Aleph and felt in his words not rebuke, but tender concern. Had this journey become more than just a job for Aleph? He did not look away. His eyes betrayed a tenderness she had not noticed before broaching some unwritten code between a stable hand and his charge. It unsettled her. The sounds of the distant band grew louder interrupting any awkward feelings that might have surfaced.

Suddenly weary of being dirty, tired, and hungry, she spoke plaintively. "But Aleph, this road leads to a palace. Surely there is food, and water to bathe and a place to rest, isn't there?" Reaching forward she grabbed the reigns in both hands.

"I am done slinking and hiding. I am not sleeping on the cold ground and eating cold gruel anymore. If I am to be a princess, as you say I am, then it is time to let people know how I expect to be treated. Let go of my horse and let me go claim what is mine."

Pain crossed Aleph's face, mingled with deep concern for her safety. He opened his mouth to speak, but Beth had already pulled the horse's head toward the oncoming throng. As the procession approached, self-consciousness swept over her. She pulled a small, metal mirror from her bag and looked at the reflection. She was shocked. The vines had left dark trails across her face, her hair hung in limp strings and red welts from the insect bites gave her the look of one with a dreaded disease. A high-pitched wail escaped her lips.

"Look! Look at me! This is horrible! How can I even let a king see me, much less the Prince! Aleph, I am mortified! Quick, give me a cloth and some water!"

"It is not the outward appearance that judges one's worth." Aleph smiled, shaking his head. "It is the condition of the heart." There was no rebuke in his tone.

"What do you know about royalty! I have letters from the

Prince! I am to marry him and be the princess! I cannot appear like this! Now, get me a cloth and some water." The moment the words fled her lips, she regretted it. She'd cast aside the admonition to be kind and gentle. Left in its place was the frantic, self-centered feeling that she looked horrible and wanted to crawl under a rock. Aleph handed her a small kerchief pulled from his pocket and the leather water bottle he carried on his hip. Snatching them from his hand, Beth began desperately to clean herself up.

It wasn't working. The black marks smudged, and the red welts became even more pronounced. In a few moments the entourage of men on horses, ladies riding in carriages, and armed soldiers on foot came abreast of the young woman. Aleph pulled the animals to the edge of the paved road. All who passed looked with disdain, even mockery, at the muddy pair, their bedraggled horse and donkey.

Giant carriages rumbled by filled with courtiers dressed in colorful silk finery. Each group giggled, pointing at the disheveled girl and her servant, then rolled their eyes at each other. Beth flushed with shame and turned her back to the traveling cortège. Then the most majestic carriage, harnessed to eight colossal draft horses, pulled beside them and, with a word from the main passenger, stopped.

"Who is this?" The voice was a high whinny, and it intrigued Beth enough to glance over her shoulder. It came from a scrawny, pale, foppish young man swaddled in ruby-colored silk and lace reclining haughtily in the pillowed carriage balancing a jeweled crown on his powdered, bewigged head. He tittered. "Or perhaps I should say, what is this?" Silence hung as Beth steadfastly kept her back to him. "Speak, creature. I am the king you know, and I shall order my soldiers to drag it from of you."

Half turning, Beth murmured, "My name is Beth, and I am on a quest. I am searching for—" In a flash she knew what was about to come out of her mouth and clamped it shut.

"A quest? What are you questing for?" the dandy asked. "In your condition you should be questing for a hot bath and a bar of soap." The gaggle of his entourage, who had been hanging on each word, laughed. He also laughed at his cleverness. "Well," he turned to one of his servants, "bring this pathetic creature to the palace, make her presentable, and she can entertain us at tomorrow's banquet with stories of her quest for clean clothes." Hilarious cackles roared from the sycophantic crowd.

He waved to the driver and the entire procession moved on, each carriage full of mocking courtesans passing by.

The king's servant stepped toward Beth and the heavily armed guard behind him prevented her from resisting. Even Aleph with peaked hat pulled low on his face, head bowed humbly, followed the lead of the servants and soldiers from Vau. Stepping back onto the broad road behind the procession, a dirty, embarrassed woman on a tired and muddy horse followed by an even more dejected-looking servant and a pathetic donkey trailed in the wake of the jovial procession. Nobody in the laughing throng bothered to look back. Ashamed at her appearance and confused about Aleph, Beth again briefly considered calling off the quest, but the phalanx of grim soldiers escorting them eliminated that option.

Hard flagstones under shod hooves and metal wheels amplified the noisy caravan ahead, but in the quiet of her mind, a cheerful thought appeared. Beth had heard the king mention soap, a hot bath, and food. Perhaps there was some good in this humbling situation after all.

For a few hours they traveled as straight as a sword-cut through the jungle. Darkness began to seep in from the trees on either side. Finally, the road pointed out of the greenery, toward the towers of a modest palace set in the center of an empty plain. Although its size was dwarfed by the castle of her Prince, Beth saw the walls were hung with bright banners, and flags waved in the sunset from each turret.

Light spilled from every window, and it seemed cheerful enough after the gloom of the swamp behind. Great cheers went up from crowds gathered at the entrance and the brightness from many torches glowed in the darkening sky.

This might not be so bad, thought Beth. The procession entered a pair of large iron-studded gates and circled the inner courtyard. Stepping down from his carriage, the king of Vau was surrounded by fawning citizens, who flocked into the wide portico as Beth was led into the courtyard.

"Aha," cried the king, "bring the wench to me!"

With legs shaky from having ridden since early dawn, Beth slid to the ground, stumbling into the circle of snorting and hooting onlookers.

"Well, here she is. The muddy lady on a quest. It appears she has been rolling with swine. Tell us what is it you are seeking, other than a bath and some clean clothes? Perhaps you can find what you are looking for by working in the castle laundry." The king looked around, laughed at his cleverness, and his courtiers laughed because they knew it was expected.

"Don't keep us waiting. Speak, wench!"

With shame flaming her cheeks, Beth mumbled; "I am a princess, and I am looking for my Prince."

"Haaa ha ha, how sweet. Ho ho ho," chortled the king. "A princess, no less, and looking for her prince. Aaaaah ha ha ha."

"Well, no," Beth said, "I am going to be a princess when I find him."

The king of Vau laughed even harder, and the crowd laughed with him. "You a princess? Haaarrrharhar. Your stable boy has a better chance of being a prince than you a princess. Maybe you already found your prince and you don't know it. Hooo haaa ha ha." And the crowd roared with mocking laughter.

Then a sinister gleam came into the king's eyes. He bowed to Beth. "Your highness, you must enjoy all the privileges of being the swine princess." Turning to the servant whom she and Aleph had followed, the king spoke again with a voice full of contempt, "The wench wants to be a princess. So be it! We will crown her the swine princess. Take her to the chambers of princess Teith," and the crowd cheered and applauded with glee. All removed their plumed hats, bowing with mock respect and shouting. "Hail to the swine princess, hail to the swine princess!"

Taken roughly by the arm, Beth was led stumbling across the courtyard. Twice she tripped and fell, but the rough hand dragged her to her feet. She was eventually brought to a wing of the palace that had missed out on the decorations. Even the windows were dark. One lone candle thrust into her hands shed little light as a massive oak door was pulled open. She was pushed inside, and the door slammed shut.

Beth clutched at her cloak with her free hand, fearful she had lost her book. It was still there. Pulling it free she balanced the candleholder on it as she pushed bedraggled strands of hair from her eyes. A long hallway stretched out before her. Ornate furniture, sculptures, and life-sized portraits lined the hall. Beth walked closer to one of the paintings. A coat of dust and cobwebs draped everything with neglect. Holding her candle up to better see the painting of a young girl with dark eyes, the word *haughty* came to mind.

The swishing of long skirts alerted the approach of a spectral figure dressed completely in black. Tall, stiff as a coatrack, with a long beaked nose, she stopped in front of

Beth. Beady eyes peered down through round spectacles from a drawn angular face. Perhaps at some time in the distant past, the face had been lovely, but some inner loss had pulled it long and grim.

"What has the phony king of Vau sent our way now?" Nasal and whispery, the voice seemed dry as the dust that coated everything in the hall. "Oh my, how disgusting."

Beth was reminded of how filthy and ratty she must look.

"Who are you and what brings you here?" the voice asked.

"I am Beth, and I . . ." The laughter of the king and the courtiers fresh in her ears caused her to stop. "I am traveling on a quest, or I was."

"Hmph, Beth on a quest." Speaking without a trace of emotion, the woman continued. "Quest or no quest, the king has given orders to keep you until he sends for you."

"Well," said Beth a little defiantly, "if I am going to speak to the king, I demand my bag, my stable boy, and some hot water."

One pencil-thin eyebrow arched a little higher. "You, girl, are in no position to demand anything." Then turning her back, the woman began to walk down the hallway as the papery voice drifted from the darkness. "Follow me."

Without a sound, the gaunt figure drifted along past massive doorways, closed rooms, sculptures on marble columns, and items of silver and gold. Few windows filtered light into the maze of hallways. Not knowing what else to do,

Beth followed the swishing black skirts of the tall woman with the birdlike nose, black eyes, and black hair pulled severely into a bun at the nape of her neck.

Up three flights of steps, down many hallways and through more doorways than she could count, Beth followed. The one lone candle she carried was the only light available. She knew finding her way out would be almost impossible.

When more light shone from an occasional chandelier or table lamp, Beth noticed the walls were lined with gilded framed portraits and icons. What became very strange was all the paintings were of the same girl or woman as she aged. Beth's curiosity began to overcome her anxiety, just a little.

Finally, they reached a door just like the dozens they had passed and gone through. Reaching into the pocket of her skirt, the woman pulled forth a weighty ring of keys and began to sort through them.

Beth's curiosity forced her to speak. "What is this place?"

Without turning, the woman answered with bitter resignation. "This is the palace built for a princess."

"What princess?" Beth asked with surprise.

The woman found the key she was looking for, inserted it into the lock, and with an angry creak, twisted the key to open the door. She turned. Dark eyes glistened in her pinched face. Her response was tight in her throat. "The princess who was too proud."

Then flippantly, she continued. "She was named Teith because she thought too highly of herself to follow the

Prince." With that strange answer she reached out, grabbed the book Beth still held in her left hand. "Give me that," she hissed, "you will not be needing it anymore."

But as the bony white hand clasped the jeweled book, anger swept through Beth. With strength she had never known, she clamped down and yanked the book away from the frail hand.

"No! Don't even touch this!" She backed away toward the open door.

"Have your way, then," the whispery voice said with some sorrow. The woman pushed Beth and her sputtering candle through the doorway into the room, and slammed the door shut, which amplified the squeal of the old key. Beth was locked inside.

There was nothing in the room. Not a stick of furniture. Not a lamp. Not a window. Not even a rug on the floor. Beth's heart was pounding, breath coming in short gasps, and anger welled up in her throat. Slowly reality replaced the anger with fear, then despair. Hunger began to chew at her stomach. The pungent odor of dust and mold assailed her nostrils. Hot tears began to run down her face. She slumped to the hard, wooden floor with her back against the locked door. Setting the small stump of candle beside her on the floor, she began to forage through her pockets for a nibble of leftover food or drink. She had nothing.

Nothing but the book! *Ahrghh*, the book! Lifting it up in the clenched fist holding it, she threw it across the room with all her remaining strength. The pages fluttered. It hit the far wall with a thump and dropped to the floor. A sparkle dimly reflected the candle flame as the quill rolled across the dusty floor. Pressed leaves carefully stored in the back scattered across the floor. For a long time, all Beth could hear was sobs coming from her own lips. *It was all a lie,* she thought. *There is no Prince. The letters are fake. I was deceived by that old Tzaddi woman. If I survive this place, I am going straight home even if I have to live with my father. I might even have to settle for Aleph as a husband.*

For a long time, she sat there bemoaning her fate. When her eyes, puffy from crying, opened, they noticed that miraculously the small stump of a candle was low but still burning. Across the room, in a scatter of leaves with crumpled pages, lay the letters. Near it the golden quill. With a deep sigh she rolled to her knees and crawled across the dusty floor to the bruised book. Lifting it with sorrow as if she was being watched, she smoothed the wrinkled pages, wiped the quill on her cloak, collected the leaves and scrabbled back to the candle by the door.

I am just too exhausted to read anything, she thought. Then turning to one of the dog-eared pages, one word at a time, the words began to flow off the page. They were words written from an honest and sincere heart. The love woven into those words could not be a deception. *I don't know how,* she thought, *but in a way I don't understand, they have to be true.* Barely able to see in the dim light, she lifted the quill with a feeble hand and began to write.

O my Prince, I need to see your unfailing love,
I desperately need you to rescue me as you promised.
I wanted to yell at those who taunted me,
because I believe your word.
No one, no one will ever snatch your word
away from me, your words are my only hope.
I will try to keep on obeying your instructions always.
I believe that soon I will be set free,
because I have been devoted to your instructions.
Tomorrow I will speak to the king about your laws,
and I will not be ashamed.
Your admonitions are a delight!
I am growing in my love of them!
I honor and love your words.
I think about them all the time.

At the very moment her fingers formed the last word, the candle flickered and went out.

Chapter Seven

Zayin

WITHOUT ANY WAY to judge time, Beth had no idea how long she slept. Her bed (the wooden floor), her pillow (the book), was not a comfortable sleeping arrangement, but she had slept deep and long. What woke her was the sound of a key in the lock. Groaning open, the ancient door revealed the white, pinched face of her hostess. Wan candlelight spilled through the door from sconces in the hall.

"Come child, Lord Vau has summoned."

That was all she uttered. Said almost without moving her lips, much like the ventriloquists that make marionettes speak. She reminded Beth of those puppets she had seen in a traveling show at the foot of the castle wall. Her guide turned and left, gliding down the hall as if pulled by strings.

Beth struggled to her feet feeling bone stiff. She slipped the book into the pocket of her cloak and hurried to catch up to the dark figure. Filled with questions about this strange silent woman who seemed so distant, her mind tangled around her, the relic-filled palace she lived in, and hundreds of portraits of the same woman. But aches, hunger, thirst, dirty clothes were more pressing. She also needed to know what she was facing next.

"What has the king called for? Am I to see him like this? What does he expect of me? How should I act?" Running all the questions together, Beth felt like she was babbling as fast as she was hurrying to keep up.

"Only this I can tell you," came the woman's voice from pinched lips, "you have an audience with the king and he will do as he pleases."

The portraits and sculptures drifted past; all of them beautiful reproductions of a woman full of life. Under some were small brass plaques affixed to the ornate frames with the one word: *Teith.*

Back down the long, dark hallways, down the flights of steps to the entryway till they reached the giant front door. Beth's guide then hesitated. Stopping in the bright warm sun from tall windows on either side the door, she turned. Her face softened in the warm light.

"Child, could I at least see the book for a moment before you go?" Her lips moved slightly with the request, a trembling, hesitant smile crossed them.

Feeling a surge of pity for the gaunt woman with the deep-set eyes, Beth reached and pulled the volume from the cloak pocket at her side. Beth's hand trembled as she reached for the jeweled book, and then hesitated. "These words were written for me," she mumbled.

Nodding her head, the woman said slowly, "I know child, but at the heart they were written for all people everywhere." Then handling it with great reverence, in white, thin fingers, the woman took the book and opened it to the page where Beth had written by candlelight during the dark night. Whispery-voiced, she read, "No one will ever snatch your word of truth from me, for your words are my only hope."

Read aloud the words seemed to float as motes in the sunbeams. Great tears formed in the woman's eyes and rolled down her face, which had become younger and more beautiful.

In a flash of recognition Beth saw the face before her, tears streaming down the cheeks, repeated again and again in the portraits, sculptures, and tapestries on the long dark halls behind her. She turned to confirm her recollection. "You—you are Teith."

The book was thrust back into her hands, and she was pulled roughly toward the door. Bending down, the face of Teith became white and hard again. She whispered tersely into Beth's ear.

"There is only one Prince worthy of our allegiance; he alone will be the one true king. Do not ever forget. Years ago, I heard of his mercy. I was told he was good. I read he was able to fill our emptiness. I wanted to follow him but was lured away by another. The promise of gowns, jewelry, riches, and fame turned my head. Listen to me! If you choose to seek him, never, ever turn back."

Thin hands with long bony fingers gripped Beth's shoulder like talons, pulled the massive door agape, thrust her out into the sunlight, and banged it shut behind.

Blinking in the brightness, Beth encountered a guard she seemed to remember from the night before. He motioned with his head for her to follow and began to lead her to another quadrant of the palace. She had to trot to keep up, feeling like a stray dog chasing for scraps. More doors, more hallways, until they reached an entrance where the sound of splashing water and rising steam indicated some sort of bath. Here, the guard turned with a shrug and went back the way he came. Hesitantly Beth slipped through the door.

Suddenly she was surrounded by coy, smiling girls who looked briefly at her ragged condition and then with a cascade of giggles, set to work. In what was to become the highlight of her stay in the palace.

She was stripped, immersed in hot bubbling waters, soaked, scrubbed, shampooed, dried, anointed, perfumed, coifed, and clothed in the most beautiful lavender gown she had ever worn. The young girls, so obviously trained in their skill, buffed finger and toenails, applied face coloring and perfume, and brought her before a giant oval mirror to see herself as she never had before.

This was what being a princess is all about, Beth thought.

She twirled to see the transformation from all sides, raising her newly plucked eyebrows coyly as if to impress the king. As a last touch she was given a glossy, lavender purse to hold the few small vials of perfume and lip coloring she had been given. *It just might be large enough to fit my book,* she thought. And indeed it was. But a fearful thought fluttered mothlike in a spider's web; would the author of her letters be impressed? Could the Prince approve? Was she breaking faith with his words?

Another look into the mirror and then one easy swipe cleared the web away.

Gliding like a marionette, as had her nighttime guide, Beth was led through the palace and at the last into a royal chamber. Filled with noisy revelers, she was brought through the crowd to the front dais.

The king, perched on a gaudy gold-and-lilac throne, turned toward her. Surprise parsed his skeptical face and widened his eyes. Two courtiers stood on either side. On his right was a tall, silver-haired counselor with elegant robes, jewels on every finger, and a haughty look under the bushy brows on his long face. Beth looked over at him to find him staring straight at her with an all-knowing, satisfied smirk on his face. To the king's left was a dark, wizened man with sinister eyes.

"Ahaaa!" spoke Lord Vau over his shoulder to his advisors. "What a marvelous change has been brought about!" Then to Beth, he said, "You, young lady, look much more princess like than you did in those rags, followed by your urchin servant."

King Vau spoke to the tall, razor-faced advisor on his left. "Zayin, I need your services." Zayin leaned close as the king, looking toward Beth, murmured something she could not hear.

A cold, reptilian smirk crossed the drawn face of Zayin. It was intended to be a smile, but it contained not a trace of contentment. Obsidian black eyes stabbed Beth's and then caressed her coldly from the jewels in her hair to the hem of her gown. She blushed with embarrassment then chilled by a dread that ran down her spine. Zayin did not look entirely human. It was the unblinking stare of a reptile. He spoke guardedly to the king while his eyes moved lecherously up and down Beth's body. All Beth could hear was what sounded like the hiss of a serpent slithering through dry grass. Zayin bowed his head to the King, oiled his way through the throng of worshipful courtiers, then in a loud, sibilant voice pronounced, "The princess is here! Come, let us adjourn to the banquet!"

A snicker of mockery ran through the courtiers as he made the pronouncement but dressed in elegance and flushed from the king's compliment, Beth did not care. Rising, stepping to her side, the king took her hand, kissed it, and tucked it under his arm, leading her in the direction of music and fragrant food. The blush on her face deepened as she felt warm at the touch of the king's hand.

Leaning close he whispered in her ear, "I hope you will forgive me the rude comments I made about you on the road. These idiot court-leeches must be entertained occasionally. I knew the moment I saw you that you were a beauty."

His warm breath in her ear raised bumps on her neck and sent a shiver down her arm. He seemed so different from the cocky dandy she had seen in the carriage. Confident and attentive, he led her into the great hall where music swelled, and the fragrance of hot food almost made her dizzy. The realization she had not eaten in what seemed to be days, made her mouth water with anticipation. Empty for such a long time, she was now being filled. The satin, lace, and velvet of her gown caressed her skin and fingertips, filling her mind with luxurious thoughts.

Wealth and splendor infused every decoration filling her eyes. Lit by thousands of candles, the room sparkled with gold and silver utensils, shimmering fabrics, flowers and peacock feathers. Sweet melodies played by a hundred musicians swelled in eddies around the room. They moved her feet to their rhythm and filled her ears. Food, drink, and delicacies piled in mounds on platters wafted fragrances that filled her nose. And hoped would soon fill her mouth.

Beth looked at the king holding her arm as he smiled to the applauding throng as he passed. Guiding her regally through the room, even he seemed to begin to touch her heart.

The meal tasted even better than it looked. She had eaten her fill and was enjoying a satisfaction she had not in a long time. Sitting beside her, the king placed two crystal chalices with a gold rims on the table between them and a servant filled them with a sparkling liquid. Its effervescence created tiny bubbles appearing at the bottom, rising to the top to burst in sprays of rainbow colors. Motioning for her to raise hers, the king lifted his chalice and tapped it gingerly on the rim with his fork. Insistent delicate chiming eventually silenced the noisy crowd. The king raised his glass. With a winsome smile at Beth, he turned his face from her to the expectant crowd. His smile subtly transformed to coy mockery.

"To the princess on a quest. May she find what she is looking for this very night."

The crowd howled with glee, raised and drained their glasses, only to fill and raise them again. The king moved his glass to his pouty lips nodding for Beth to do the same. As the golden rim rose toward her mouth a totally unexpected shock jolted her.

Gazing contentedly across the crowded room, her glance locked on the dark, intense eyes of Aleph. Aleph!? The stable hand, her lackey? *What is he doing here at the banquet?* He was dressed as one of servers and carried a tray of dirty plates, but his look was not the humble look of kitchen staff. Stricken with concern, he shook his head slowly from left to right, indicating clearly she should not drink of the chalice in her hand.

A rebellion rose into her heart. This was her moment. She had endured weeks—or months—of deprivation. Being treated for the first time since she came on this ill-fated journey as she had expected to be treated: a rightful princess. She looked directly into his concerned eyes, looked away, and drank.

It was sweet as it caressed her tongue, tingling as it slid down her throat to warm her insides, and it immediately began to whirl her wits. Her hand tilted the chalice until the last drop drained across her lips.

She may have drunk more than one chalice full. It may have been many, she could not remember, but the light became more golden, the delicacies tasted better, and the music was more spirited. She laughed with the king and his wit became sharper, until it seemed everything he said was hysterically funny. The caress of his hand on her arm became more often and insistent.

They drank, they ate, they danced, and as he escorted her around the room as a trophy, his courtiers bowed and doffed their hats. Many of the young, handsome men kissed her hand. She floated in the golden moment. Her head spun.

The music then began to fade, and the merriment died out slowly behind her. Drifting down a hallway on the arm of the king, they approached a set of elegant carved doors. Stern guards stood at attention on either side. Beth reached over and poked one guard with a giggle but got no response. As one, the guards opened the doors, and she was ushered in by the demanding arm of her escort. In a moment she realized it was a bedroom, the largest she had ever seen.

"Welcome, welcome princess . . . tonight you will find what you seek. You have reached the end of your quest." With a bow the king then threw his head back and laughed. His crown fell from his head and rolled across the room to the foot of an elegant four-poster bed. Discarding his cloak and doublet, his glazed eyes narrowed down to evil cunning.

Uncertainty straightened Beth's shoulders. She became confused. This did not seem right. With a stumbling clutch at her arm, the king fell forward, grabbed at her sleeve, and Beth heard the delicate fabric come away with a noisy rip. Backing away, she cried out, "What are you doing?"

Still laughing, the king clutched at her arm again, pulling her to him in a clumsy embrace. Drawing close, he attempted to kiss her. Suddenly, his laughter sounded like the foppish dandy she had first seen in the carriage. His breath smelled rank. The texture of his skin seen up close, was pocked and pasty with powdered makeup. Disgust enveloped her along with his over sweet floral perfume. She felt herself gag. Bracing herself against the bedpost, she pushed him away.

"Oh, don't push away from me, you little priss," the king sneered. "If you want to be a princess you have to be with a king!" He giggled, holding her fast around the waist. As lanky as he was, his arms were like bands of steel.

Terror flooded her groggy mind. With a show of

strength, she burst from the king's embrace. His majesty stumbled after her. She ran toward the exit. Hitting the door with both hands, a small budge gave her hope. Before she could push farther, the grasping hands of King Vau were around her. The massive door gave a little more, but the clutch of the almost insane king held her tight.

Still he giggled. Breathing heavily, the mad king pulled her back into the room. In frantic desperation, she turned and with all her strength, swung the cackling monarch against the doorframe. A solid thud released his grip. Beth again pushed at the door and saw it reluctantly open just enough to allow her to begin to squeeze through. Then with a breathy croak, the maniacal creature behind her foiled her last attempt to escape.

Dragged toward the high poster bed, she heard the door slam shut, followed by the unmistakable clack of a bolt on the other side. Dizzy, drained, and fearful, she was flung on the bed by the mad king. The room was spinning crazily. Her brain reeled in her skull. Still snickering, the king flopped down beside her. His arm landed heavily on her chest and leg pinned her to the mattress. Paralyzed, her brain, refusing to accept what was happening, just shut down.

Merciful forgetfulness draped the scene in black. When Beth finally returned to her senses, the candles around the room had gone out. What she hoped would be silence, was interrupted by the king's long gurgled snore. His sweaty arm was still draped across her breasts. A far away clock, chimed three in the morning. There was no sleep for Beth.

Flocks of colorful, dizzy memories of the enchanted evening spun in her head. The allure was gone. Memories of the glitter and glamour came back flat, tasteless, artificial.

Blaring music became tuneless clanging. Loud chattering conversations, like screeching macaws, echoed in her thoughts. She was ashamed for allowing herself to be hypnotized by the heady riches of the party and lured into the king's bedroom.

A lonely tear traced down her temple and puddled in her ear. Now she lay in the dark wondering what was next. Hours crept by, marked by the cool moonlight that silvered through the window and across the floor. Words Tzaddi had spoken came back to her. "*You will find him when you look for him with your complete heart.*"

The memory of the good people of Daleth gradually replaced the noisy clamor of the ball. Her mind, now quiet, remembered the soft songs sung by simple, joyful people. Moving in silent harmony, her lips whispered worshiped for the true Prince. His promises gave her hope. Fumbling around in the dim, cold light she dragged herself from under the king's dead weight. Attempting to straighten the ruined gown, she almost fell from the bed in the darkness. She found the clutch purse, casually tossed amidst the pillows in the scramble. Then pulled by a silver beam of moonlight, she slipped off the bed and padded silently to an ornate chair in the blue-white light. Heavy of heart, shamed by guilt, drained in her spirit, droopy-eyed and weary of hand, she pulled her precious letters from the purse. Too spent to read, she sat looking at the book, knowing her failure loomed large between her and any hope of being accepted by the Prince. *Is this the end of the journey? I can't believe anyone, especially the Prince, would want me now.*

At long last, remembering how she had been lifted by his words before, she opened the pages to read a line or two. Unbelievable. In those very lines he had written of his own failure. Wounded by an enemy lance, lying face down on a muddy battlefield, he told of despairing for his life. What lifted him was thoughts of Beth. He could not fail. The story would not end there! Wracked with unimaginable pain he rose from the earth, limped back to the fray, and his soldiers moved onward to reclaim the victory. Before even seeing to his wounds, weeping with pain, he took quill in hand and wrote of his love for her. The pages in her book bore stains of his tears.

I must write to my Prince. He doesn't need to know. Even if I turn back now, even if his rejection is sure, I will still carry the memory and the sweetness of his words.

Then knowing she had to write something, even if it was all wrong and too late, she withdrew the quill and wrote.

O my dear Prince, please forgive me;
you are my only hope.
Only your promises can revive me;
they can comfort me in all my troubles.

I have been defiled by these arrogant people
who treated me with utter contempt,
but I don't want to turn away from your loving words.
I remember your wise and lasting wisdom;
O my Prince, it refreshes me.
I am devastated by these wicked,
proud people because they reject you.
Your sweet words will be the theme of my songs,
wherever I may have to stay.
In the middle of the night I remembered you,
O my Lord; I listened to your instructions.
This is how I want to spend my life:
honoring your truth.

Finished, Beth leaned forward to slip the golden quill into the spine of that special book. Bright shafts of moonlight crossed her shoulder, highlighting her pendant casting a shadow on the blank page. Expecting to see the shadow of uplifted hands, or the graceful wings of a dove, she was puzzled by the odd shape of a letter. It looked much like one of the mystical runes she had seen scribed by her father. Then quickly the memory came of the guiding marks Aleph had fashioned in the sand. *What sign was that? I know it was shown me by my father.*

Just as quickly, the pendant turned, the shadow changed to a different symbol. What did they mean? Her exhaustion layered over the throbbing ache of the brutal attack intervened and her drooping head rested on the padded arm of the chair. She lay in exhausted grief until her mind, reliving the recent horror, thrust her into the darkness of a nightmare.

Chapter Eight

Heth

FULL SUN STABBING her eyes, Beth woke. A harsh acrid yellow glare replaced the blue-white of the night moon. The chair had not made a comfortable bed. Her body ached. Across the room, an oval full-length mirror reflected the sunlight and tempted her to see what she looked like after the wild night. Shuffling toward the mirror, the empty bed, discarded crown, and embroidered coverlet, revealed the king had gone.

Her reflection was not pretty. Lanks of disheveled hair, matted on one side, smeared face paint and pale skin, emphasized the purple bruise under one eye. The color seemed coordinated with the stains on the lavender gown. A torn sleeve, sagging hem and wrinkled taffeta completed the look of someone who had been attacked by a dog, instead of a princess returning from a ball.

She had been attacked—by a cur.

As Beth began the futile effort to repair her looks, the door opened behind her. The nasal, whiny voice of Zayin, advisor to the king, preceded him into the bedroom. His appearance matched his smarmy voice. Sinuous and swathed in flowing robes, he moved with a reptilian ooze.

"Oh my! How totally tragic. What happened you, pooooor, disgusting little waif? Did you fall off your horsie? Tsk, tsk. Well, don't keep me waiting. The Lord Vau has given me instructions for you. Since you failed him miserably as a bedmate, you are getting demoted to the cleaning crew."

"You can't make me go anywhere like this," Beth said. "I need to get cleaned up."

"Oh, rubbish! Nobody gives a rat's bottom what you look like. Now, don't be tiresome and follow me. They will provide you with proper attire. Something more suitable for your lowered status."

"Who are you, ordering me around, anyway?" Beth said, trying to assert herself. "The king invited me here to be with him. You can't contradict the king."

"What are you saying? You are addressing Zayin! Grand Vizier. Fountain of wisdom. Advisor to King Vau. Giver of favors to the submissive and dispenser of judgment on the rebellious. I recommended you, you miserable piece of dirt. I was thinking you might make a fun plaything for his majesty. But you have proven irksome and stubborn. Now move along, or I will gladly call a guard and have you dragged down to the basement like a dirty mop." Zayin spoke with the puffed arrogance of a petty official.

More hot air than confidence. More bluff than assurance. His was the worst kind of servitude. Sucking his status and self-importance by groveling before his liege. Pandering to royalty for every crumb. He would do the king's bidding, no matter how onerous, for the smallest scrap of reward.

He even looks like a worm, thought Beth. But with no defense, no argument, not even Aleph, her servant, to stand with her, she had to hang her head and follow. At the last moment she remembered the purse and grabbed it on the way out of the king's chambers. Watching Zayin's back was like following a snake as he oiled his way down flight after flight of stairs. He made no sound other than the sibilant hiss of his robes.

Finally standing arrogantly before a door dingy with the marks of many dirty hands, Zayin pointed a bony finger to the wooden latch.

"This is the only place you will be of any worth to this kingdom. Until you learn to submit. But you will bow, you proud little wretch. They all do eventually." He sniffed haughtily. "Sensuous silks, pampering baths, and the lure of lace will bring you groveling back to the tantalizing dream of fame and glory." Head back, lips twisted in a haughty sneer, Zayin issued his proclamation: "In the end, like all your kind, you will become a prisoner of your own desires. Trading your virtue for any crumb of royal attention."

Beth shuffled forward, head bowed, hands grasping her purse and the ragged remnants of a once-elegant gown. She turned toward Zayin, faint hope urging her on. Perhaps if Aleph could help. Perhaps he could bring her clean clothes. It seemed unlikely, but he might even find a way for her to escape. It came out as a feeble croak: "At least tell me where my servant is. He cares for my horse. In my saddle bags are clean clothes. Can you tell him to find me?"

"Pshah!" The sound exploded from Zayin's flaccid lips, launching venomous flecks of spit in her direction. "The mare was the only thing you brought with you of any worth. She has been taken to the king's stable for his use. Your stupid, worthless lackey however, has abandoned you and fled to the forest."

That last statement stabbed her heart. Aleph—gone! Now it was too much to bear. She was truly alone. Abandoned in a place where she knew no one, and no one cared. A great cry rose in the back of her throat, on the verge of exploding into a torrent of hysterical wails. Looking into the malicious black eyes of Zayin, she saw an evil contentment spreading across his face. His lips stretched as if ready to laugh.

A childhood memory at that moment surfaced. Not paying attention on the cobbled market street of her hometown at the foot of the castle, she had tripped on a curb and fallen heavily on her face. Knees scraped, dress ripped, purchased goods spilled across the path, she pushed herself to her hands and knees. Tears spilled out, shivering gasps for air bracketed between sobs. Her cry for help echoed on the stony path, hoping some kind hand would reach out to help.

Then she heard a snicker. When she turned her mud- and tear-stained face upward, through blurry eyes she could see the mocking faces of three local urchins making sport of her calamity. Realizing she was not hurt badly, indignant eyes squeezed the tears away, lips clamped into a thin line, she stomped to her feet. A two-handed wipe smeared away most of the mucus and tear tracks. Then giving the three tormentors an angry stare, she began picking up the spilled groceries. She had not been paying careful attention on the rough path. No one had pushed her. It had been a fall of her own doing. Sobbing in the gutter was not going to make her feel any better. Taking ownership of her own carelessness was the only option.

The faces of the three snickering urchins faded, replaced by the leering face of Zayin. She remembered she had chosen this journey rather than the comfort of home. No one forced her to go with the king. The memory of last night's horror and misery would get locked away forever. One blink cleared away any trace of moisture in her eyes. A deep breath squared and pulled her shoulders back, chin pushed out, and through narrowed lids, she returned Zayin's look with a haughty look of her own. Head up, jaw clenched, chin forward, she then turned her back to him, pulled open the heavy door and stepped beyond.

The hall was huge, clean but dim, with high windows

looking out on a gray sky. Long wooden tables surrounded by young women cutting and preparing food, filled most of the room. Stoves covered with steaming pots; ovens lined the walls. Young men carried bags and boxes of vegetables, fruit, trays of spices, slabs of meat and fowl of every kind. Each open door in the great hall seemed to be a storeroom filled with foodstuffs.

Presiding over it from a high platform in the center of the room, much like the imperious King Vau, stood a massive, ogress-like woman looking much like a wall, a pillar. The ogress was wearing an immaculate white apron big enough for a ship's sail. A pile of bright orange hair braided into a ponderous turban, capped a round face with harsh sunburnt cheeks, intense eyes, and lips puckered into a permanent, full pout. In her right hand, held up and brandished like a scepter, waved a long black whip.

Behind her the sharp hiss of Zayin's sarcastic voice introduced Beth to the room. "Here, most noble Heth, is another reluctant worker. She will have to be humbled and trained, for I doubt she has ever done an honest day's work in her pathetic little life."

For a moment, all eyes in the room turned toward her. Most reflected sorrow, an unspoken apology for what she must endure, a resignation to their own fate. And terror.

"Pause? Who gave permission to pause?" the massive Heth roared. "Nothing to see here, wretches. I will inform you when it is time to rest, and no sooner."

Eyes snapped back to their knives, graters, and mixing bowls. Vegetables were to be pealed. Cooked hunks of meat needed to be sliced, geese and chickens plucked and pinioned. Cheese to be grated, dough to be kneaded, and sauces mixed as the ogress stared down on her slaves.

The cold amber eyes turned and impaled Beth with a vicious, imperious glare. "*Scullery*! Are there ever enough pot scrubbers?" Words, instructions, and mandates belted across the kitchen.

"*Uniform*! Why are you dragging that ridiculous costume through my kitchen?" Pointing to a closet behind her filled with folded white clothing, the imperious Heth continued. "*Move*! Is stepping quickly too difficult for your dainty toes, dearie?"

Beth began moving toward the closet. As she passed the dais upon which the giant matron stood, the whip sliced through the air and caught one bare shoulder with a burning slash. Sudden pain brought tears to her eyes, an instant red welt, and a trickle of blood down her pale skin. Leaping quickly sideways and into the closet saved her from a second strike of the whip. Without waiting, she grabbed quickly at rough cotton clothing and with nowhere else to change, Beth removed her tattered gown and pulled on the humble outfit of a scullery maid. With her back to the open room, she tied her gilded clutch purse, which held her treasured book, to the inside of her shift and tucked the silver amulet that hung around her neck carefully under the rough neckline. Then she turned to face her tormentor.

Pointing with her black instrument of torture, Heth indicated a far corner of the kitchen, to a sink where piles of pots and dishes were waiting.

"*Wash*!" she bellowed.

Most were crusted with burnt-on food that required repeated scrubbing and washing with a black pumice stone. Beth began to wash. Endless hours of scouring soon chaffed her hands into raw open sores.

On occasion, Heth the malevolent ogress would tour the giant room, dispensing criticism and punishment. Many of the cooks, scullery maids, and serfs were victims of her slashing. Many bore scars and bloody welts from her brutal ministrations. She stopped at Beth's corner sink.

"You! You are a worthless piece of garbage. I have been told how in your foolish arrogance, you rejected the king. An ugly and scrawny wench like you needs to be humbled."

Once more Beth felt the lash. Twice she flinched in pain as Heth raised her voice in recriminations. Three times she saw her whip some unfortunate serf into semiconsciousness. But more than she could count were the number of pots and pans that landed on the counter beside her sink for her to wash. Thoughts of her easy life back in her father's home came to mind. Reminders carried upon distress. Pondering the direction her life had taken gave clarity to former childish dreams. The longing brought silent words to her lips. *I never appreciated how good my life was, how kind my father was, how sweet my mother*. How she missed them.

Finally, the pace seemed to slow. As Heth stalked from the room, she passed the sinks where Beth washed endlessly. "*Finish*! Do you think you are done? Every pot, every dish, every tray, every utensil must be scrubbed clean. You do not leave anything dirty in my sink!"

When the march of her boots on the pavement had drifted into silence, a bent-over, snaggle toothed, old cook tugged at her dress. "Come, child, fret not about the pots. There will always be more at the dawn. The ogress will never notice. Come, I will show you where to sleep."

Wiping her reddened hands on the front of her frock, Beth, grateful for the small kindness, limped slowly behind the old woman. Wending between two armed guards quickly dissipated any thought of escape.

A group of worn and sweaty kitchen workers pushed passed them, one calling out to Beth in a coarse voice, "Come with us," she said, "we have some wine to dull the pain, to give us courage to mock the ogress and forget for a short while. Come join us!"

Beth was tempted to follow the laughing group. Some mind-numbing drink sounded appealing, but words she wanted to write for the Prince pushed into her mind. *I have pondered the direction of my life and have continued to follow you and your words.*

The old woman was leading her down a different hallway. It was dark, but not so dark she could not see crossed welts on the bent back and wrinkled arms of the shuffling form. Beth saw no paintings, no tapestries, no finely carved furniture adorning these halls. Stone, dust, grime, and mold were everywhere on display. Finally, a room with no door, dim light, and rows of bunks stacked as high as the ceiling, opened alongside.

"Here," croaked the ancient one. "Rest quickly, dawn comes early." Then the scratchy voice echoed back to her, as she shuffled into the darkness, "Forget not the words of the Prince." The voice, the bent-over form seemed familiar. Was this . . .? It could not be, so far from her home and the castle.

"Wait," Beth called out wearily, reaching out to the old woman. "Have you seen, do you know of the Prince? Do you know where I can find him?"

The woman turned. Tears welled up in the rheumy eyes. She nodded her gray head. "He promised," she said, nodding. "He promised he could be found when you seek him with all your heart. He also promised to return someday, victorious, and set us all free."

It was the words Tzaddi had spoken. Affection for the woman overcame Beth. She knew this woman. A million questions filled her mind, but the old woman had gone. Thoughts of home brought back the memory of the first moment Beth laid eyes on the book. She recalled the good people in Daleth and the resentment she felt at their longing for the words of the book. How strong men and mighty warriors had humbly bowed at the reading of those powerful words. The kindness of this old woman marked her as one of his own. She was sure of it. Her spirit fluttered weakly with the sympathetic vibrations that bonded them together. It was not Tzaddi, she knew, but wondered if her eyes would ever see the old nursemaid again. Perhaps not, but her words still admonished her, *Forget not the words of the Prince.*

Beth climbed the rickety ladder leading to one of the few bunks left on an upper tier. Her brain was too tired to make any connection as she thought of those last words. They would come back to her. But for the meantime, she had been reminded of her precious book. It was very dim; the smoky oil lamp hung in the ceiling was not enough, but the pages glowed with a light of their own. They whispered as she turned them. Her wounded soul drew hope from the life-giving words recorded there. It was strong analgesic for her pain; strength for weakness; courage in fear; oxygen for aching lungs. They were nourishment for a starving soul; sweet music for deaf ears. They became the colors of a rainbow for blind eyes. The words of her beloved now meant more than life to her. She was grateful. In a small measure spiritually refreshed, sleep dropped down upon her exhausted body.

The hours seemed like seconds when she awoke. Still dark, the flickering lamp cast its feeble light on the dozens, perhaps hundreds of sleeping bodies around her. What had woken her she did not know. She was reminded she had recorded no words for her Prince. Lying in the semidarkness, she located the book in the bedclothes, running her red, chaffed fingers across the precious jewels on the cover. Feeling each smooth stone, counting seven in the row. Regardless of the fatigue that weighted her body, the burn of the lashes on her back, and her aching feet, she opened her volume and in the faint lamplight stared at the blank page. Even with her failure stinging more than the welts on her back, she knew the request of the Prince had not changed. She was duty bound to write something in return. No matter how little.

Prince, you are mine!
I promise to follow your words.
With all my heart I long for your blessings.
You promised to be merciful.
I am in anguish with all this pain,
but I still want to seek after you.
So, I will try as soon as I can to keep seeking you.
These evil people dragged me into sin,
but I am still anchored to your instructions.
I am awake at midnight to thank you
for your righteous warnings.
I have found an old friend who fears you—
she listens to your watchwords.
My sovereign, your unfailing love fills the earth;
teach me what you want me to know.

Chapter Nine

Teith

EACH DAY, FOR Beth, was a nightmare; each night was filled with dread for the next day. Endless piles of pans, baked black with grease and burned food, filled her workstation. Scrubbing the same pots, only to have them sent back to be scrubbed again. The word of the ogress taskmaster, Heth, was iron. But she and her demanding, imperious commands were a goad, in some way driving Beth to find a way to continue searching for the Prince. She spoke of cruelty; his words were grace. She imposed affliction; his message brought comfort. Her voice was callous; his whisper was kind. Under her was bondage, darkness, cruelty, and hopelessness. Her law was death; his words were life.

In the haze of misery, days faded into one task after another. She hated herself for choosing the journey, but the guards were at every door. There was no escape. Feeling worthless for being foolish, guilty for falling prey to the king's lust, depression weighed her down. Trying to hide it all made her numb. Eventually she withdrew into a place where she felt nothing.

The grind wore her down. In time her book, the love letters, lay neglected at the foot of her pallet.

The pit she was in was the darkest depression she had ever known. Like the hiss of Zayin's robes, a vile thought slithered in.

I could take my own life.

The first time it happened, it was an accident. A pan still burning hot from the oven slid off the pile of dirty dishes and seared her arm just above the wrist. Blinding pain shot up to her shoulder. The skin immediately blistered. The sudden agony yanked her awake. In some way it seemed to atone for her failures. She deserved this. Her mind twisted the laceration into something she needed, something that gave her control. Facing her real pain, the pain within, was hopeless. There was no way out, nothing she could do to alleviate that pain, save swaddle it in darkness. This external pain, she could choose. Or not. She had control. On days where the hopelessness pressed hard, there was always another burning hot pan, another open wound, another way to forget the pain within. Her scullery garb covered her damaged arms. No one knew. No one cared.

Days punctuated with misery dragged into wakeful nights of regret and a few fitful moments of sleep. Ending it all loomed as an option. Knives, razor sharpened, used briefly, and carried to her sink, were always available.

Perhaps now was the time.

Lying in her miserable cot, a wicked paring knife hidden beneath her pillow. In the darkness, waiting for the right time, a silent cry came to her lips as she drifted off. *Oh Aleph, please Aleph, would you come? Aleph, come rescue me.*

‡ ‡ ‡

IN THE DEPTH of that blackest of moments, a hand on her shoulder shook her awake. "Milady. Milady Beth, it is I, Aleph."

Groggy with fatigue, Beth could hardly comprehend what was going on. She sat up, blinking crusty eyelids. It was certainly weeks, if not months, that no one had called her by name. *Scullery slave*, *wench*, *urchin*, *scum*, were the words thrown at her. Cursed, maligned, insulted, abused—but never called by her name. It was a delight to her ears. *I can't believe it. Aleph called me by my name!*

"Come quickly! I have found a way of escape!" Aleph whispered urgently as he helped her climb down the ladder to the floor.

"Oh, Aleph," she choked out in a whisper, "I don't think I have ever been more relieved to see someone than you." The mysterious talisman *yohd*, hidden around her neck, and the well-worn ragged scullery uniform, went with her.

"I also have been anguished to see you, my princess. I will

lead you on the right path." Taking her by the hand, he guided her into long, dark, smoky hallways, dank tunnels, low doorways—always, Aleph leading her on. His hand felt warm and strong entwined in hers, guiding her, helping when her steps faltered. Many times they ducked into hidden rooms, alcoves, and behind furniture to avoid soldiers guarding the way, but onward they went. Often confined spaces forced them to press together. The warmth of his body comforted her and calmed her fears. Up winding stairs, down ramps and finally a small door opened out into a silent, fragrant garden.

It was a still night, but Beth could tell by the stars twinkling above, they were out side the palace. Cool air brushed the hair from her face. Falling to her knees, she dug her hands into the dewy moss at her feet. Even lit by the stars alone, she could sense the lush growth of a garden around her and smell the heavy scent of unseen flowers. With hands soaked with dew, she wiped her face. Fresh liquid on her lips. Clean air to breathe. No fetid heaviness laced with the smell of rotted food or burned pots. She breathed again deeply, and again, becoming lightheaded by the aroma of the night.

With gentle hand, Aleph, her stable boy, touched her lightly on the shoulder. "It is time to go, Milady, dawn will be here soon."

Suddenly, overcome with appreciation, Beth took that hand, pressing it against her moistened lips.

"Oh, Aleph, thank you, thank you!" It was a long grateful

kiss, surprising herself at this rush of passion for the servant who had so faithfully followed, cared for, and rescued her. "You did not forget me. You did not abandon me. You were there for me the entire time. Waiting for the right moment to find me and set me free." Her eyes rose to meet his. Pools of kindness drew her in, opening her soul. Held in his gaze. She could not look away.

A sob rose up in her throat. Self-consciousness fought gratitude and these new uninvited warm feelings for Aleph, but the reminder that he was, after all, just a stable hand, set her back.

It was quite unseemly to be on her knees, covering his hand with grateful kisses. It was more than just appreciating his loyalty. Suddenly embarrassed by her emotional outburst, she realized it was a trifle overdone. Averting her eyes, she stood. Released his hand. Wiped her face on her sleeve, then said a bit more stiffly, "Thank you, Aleph, you have done well." Turning toward what she expected was the way out, she added, "Where is our horse? Or must we walk?"

Aleph, head bowed to hide a tender smile, murmured softly. "I am so sorry Milady, the mare is still being held captive in the stables of Vau, the puppet king. We must go find her and set her free."

Oh, no, not back in that wretched palace, she thought. Then she straightened. "How can we do that, Aleph? They have guards and the keep is enclosed with walls too high to scale."

"We cannot go on without the steed, Milady," Aleph said. "I could try to release her but if you would be willing, help might be found with the Countess of Teith. Her confinement is right across from the stables, in the wing of the palace preserved for her."

Shaking her head back and forth, arguments began to form, but Beth was too weary to contest his suggestion. "Do you really think that sour woman with the bony fingers would even speak to me? She was not kind when she locked me in her palace for the night."

"You must try, Milady. I cannot go to her, for she does not know who I am, but you . . . you would appear harmless and needy. You could win her over."

The fatigue was instantly flushed away by indignation. "I don't need to appear to be anything! I *am* needy. I am harmless. Look at me, Aleph. I don't have the strength to bend a flax straw, much less break one."

Aleph bowed his head but spoke with conviction. "You are stronger than you know, Milady, and it is meager hope."

With great reluctance and a deep sigh, Beth shrugged her shoulders and shuffled towards the metal gate at the end of the garden. "Well, show me how to get there."

Suddenly she turned, running back into the garden. "My book, the love letters!" she cried. "I have left them behind!"

In her haste she ran headlong into Aleph, who embraced her to prevent a fall. Struggling to get away and return to retrieve her forgotten book, there was no thought of the madness of trying to find her way back to the dormitory and empty cot where it had been left behind.

"Aleph, let me go! I have to get my book!"

"Wait, wait, Milady," Aleph said. "Your book was not left behind. I carried it out for you."

Then for a second time, Beth clutched Aleph's hands holding the forgotten book, and brought them to her lips.

Chiding her gently, Aleph said, "These words are precious. They were written to you, Milady, with great care. Keep them with you always."

Brushing her dirty hair back from her face, Beth looked at him, not knowing what to say.

"Thank you, thank you, Aleph." She leaned her head wearily on his chest as he patted her shoulder.

Finally, Beth, retrieving her composure with Aleph leading the way stepped out of the garden.

By some route Beth would never remember on her own, the two furtive shadows managed to return to the massive oak door where she had last seen the face of the lady Teith. Before she had a chance to ask for or suggest a strategy, Aleph lifted the massive wrought-iron knocker and dropped it against the door. Once, twice, three times. Beth reached out to stop him from striking the door again, but he had already melted into the shadows. Fear, she thought, was going to make her flee. Perhaps because of exhaustion, or the days of being abused by the kitchen ogress Heth, or the image of the frail woman, Teith, who did not even have the strength to snatch her book away, no fear came. Perhaps it was the words of the Prince, who had assured her in his letters he would, in due time, rescue her and set her at his side. She stood firm and waited. Sounds like slippers on a marble floor approached on the far side of the door, then it opened. Teith stood, her face and hands pale in the blackness.

"Why," she said without moving her lips, "have you returned to trouble me?"

Beth stepped closer and saw the woman Teith, as if for the first time. No cloak covered her shoulders. The black shift she wore emphasized her thin frame and protruding belly. She looked wan and sad.

"No, Lady Teith, I have come because I need help. I was told by my servant you might be willing to assist us." Her words caused the black eyebrows on the pale face to furrow in puzzlement. She stepped back into the gloom and beckoned her into the hall.

"Come, I will listen to your request, but it is night, and you must not be seen here, for a warning was sent out about your fall from favor with King Vau. His anger is still hot and he intends to humiliate you." The countess reached for a lamp on a hook by the door and turned it up to create a puddle of light. She then closed the door and led Beth into a small sitting room. Two chairs faced each other near an empty fireplace. Lowering herself to one, she waved her pale hand to the other. Beth sat on the edge of the chair facing her and spoke immediately.

"Our steeds have been taken from us and are stabled nearby. My servant informed me of this. He also spoke, saying you are good. That you would help us. I . . ." Beth hesitated, wondering how much to reveal to this woman she didn't know. Then with a rush, trusting Aleph's encouragement, she said, "I am trying to resume my quest for the Prince. He has called me to come be with him. You told me, I remember, if I was to follow him, I should never turn back. My horse alone is the way I travel. I don't know why you would, but . . . would you be willing to help?"

The lamplight wavered as if from some invisible breeze. Silence from the gloomy palace pressed in around them. Beth thought she could hear the ticking of an ancient clock in the distance. This was confirmed by deep, mournful chimes within. One, two, three, four, five . . . Dawn would arrive soon. The guards would start stirring and they would never let them escape. She must press for an answer. By clasping her hands to her chest and leaning close to the still, pale figure, she indicated her need for urgency.

Finally, Lady Teith spoke. "Yes, I will help. But first I must tell you my story. It will instruct you on your way." She paused and looked up at the darkened ceiling as if looking into the distant past. "Seventy years have I been a prisoner here. Seventy springs have brought the rain. Seventy summers have blistered the roof of this palace. Seventy autumns have piled leaves in the gutters. Seventy winters have I watched the snow fall and shivered in dark, lonely halls. At times it has been too much to bear.

"Those many years ago, a basket was abandoned on the steps of this palace. A foundling infant. A rejected child. Countess of Teith the sixth found me on this very stoop. She raised that newborn and kept me here until her death. I then succeeded her, for I am the seventh to be declared Countess of Teith. Each of the seven in turn was given a choice: to cling to the silver and gold, relish the pleasures and riches of this foul and depraved kingdom for a season, or endure the sufferings of following the true Prince. Each in turn chose badly. I also. And each in turn proved barren and rejected for being childless and banished to this palace."

As each word dripped bitterly on her ears, Beth felt the chill sink deeper into her bones. The Countess of Teith then took Beth's hands, gripped them in her cold fingers, and looked deeply into her face. "I assure you, my child, it is far better you have suffered, that you have endured afflictions with the loyal followers of the true Prince, than be lured into the golden cage of the arrogant false king. My suffering has been good for me. It taught me of the folly of wealth and the foolishness . . . the weariness of chasing after what will never last." She sat in silence for a moment. Tears coursed down her wan cheeks. Then in a rush her words spilled out. "Go, seek your Prince, be fruitful, find the happiness you pursue."

She stood. Spoke tersely. "Wait here."

Moving swiftly to the door, she stepped out into the gray

pre-dawn. Behind her Beth peeked out, looking for Aleph in the shadows. The dark form of the Countess Teith slipped silently from the portico toward the stables. In a shorter time than she imagined, the *clip-clop* of shod hooves echoed across the stone courtyard, and Countess Teith, dwarfed by the mare behind her, stepped through the arched entrance.

The mare had been curried, combed, and cared for well. Glossy, shimmering, even in the early light, her black hide stood out from the gray stones. Her livery was polished. The way she lifted her hooves and arched her neck seemed proud but not arrogant. She tossed her head, shivering her mane. The flick of her tail cast out sparks of light.

Beth ran down the steps and embraced the massive head. Her soft muzzle pushed against Beth's neck as if to say, "Greetings, Mistress."

Turning her head, Beth opened her lips to call out for Aleph, but as always, he was already standing beside her waiting patiently to lift her into the saddle. A door opened across the courtyard. Two early risers of the king's guards stepped out, surprised to see the mighty horse held by the Countess, a stable hand, and the young woman they had seen working in the galley.

"Quick, Aleph, boost me up. We must leave now," Beth said urgently through her teeth. Aleph, at her side, took her knee and hoisted her into the saddle.

Standing straight, at the horse's side, gripping her halter, Countess Teith spoke across the courtyard. "Let these travelers pass, they have my permission." Then in a lower voice, looking up at Beth, she said, "I am a prisoner, but those minions still do my bidding." Satisfaction lifted her voice. For the first time, Beth could see a smile on her lips.

Then with a weight of wistfulness, Teith spoke again. "Go, child. The afflictions you have faced and will endure are needful. The scars might remain, but they will serve to keep you on the right path and teach you what is true. May your journey be fruitful."

Aleph, leading the black mare followed by the little donkey, walked past the guards, through the portico, beyond the gate, onto the road leading away from the Castle of Vau, and into the woods beyond. No cry was raised. No one pursued.

As the gray sky feathered into pink, Beth looked back at the towers receding in the distance. She pondered her experiences in Vau's palace and the words spoken to her by the Countess Teith. The pain from the beatings and self-inflicted wounds persisted. It would be a long time, if ever, before the scars on her arms would fade. Ugly memories might never heal. That memory of a warm hand guiding her through the castle maze which she had kissed so gratefully brought an unbidden flush to her face—then faded quickly, remembering the words in her treasured book.

Pulling it out, she began to read. It had been long, too long, since she had read the letters from her Lord, the Prince. Her soul was starved for the affirmation and love that carried such weight, such insight. Truly he seemed to understand what she had and would endure, before even the events came to pass. His words presented her with a true and genuine understanding of her experience and the rebel pride that desired to conquer her own soul. He wrote about hard and callous words that had been spoken about him; he knew the feeling of being lied to and mistreated. His gentle words of direction provided the soothing, comforting hope in this dark time. After many miles, she retrieved the quill and began to write.

Please continue to be good to me
according to your word, my Prince.
What you have written teaches me knowledge
and good judgment, for I trust you.
Before I suffered, I didn't understand what to do,
but now I am following your word.
You are good, and what you have written for me
is good;
keep teaching me your decrees.
Though the arrogant smeared me with lies,
I tried to keep your precepts with all my heart.
They are callous and unfeeling,
but I delighted in your precious instructions.
It was good for me to be afflicted
so I would learn from your wisdom.
The words from your mouth
are becoming more precious to me
than thousands of pieces of silver and gold.

Chapter Ten

Yodh

PULLING TO ONE side of the road leading away from her time of misery, Aleph helped Beth dismount. A cool stream running along the road provided her with water to wash, and in a great stroke of fortune, her mare's saddle bags still contained some of her clean clothes. Removing the greasy scullery shift, pealing it away from the still-open wounds, caused such pain she almost fainted, but it was a great relief to discard it. She was pleased the clean dress and travel cloak covered the wounds and burn scars on her arms, but they still throbbed painfully. It would be a long time before they healed. Feeling light-headed but much revived, she sat on a fallen log for a few moments longer, enjoying the quiet of the forest around them. Aleph bathed also; he came up from the stream looking refreshed, but as he reached the for the saddlebag to retrieve a clean jerkin, Beth gasped and felt the blood drain from her face. His back was a mass of welts and open wounds.

"Aleph!" Hands at her lips, she cried in a choked voice, "They beat you too!" It had not even crossed her mind. He also had been abused and mistreated. "But why?"

"It was to be expected, your highness," he said as he quickly turned to hide his back and slip his jerkin on. "I was forced into labor, but they knew my solitary desire was to serve and protect you." Then with a rather lighthearted laugh he said, "And although they did keep me prisoner, I found ways to escape numerous times before I managed to come to your rescue."

"Oh, Aleph, I am so sorry for my foolishness." A guilty knot formed in her chest at the sight of his wounds. Impulsively she wanted to reach out, touch him, and tend to the lashes on his back. The horror of them kept her back, yet the emotion was strong. "I know it was all my fault for not listening to you."

"Do not fret, my lady. I would endure it all again and many times over, even unto death, if I could have prevented damage to a single hair on your head."

His confession of loyalty impressed her even more deeply. Her stable hand, her companion, her friend was reaching places in her heart never touched before. "It is but a small thing to offer myself for your freedom."

The weight of her bad choice that had caused such suffering, both to her and Aleph, was lifted significantly by the words of the Prince reminding her that he, too, would give himself and love her even at her very worst. She wondered, *Would the Prince show appreciation to a stable boy who had suffered to rescue me?* She purposed it would be one of the first things she would tell him about. If she was given any power as queen, she would reward Aleph for his sacrifice.

Aleph finished dressing and began pulling food from one of the bags. Beth sat watching him—in wonder at his steady servanthood. He provided a delicious meal of cheese, bread, fruit, and slivers of smoked meat. It was a delight to eat something fresh, after the greasy leftovers ladled into her bowl in the scullery.

Trying to ease away from an awkward subject she asked, "Aleph, why did the soldiers not pursue us? I really thought we would be running for our lives, with the whole garrison on our heels."

"I am sure, your highness, the king has not been informed of your escape. In his palace, all dread his rule. He can drive his servants with fear, but only so far. Unless a direct order is given, no initiative is taken. The Countess Teith, perhaps, has some power yet. Her silence has kept us safe for a time."

Speaking quietly, Beth, always aware of his caution to be quiet, asked, "I would not want to follow an order from him either. But how can Gimmel and his men be so loyal as to follow and give their lives in obedience to the Prince?"

"It is because they know him," Aleph answered with

confidence. "He is their friend. They love him. No greater love can be shown than if one would lay down their lives for a friend."

"Has the Prince given them words of hope and encouragement too?"

"Yes, Milady, all who have been touched by his words have the same hope."

"And the people of Daleth, they, too, love him?"

"Even under fear of great persecution, those who have heard and been touched by his words love and follow him. They, too, would give their lives."

"One of the cooks in the scullery told me she believed the Prince would return and set all his followers free. Are there many under the rule of the kings of Vau who follow the Prince?"

"More than you would believe. The followers of the Prince are everywhere."

"What happened with Countess Teith? She seemed a tormented soul."

"Turning back from following the Prince weighs heavily on her. Living for years in a shrine dedicated entirely to herself also carries a toll. The Prince does not condemn her disobedience, but the price she places on herself is high. She must learn to receive his forgiveness."

"But I still don't understand how those who have never seen him, can endure such persecution and still love him. I mean, I can at least look forward to being his bride and ruling with him, but what do all these others get out of it?"

"His kingdom will be a glorious place of peace and freedom when he is finally on the throne."

"Aleph." Beth paused, forming the awkward question in her mind. Then with a catch in her voice from uncertainty she felt deep in her heart, she asked, "Will I . . . will I be able to endure until we find the Prince? Will he still accept me and speak comforting words to me? Will He . . . will He still love me?"

Aleph, with head lowered, remained silent. Then thoughtfully, in measured words, he spoke. "The journey is yet long. You must continue the quest to seek him with your whole heart, but the words of the Prince have begun a good work in you. They will continue their work until he lifts you up and welcomes you into his kingdom." Aleph's face raised towards her with kind eyes. "Yes, his love endures forever."

Beth believed it.

Then, with humble efficiency, the stable boy cleaned the remnants of their meal and prepared to leave. "The danger from behind might be delayed," he said, "but they will come soon, and there are more enemies ahead, so we must move on."

Saddled up and continuing the journey, her mind went back to her home at the foot of the castle. She thought kindly of her stoic father. She thought of old and wizened Tzaddi, who had assured her she would keep her father informed of her journey. Beth was certain he was afraid for her safety.

The longing for home ached in her chest: Memories of the good times in her family's humble cottage, with a fire on the hearth, fragrant smells drifting from the pot hanging over it. Her mother humming sweet songs as she cooked before the plague took her. On the rough table in the center of the room and in his workshop she remembered her father teaching her the craft of forming letters, runes, shapes, florets, and mythical symbols on scrolls of parchment. The smells of ink, paint, and paper reminded her of his admonition to "learn the ways and words of the Prince."

It had been a safe, comforting place until the quest began. Now, on a journey she could not explain, motivated each day with letters written by one whom she had never met, searching for a place she had never been, there was hope in a dream that might not become real. The longing to be with the one whose words of love for her were pure continued to pull her forward. Now, perhaps because of the pain she had endured and the struggle against temptations to turn back, the letters tugged her onward more strongly than the longing to give up the search and return home, even when the urge to turn back had been so strong.

Thoughts of wealth, power, and lavish banquets on the arm of the king of Vau no longer enticed her to turn back. She had no stomach to endure his brutality. She would do everything she could to put it behind her and forget.

It was delectable to imagine being with the Prince. Beautiful baubles, jewelry, velvet and silk garments would no longer tempt her, luring her away from the narrow path ahead. Every time she felt the urge to give up, to return, dark memories of what she had suffered floated into her mind. Terror clutched her throat, remembering the bloody and dismembered bodies of Gimmel's faithful, courageous soldiers. Shame echoed in her mind at the mockery thrown in her face by the courtesans of Vau. Disgust forced her head sideways from the memory of the foul breath of their king as he drunkenly ripped at her gown. Wincing in pain at the lash of the angry ogress. Loneliness in the darkness. It all became galvanized steel in her resolve to continue the quest.

Then, as if the sun had come out from behind the clouds as she read words from the book, she saw the united throng of expectant faces that looked to her in the village of Daleth. She remembered their lofty songs of worship and kind words of gratitude spoken to her by their shepherd. Recalling the admonition of the white-haired cook in the kitchen hallway, wistfully hoping that *Someday the Prince will return victorious and set us all free.* And Countess Teith, with pale face and tears in her dark eyes saying, *if you go on this journey, you must never turn back.* The deep voice of Gimmel warning her of straying. Then, too, as if a hundred years ago, the gravelly voice of Tzaddi, speaking stern words of inspiration to follow. *I must continue to seek him with my whole heart.*

She had put her hope in the words of the Prince. She wanted his unfailing love to comfort her. She was now more committed to find him and be with him forever. It was curiosity at the beginning. Thoughts of a royal marriage and the thrill of sitting on a throne that continued it. But meeting those committed to the Prince and even the scurrilous treatment from those who hated him had forged in that kiln, a commitment to continue the search for the one who had written of his love for her.

It was now settled in her soul.

‡ ‡ ‡

THE PACE WAS steady. Her thoughts drifted. Then the sound of shuffling bare feet and the clink of chains caught her attention. Ahead, a tethered string of prisoners moving toward the place she and Aleph had just left, lined one side of the road. Burly guards wielding whips and goads prodded the captives forward. They were skeletal-looking men, women, and even children. shuffling past them toward the palace of Vau. Fifty, a hundred or more—she counted until the number boggled her mind. The last few in the queue looked too weak to carry the weight of their own ragged clothes.

As the sound of the chain gang receded in the distance, Beth called out. "Aleph, who are those poor people? And why are they in chains?"

Aleph turned, waited for the mare to reach him. He shook his head. "They are slaves, your highness, captured by Belial the deceiver, the destroyer, prince of darkness. Kidnapped from their homes and villages, they are sent to the palace to serve the rulers of Vau."

Shaking her own head, Beth could not believe people were being treated so cruelly. "Is the king of Vau, Belial?"

"No, Milady, he is merely a puppet, a slave as well—a slave to his own fancies." Beth opened her mouth to ask more questions, but Aleph had already returned to lead them farther from that gloomy palace, the king, the slaves, and the wretched memories that lay behind. It was a relief.

The road was level and smooth, easy to travel. She rocked back and forth with the steady sway of the mighty horse beneath her. The motion seemed to hypnotize her. Sunshine streaming over her shoulder cast a moving shadow on the flat pommel of the saddle. Swinging back and forth, Beth noticed the silver charm had come loose from her cloak and its shadow was forming shapes as it swung.

They were the shapes she had noticed before in the king's bedroom by moonlight. From the time she first slipped the silver chain around her neck in the village of Daleth, she loved it but knew nothing of its true value or purpose. As the charm twisted, the shadow changed. First it appeared to be a letter, then a rune or a glyph of some sort.

Pulling the book from her pocket, she took the quill with the decision to copy the letters. Not wanting to use the blank pages reserved for her words for the Prince, she took one of the pressed leaves stored in the back and began drawing the strange shapes. It was a joy creating the images. Art learned at her father's knee satisfied deep longings for beauty. She drew each shape on a separate leaf. Every shape formed a letter. Each different. Yet she was sure each had a meaning. Perhaps together they would spell something. They were graceful, but not the common letters most knew. Each moving shadow, repeated in sequence, began to hint at a story, a message, a series of letters spelling out danger a warning or . . . a meaning she could not grasp.

Something important lay in these shadows just beyond her understanding. She scribed them as carefully as she could on a moving horse, but there was no sense to the order she could see. Just as some pattern or semblance of context approached the surface, it would fade away. Swinging like a pendulum, forward then back, forward and back, then repeated again with the movement of her horse. Staring at the shadows began making her eyes heavy. Sleep was just beneath her thoughts. As the sun began to sink toward the horizon the fading light diminished the shadows until they finally disappeared. Stacking her leaves neatly, she tucked them back into her book.

Aleph pulled the donkey's lead and her mare to one side where a small glen opened off the path. Gratefully Beth slid from the saddle and dropped to the ground. She was weary, however her newly forged resolution remained strong. Without waiting for Aleph to light a fire and prepare a meal, she began to help. Collecting small bits of kindling and wood, she assembled them the way she had seen him do it. Watching closely as sparks flew off the flint as it struck steel made her want to learn. How clever it was to watch the way a small spark could be coaxed with soft breaths into a steady flame. Beth even helped with the preparation of the meal and began to clean up afterward.

"No, my lady," murmured Aleph, "my purpose on this journey is to serve you. I know you must be tired. Prepare to take some rest." This continuing kindness from a young man was something she had not experienced before. She marveled how he had been a constant servant for these many days and nights. Never having given her heart to anyone, Beth wondered about that feeling. *I know it can't be love, because my heart is committed fully to the Prince.*

Settled on a nearby log, shadows of shapes, runes, and letters swarmed into her head. Not sure what they meant, she opened her book to the back where the leaf drawings of shadows had been stored. Laying the leaves on her lap and leaning forward, the light of the fire cast the shadow of her silver pendant, whether hands lifted in prayer or a dove in flight, depending on the way you looked at it. The same letters began to form. Now sitting still, she could see them more clearly and copied their shapes with more precision.

At the last, with her eyelids becoming heavy, seven shapes had been drafted onto leaves in her collection. Suddenly one of the shapes became clear. It was a letter, the smallest of those she had traced. Not from the language of this kingdom, but from an ancient mysterious language, a rune her father had taught her as a child. *It is the letter yodh.*

That was the name the shepherd had called the charm. It looked very much like the silver talisman hanging from her neck. As she recalled her childhood teachings, she remembered the meaning. The yodh represented worship of the creator.

The world and the heavens were created with the utterance of yodh. Silently she mouthed the letter: *Yodh.* Now she was certain these shapes were letters. *I wonder what is the right sequence? Or is there any order to them at all?* Beth had a sense they were intended to convey some message. This charm was going to help guide her. Some truth was waiting to be revealed through the lovely talisman given to her by the shepherd of Daleth.

Longing for sleep, she eased off the log, which had become as hard as a rock. She stretched out on the cloak Aleph had spread over a fragrant mound of balsam branches. Closing her eyes for just a moment would usher her into a dreamless slumber she was sure. Yet the conviction to be strong caused her to resist. All the pain, suffering, rejection, insults, loneliness, had changed her. Scars from wounds just now beginning to heal were tougher than surrounding skin. Callouses became harder than the flesh underneath.

Fatigue or not, it was critical to open the treasured volume, pull the quill from its hidden chamber, and write to the Prince what was in her heart.

Your words formed me; they have shaped me,
now give me the wisdom to follow you.
May all who fear you find in me a cause for joy,
for I have put my hope in your words.
I know, O Prince, your regulations are fair;
you taught me because I needed it.
Now, let your unfailing love comfort me,
just as you promised your subjects.
Protect me with your tender mercies so I will be safe,
for your instructions are my delight.
Bring disgrace upon the arrogant people
who lured me away from you;
meanwhile, I will concentrate on your truth.
I would like to join with all who respect you,
with those who know your laws.
I want to be blameless in keeping your decrees;
then I will never be ashamed.

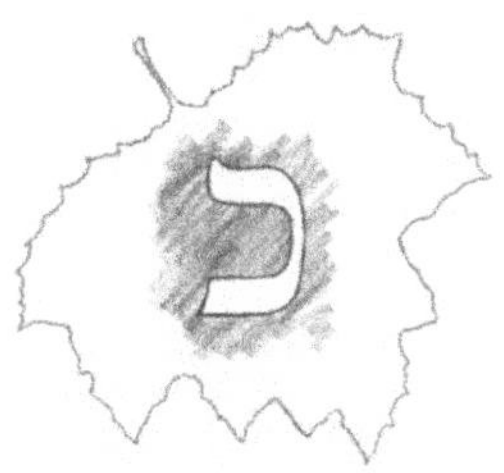

Chapter Eleven

Kaph

WHAT WOKE HER was the huff and munch of her horse. She was eating grass right by Beth's head. The warm breath of her nostrils fluffed Beth's hair. Reaching a hand over, Beth stroked the velvet-soft nose. The mare pushed against her hand and then nuzzled her cheek, so gentle for such a giant. The majesty of this creature was even more evident when she was this close. In the morning quiet a thought came to her. She did not know her name. This patient steed who had carried her for many miles and through untold dangers, still showed her mighty strength. They had walked, trotted, cantered, and galloped uphill and down through rocky valleys and marshy wetlands. Never a hesitation or whimper of complaint.

What did they call this striking black horse, at least seventeen hands high, with a long, full, flowing mane and tail?

Silk smooth to the touch, her hide was black as midnight, with shimmering blue highlights. They had obviously cared for her well in the stable. Washed, curried, combed, even her hooves, each the size of large platter, had been polished to a burnished charcoal patina. Some caretaker had valued this wise and powerful animal that served humans so faithfully.

The graceful head nuzzled closer to her face, inches from the large liquid eyes, Beth studied the black pupil reflecting her face. There was patience, wisdom, and kindness reflected back at her. As she scratched the downy muzzle, names floated through her mind: Midnight? Nightshade? Charcoal? Blacky? Dark Star? Nothing seemed right. She would have to ask Aleph what they called her. Thinking of Aleph, where was her companion?

As if summoned, her servant rustled into the clearing with food and provisions for the journey onward. Beth climbed to her feet, stretched, and accepted two hard-boiled eggs, a small loaf of bread, and an orange from his hand and gratefully began to eat.

"Aleph," she said through a mouthful of food, "what is my horse named? I mean, not my horse, I guess. Perhaps someday it might be mine if the Prince and I ever get together. It is the Prince's horse, isn't it? What did he name her?"

"The horse, Milady, is yours. She is a Friesian, bred in the far northlands with a small infusion of the warm blood from southern stallions. She was born as a set of twins, which is exceedingly rare in all horses. Never had it happened in the annals of the history of this breed. At birth there was great concern they would not live, much less thrive, but beyond all expectations the pair have become king and queen of the Friesians. The Prince named and designated the mare at birth, for you. The stallion he reserved and trained for himself. They are a matched pair. Raised together, her hesitance on this journey has been longing to be reunited with her twin."

"Were you there at the birth, Aleph?"

"Yes, Milady, I watched as they took their first steps and delighted in their growth and strength."

"But what did the Prince name them? What do I call this magnificent mare?"

Aleph paused and reached out with tenderness to stroke the long fetlock on the nearest giant hoof. "The pair were given names no one knows save the Prince. He indicated the names will revealed at the appointed time. Those who care for them call the mare Ashes and the stallion Blackstone." Aleph cocked his head, listening to something Beth could not hear, and abruptly began to pack and prepare to move on.

Beth was still a little in awe at the story of the twin horses and surprised at Aleph being so connected to them. As they moved out, she patted her mare on the strong neck and whispered, "Thank you, Ashes, for your strength, gentle nature, and for carrying me all this way. And thank you, Prince, for this majestic gift. It is tangible evidence of your love."

The trail led over a ridge into a giant valley full of rust-colored stones. It resembled a bowl filled with pebbles. Pebbles, perhaps, but the size was deceiving. As they approached, the pebbles loomed larger and larger until they became massive brown boulders. The full scope of the valley stretched off into the distance, where mountains stood high on the horizon. No path guided them, but between them wound dusty paths leading in all directions. But there was some confidence in the leadership of her companion, who now looked even smaller, dwarfed by the giant stones, kept them on track. Back and forth they traveled, around rocks the size of dwellings, through gullies, down narrow chasms. It all seemed carved from frozen stone.

"Aleph," Beth called ahead, "where is this winding path taking us?"

Calling back over his shoulder, Aleph pointed to distant crags on the other side of the bowl. "To the far side, Milady, at the top of that cliff where the army of the Prince is gathering, is the citadel called *Samekh*, which means the fort of safety. It is also called *Salaj*, the place of forgiveness."

"Am I finally going to meet the Prince there?" Beth asked wistfully.

"No, your highness, he will be revealed to you beyond Samekh at the broken palace on Mount Shin. The horn of victory or surrender will be blown there, with the hope of ultimate peace."

"I understand the citadel being a place of safety, but why forgiveness?" That word unsettled her.

"In truth, Milady, all need to receive and grant forgiveness. All must give and also find forgiveness before victory." He pointed toward the mountain. "That is the place of the final battle. There you will meet the Prince."

Finally, a definite place! Her mind clung to the thought.

"Will I see him? Is he fighting now? How long before we get there? Have you seen the Prince? Do you know him? Aleph, tell me about him! I don't know if I can wait much longer."

"It is not time yet, your highness. We must first go to the Citadel Samekh, Salaj the place of safety and forgiveness." Then, leading the donkey, he continued the walk. Beth knew it was pointless to keep asking questions he could not or would not answer.

The thought of safety was appealing. After being on the run for what seemed like months, a place of security sounded wonderful. Perhaps there might even be water that could be heated for a bath, cleanse her face, do her hair, she might even be able to find some nicer clothes. Then she could try to make herself presentable for the Prince. As she thought of him and his words, the letters, the runes, came back into her head. She opened her book on the pommel and studied the shapes drawn in the past days. The discovery of the letter yodh encouraged her to look for more.

As she analyzed the shapes, she refined the grace of each

as her father had taught her. Each curve and parallel increased the surety that some underlying substance existed in each individual letters. Yes! The letter on the fourth leaf was shaped like a door! Another memory returned from her father's teaching. Excited, she refined the shape slightly and it looked exactly like the gate, the door entrance to the town of Daleth. Two shapes had become clear. More, she knew, would follow. In the valley, sunlight was regularly blocked by the stones and cliffs, making it impossible to see the shadow of her dangling charm. She would have to wait for better light.

Her thoughts reverted to the resolve that had grown in the days before. Setting all her doubts and misgivings aside, Beth reasoned this man, the Prince, loved her. His words were true. The gift of Ashes testified to it. He said he wanted to marry her. If she became queen, she would sit at his side to lead the kingdom. Our kingdom. Then came a startling thought: *This war raging around us is a battle for my kingdom! If I am to be a part of the victory or defeat, I might have to fight!*

Now, that thought was exciting! Memories of the jousting clashes and sword combats she had witnessed outside the castle walls thrilled her. Sitting passive on her horse did not, nor had it ever been her idea of excitement. Friesians had been bred for battle. Perhaps she, too, was intended to be in the conflict. Her temperament was not of a bystander. *This is something I need to find out about.*

"Aleph," she called out. "Stop, I need to ask you something."

"Now is a good time, Milady, to pause for water and rest."

"No . . . yes, we can do that. But I have to ask you something important."

"Yes, Milady." He answered amiably as he poured some water out for her, the horse, the donkey, and lastly himself.

"Aleph . . ." Beth pondered on how best to ask the question. "Do you think the Prince wants me to be in the battle? He was sent off for a time into war as a soldier to defend the kingdom. I mean, if the battle needs warriors, I know fighting someone like Gimmel would be pointless for me, but could I train for a fight? If the Prince had to, should not I, as well?"

Standing in the shadow of one of the boulders, with his peaked hat low on his forehead Beth could not see the expression on his face. Yet the tone of his voice seemed to convey it all.

"The battle is for everyone, Milady. For the kingdom to be liberated, as many as are willing must fight. You . . . forgive me for casting any doubt, perhaps you might be unable or unwilling, but the Prince longs to have you at his side in the battle against the forces of Belial."

"What!" Beth stomped her foot in the stirrup angrily. "Are you saying I am too feeble or scared to fight? I don't know how to use weapons, but I can learn! I am not feeble, and I am not scared! And if the Prince wants me to fight at his side, I will!" In her huff, she had yanked the reigns, which caused Ashes to turn her head toward Beth with a curious snort and what seemed to be a skeptical look in her eye.

A questioning sound came from Aleph as well, but she decided to ignore it.

"Look," she went on with some heat in her voice. "You are a stable hand. I don't know if you have any knowledge of weapons and warfare. I guess in taking care of the horses, you are contributing to the battle. But if I am going to be a monarch, then we better win, or there won't be any kingdom to reign over. Can't I do something?"

Aleph stepped closer to the mare. His voice was still amiable but he spoke firmly.

"Yes, Milady, weapons are available, and you can be taught. It is also critical to know that much of the real battle is fought in the unseen world of the soul. This battle is against powers, authorities in spiritual places. It is a battle of words and thoughts and feelings."

"Well," Beth said, lifting her head back and furrowing her brows. "I don't know about the spiritual battle, I don't have any knowledge about those things. But I would feel better if I had a sword, a helmet, a shield, maybe, or even a dagger. Can you take me somewhere I can learn to use these weapons of warfare?"

"It is appropriate that your interest should surface with this stage of our journey, Milady. We are within half a day's travel from a place that can provide every weapon you could want and the instructions in how to use them. The inner battle, you must learn from the spirit."

"What, then, are we waiting for?" Jingling the reigns and urging Ashes to move forward with her heels. "Show me the way." Aleph nodded agreeably and turned again to the maze of boulders where no roads and no straight path guided them.

Two phrases came back to her from Aleph's starling conversation. *The Prince longs for me to be at his side in the battle.* That was a revelation. The words he had poured out in the letters convinced her of his love. They spoke of a battle, but she had no idea it involved fighting with him at his side. She could do that. Her resolve to continue the journey strengthened that conviction. Yet, *what is this about fighting an inner battle learned from the spirit?* What unseen forces, what powers in high places? It made her dizzy. *How does that work? What weapons will be available for that? A sword, a shield, a spear, I can understand—but how do I fight something I can't see?*

The boys she played with in her neighborhood tolerated her as she charged into battle against them using wooden sticks as swords, pot lids as shields, and broom handles as spears. A real battle, she knew, would be totally different than the *whack-whack* of wooden sticks and the *clang* of tin. The sting of getting poked with a broom handle was not like the bloody wounds she saw on Gimmel and his soldiers. Could she handle the real thing? She thought about that for a long time. *I guess,* she thought, *I am going to find out.*

As they wove their way in and out of the pillars and boulders of the natural bowl they were traversing, up near the rim they began to see people digging, chopping away at the rocks. Loads of stones were being transported in baskets carried on their heads.

"Aleph, what are these people digging for? Are they mining for something?" Without stopping, he called over his shoulder.

"These are the mines in the valley of Kaph. Stones for building, iron for weapons, jewels for decorating the palaces and clothing of kings. Gold and silver are the prize. These miners also are slaves of Belial; they are never given rest."

Turning a corner in their meanderings, Aleph at last entered the mouth of a mammoth cave. Hay, straw, and the familiar smells of a stable made it clear it was used as a natural barn. Cool air flowed from the darker recesses. Other animals stirred and munched around them. Iron rings provided places for tethering the horses and wooden troughs lined the walls for feed.

Always setting the needs of others first, Aleph started scooping out feed and water for the mare and donkey and offered his hand for Beth to dismount, but she was too excited to wait and dropped to the ground on her own. Off in the distance below she heard the clang of metal hammers on anvils and saw fires, torches, and sparks flying around what must be the work of many blacksmiths. As she started to edge toward the sound and fire, Aleph halted her.

"Wait, Milady, I am known, but you are not. These metalsmiths are secretly loyal to the Prince, yet they might not recognize his choice of bride." After removing saddle and bridle, scrubbing down horse and donkey with a burlap cloth, he picked up his small rucksack along with Beth's bag and moved into the darker part of the cave. Not more than a few strides into the tunnel two sentries stepped from the shadows carrying torches and long spears.

"Halt, what purpose do you have in venturing into the caves of Kaph?" the sentries asked Aleph.

He pushed his beaked cap up onto his forehead the torchlight shone directly on his face. "It is I, Aleph." He spoke with authority.

In that moment a look of awe and surprise crossed the faces of the sentries. They looked at Beth, back at him, then at each other, and began to back away.

"Wipe the surprise from your faces," Aleph continued quickly. "Make no indication we are different than any other seekers of armament. Say nothing of this to anyone. This is the Lady Beth, chosen by the Prince to be his bride. She has left the castle on a journey to the battlefront. We are traveling to the keep at Samekh, on the slopes of Mount Shin."

The two straightened to a more soldierly stance. The first spoke crisply. "How, then, can we be of service?"

"The Lady Beth will need armor and weapons." Aleph

pointed at Beth. "Those fit for her size and designed for her exalted position."

"It will be our pleasure," the two sentries spoke as one, and a well-oiled machine went to work.

With a whistle, a rather hefty, stern-faced matron appeared with a young woman behind her. They looked so much alike as to be mother and daughter. The girl seemed shy, yet her mannerisms exhibited some handicap that must have come from birth. They stepped from around a stone pillar and stood beside the sentries. A brief intense conversation was whispered to the women, causing their eyes to open wide. Instantly they bowed, took Beth by the hand, and led her into a well-lit cave obviously suited for measuring and sewing.

The woman introduced herself. "I am Kaph," she spoke proudly. "I was born in this valley and named for it. This is my grown child, Kaphet." With some clumsiness but very gently, the young girl indicated she wanted to remove Beth's cloak and dress. What became immediately visible as she unlaced and removed her clothing were the open wounds on her shoulders and scars on her arms.

Taken aback, a small gasp slipped from Kaphet's lips. She turned to her mother, a look of anguish on her face. Pain filled her eyes. The matron looked over and breathed a long deep sigh. She knew exactly what needed to be done. Gone for less than a minute she returned with a bowl of water, basket of ointments and an armful of cloth that resembled bandages. As she cared for her wounds with sure hands and nimble fingers, Beth could tell Kaph had done this often before. Without interrupting her mother's ministrations—cleaning, applying soothing ointments, and bandaging—the girl Kaphet began taking Beth's measurements.

"Wounds of war," Kaph muttered. "Burns for certain, but wounds and scars from the battle fought within." Then speaking sternly to Beth, Kaph with a great wellspring of compassion murmured, "These wounds on your arms can be healed. Wounds I cannot see must be healed by the spirit." Looking directly into Beth's face, she said, "Those are the wounds you carry on your soul."

There it was again. Wounds of the spirit. What were they, and how did this woman Kaph know? Memories, masked and cauterized for a time by the burns on her arms, surfaced quickly. They had been forced down by shame and fear. Beth had told no one. Images of her defilement she had vainly hoped would drift quietly into forgetfulness returned, tightening her throat. Bile rising from her stomach lurched with the feeling of wanting to throw up. A forced swallow pushed it down again.

Beth, startled at Kaph's insight, asked in a choked voice, "Lady Kaph, how, then, can the soul wounds be healed?"

Still looking open-faced into Beth's eyes, Kaph responded softly with just one word. "Forgiveness."

Revolted at the impossibility of that thought, clenching her teeth, Beth shook her head. *Well, that will never happen.*

She looked toward Kaphet. With lips pursed tight and tears streaming down her cheeks, the young girl nodded in agreement with her mother. Wiping her nose with a delicate hankie, Kaphet continued to measure every part of Beth's body, head to feet, in three directions. Beth longed to reach out and comfort Kaphet but did not know how.

Attempting to get past that terrible word rolling around in her head, Beth cleared her throat. "Lady Kaph, I know Aleph, my servant, also has wounds that need tending." Beth noticed a pained expression flicker in Kaph's eyes, although she looked down to cover for it. "Could you see to his care as well? He does not complain of his ailments, yet they are severe. He was beaten—" Beth's voice cracked, exposing feelings for Aleph that had been sown and taken root during their journey. "He was beaten, because of my . . . my stubbornness."

A surprised look came from Kaph. She raised her brows then responded. "Thy honesty is noted. I will see to it immediately, Milady."

Measuring complete, Kaph announced "Weapons and armor for you will require more than a fortnight to forge."

"Fourteen days?" Beth sighed. "That is an eternity. Don't you know I am on a quest? The Prince is waiting for me. I must return to the journey."

"It cannot be helped, Milady, the protection you need and weapons worthy of your hand, take care and skill. They cannot be rushed." Beth could not see the expression on

Kaph's face as she packed and quickly left.

Kaphet, guiding her back to the stable cave, veered into a side cavern to show a small smoky alcove prepared for her.

"I, I must say," she said with a stutter, "I will, I will return d–daily to salve your wounds. To re–replace the bandages, I, I will. My mother, I must say, has prepared a healing draught for you, m–my lady. You must drink it, you must." Slowly Kaphet poured a wine-colored liquid into a cup and watched Beth swallow it all. Beth lay back on the pallet and almost immediately fell into a profound, dreamless sleep.

‡ ‡ ‡

BETH SLEPT A long time. With no sunlight, no candles, the gray light filtering in from the barn, when she awoke gave her no idea what time or day or night it was. She had faint, numerous recollections of Kaphet replacing her bandages. More times than she could remember she swallowed the healing draught. And somewhere in the background was always the anxious face of Aleph.

When Beth finally came fully awake, she stood and walked to a lighted torch in the main barn, lit some candles in her niche to look over her condition. In the corner was a shelf with basin, pitcher, cleaning cloths, and a small mirror hung on a protruding rock. She was significantly rested. Her arms no longer stabbed painfully when she moved them but she felt disheveled, like an unmade bed. What she saw in the mirror confirmed it. Matted in clumps to her head, her hair looked like it would never be clean, straight, or smooth again. Eyes sunken with dark bruises underneath were bloodshot from the smoke in the air, haunted-looking windows into a damaged soul.

The bandages were gone but large red welts remained, slashing down her arms and reaching to her red and still-chapped hands. Weeks, perhaps months of scrubbing burnt pots had reddened and dried out her flaking skin, broken her nails to the quick, and perhaps permanently injured her fingers. The Prince would be horrified seeing her now. Embarrassed by what he saw, he would walk away from the wretched, ugly, scarred, and soul-wounded creature who stood before him. These thoughts were testing again her resolve to continue the journey. Lady Kaph had spoken a word for healing that soul wound, but she could barely think the word, much less speak it or act upon it.

What warred against her was the feeling that if the Prince ever found out, if he knew what had happened, what had been forced upon her, the quest, the dream would be over. Branded as tarnished, damaged goods, he would assuredly reject her as his bride. A great sob was rising into the back of her throat. But something unexplained choked it off.

A voice—as if rising from the spirit charm around her neck, rising into her mind like fresh spring water flowing into a dark scummy pond. *I will never leave you, nor forsake you! The book! Where are my letters?*

Almost tripping in her haste, Beth ran to her sleeping

ledge. The book was gone! Throwing the blankets aside. Snatching at the cloak. Digging through the straw that made up her sleeping pallet, she found nothing. In a panic she ran towards the exit. One last glimpse on the way out. There it was!

Relief poured in like a healing balm. On the shelf behind the pitcher was the book. Her letters from the Prince. As so often before, she quieted her damaged spirit, soothed her wounds, calmed her fears of abandonment, covered her wretchedness in the cleansing, mending words of the Prince. He had written about his own suffering, sacrifice, and healing. At each time of conflict, it was clear that in the middle of the pain, his thoughts were of her. His long days and sleepless nights were spent thinking of how dear it would be when they were together. The words came off the page as if breathed.

After long, hours refilling her dry, fearful, damaged, empty soul, she pulled the quill from the spine with quivering fingers and wrote.

I am heart sick waiting for you to rescue me;
but I still believe in your words.
My eyes are getting heavy watching,
waiting for you to fulfill your promise.
How long will I have to look for your comfort?
Smoke has burned my eyes, they are blurry with tears,
yet I fixed them on your instructions.

How long do I have to wait for you
to judge those who persecuted me?
My arrogant enemies are still pursuing me
but they don't understand about your protection.
I believe that safety with you is a sure thing
but the enemy is chasing me down with lies; please help me!
They almost made me end it all,
but I remembered your sweet encouragement,
and your steadfast love kept giving me life,
So, I will keep all of your words in my mouth.

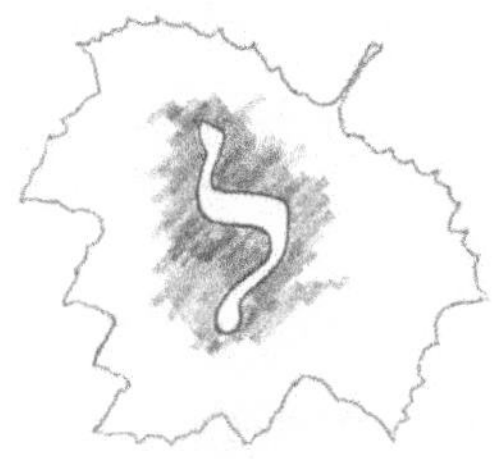

Chapter Twelve

Lamedh

AS THE LAST word of her meditation was written with passion on the page a soft voice spoke from the entrance to the alcove. Beth looked up. Standing, hands clasped behind her back, a curious smile on her slightly misshapen face, was Kaphet. With an awkward curtsy, head tilted to one side she asked,

"Is m–Milady feeling, I should say, f–feeling better?"

"Very well, Kaphet," replied Beth in a much softer tone than she would have used in former times. How could she speak harshly to this kind person who had daily cared for her and dressed her wounds? "I could use a bath and some clean clothes. And I have to do something with this tangle of hair. Dear Kaphet, is that something you can help with?"

"Y–yes, Milady. I will say, th–there is, I mean to say, I will lead you to the d–delightful hot s–springs in a lower cave where, I will say, a b–bath, and clean clothing await you. They are not the attire worthy of a p–princess, but it, it is all we, I will say, all I have. Shortly, your excellency will be fit, I will say, fitted with the armaments designed and made just for you."

With a crooked grin, Kaphet lifted her shoulders and led the way. As they walked, Kaphet spoke again with deference and a small nod of her head. "This is a g–great honor, m–Milady, to be in your presence. We are fearful here in the c–caves and the mines below, I will say. Many foretold of the coming war, b–but not certain of th–th–th . . ." Unable to finish, she turned with embarrassment on her face. "I will s–say, not sure of the ending. But the coming of the princess has given us hope."

Fresh in her mind from her meditations that morning, Beth repeated her earlier thoughts. "Well, sweet Kaphet, I am of no consequence, princess or not. The words of the Prince, they are our hope, and he wrote to me or rather, he has written, "In this world, you will be trouble, but don't be afraid, I have overcome the world."

A big wide grin opened Kaphet's face. "I w–was assured you would g–give us hope. One–one thing I must confess, Milady. Your book t–tempted me while you were sleeping. And I read, I must say, read some for myself. Would, could you f–forgive me?"

There was that word again. Beth swept it aside, laughed, and approached Kaphet, embracing her with a tight hug.

"Oh, my friend, you can read from my book as long as I am here. It is written, I am told often, not just for me. It is for you as well."

Kaphet blushed fiercely. "Not true, m–Milady, the words are yours, b–but they do encourage us all. I would say, I would ask one thing I find m–most curious. Might I ask it?"

Beth nodded curiously, wondering what sort of question Kaphet would ask. "Of course, Kaphet, what do you want to know?"

"I did, notice, I would say, in the words you write, you speak of him, The Prince, I would say, you speak of Him as your lord, and his words as rules and laws. Is this the way a wife will, must, I would say, should so speak to her husband?"

Beth laughed again, then turned thoughtful. "You are right in asking, Kaphet. It is a good question." She frowned and looked up at the ceiling, thinking about how to explain what she felt inside. "See, Kaphet, if these letters and words are really from the Prince himself, he is one day going to be the true King of the entire land. He will rule everything. What he says will be the law of the kingdom. If I am ever his wife, I will be at his side as his partner till death parts us, but he will always be the master of his domain. I will also be a subject in his realm, and humbly respect him as King. That is what a wife does. She loves her husband but honors his role in the world. Do you understand, dear Kaphet?"

Kaphet was hanging on Beth's every word. Whether she

could fathom any of it, Beth did not know. But with an understanding beyond intelligence, a wisdom above intellect, Kaphet nodded assent. "I do, it does, Milady. Th, it is a good word. Now how about a bath and c–clean clothes?"

Down multiple flights of stairs, endless landings, and into wandering tunnels, Beth followed Kaphet's careful steps into hotter and hotter caverns with steam rising off the floor. A door appeared before them, an actual door with hardware, hinges, and a handle.

"This, m–Milady, I will say, this is the bath. Some clean clothes of mine. They have been w–worn, but I will say, I, I washed them well." Pulling open the door, a cloud of steam billowed out. "They are f–folded on the shelf."

‡ ‡ ‡

OH, HOW SHE would have loved staying in the natural hot water pool and steam bath until all her skin wrinkled like Tzaddi's face. But the third time Kaphet opened the door to peek in, Beth resigned herself to face the fitting of the armaments.

Clothed in Kaphet's soft, worn but carefully handmade shift, feeling so much better, Beth allowed her guide to lead her to a fitting room designed, she could tell, to impress. High ceilings arched over walls sloped outward to emphasize the size of the room. More lit torches than were necessary reflected off hundreds of shields, helmets, swords, lances, suits of chain mail that covered the walls. Next to a table at one side of the room stood a screen for changing and Kaphet's mother. Behind her lounged a tall whippet of a man, with pins sticking into his foppish hat. On his hip rode a holster fitted with large scissors. Off to one side, a strong, handsome, muscular warrior caught Beth's eye. Standing a little straighter, she wondered, *Could he be my Prince?*

No . . . her shoulders sagged. I am sure when I see him, my heart will explode. I will know immediately.

Then Kaphet stepped in behind her mother, patting her hands together with obvious excitement. The other item in the room was some sort of a large wooden figure, outfitted with armor and mounted on a complicated swivel device. Oh, and Aleph, a quiet presence who cared for the horses, shoveled manure, and would fetch anything necessary when needed. Yet something in his manner indicated his presence was no longer just as an impartial observer.

"This," Kaph said, pointing to the tailor, "is my assistant and that"—she gestured toward the soldier—"is Master Lamedh. He will instruct you in the use of armor and weapons."

The fitting process was tedious, but incredibly meticulous. Behind the screen she slipped on the undergarments which fit perfectly, and the protective armor amazed her with its beauty and craftsmanship. It began with the helmet. What seemed like a fragile, delicate swoop of silvered metal with a chin strap in fact, proved to be practical safety, as demonstrated by Master Lamedh when he banged a sword handle on it after placing it on Beth's head. Chain mail so fine as to appear woven, covered her from neck to thigh. A belt with scabbard of flexible metal strips around her hips, and there were sturdy leather boots. A rounded shield with the crest of the Prince emblazoned in the center. And the sword, *Oh my!* What a dainty, exquisite, subtle weapon, almost the size of a dagger.

Beth lifted it and looked at it with a frown. "Is this my lone offensive weapon I get? It looks just a bit . . . a bit ineffective."

In a move almost too quick to follow with the human eye, Lamedh snatched the dainty-looking sword from Beth's hand and swung, sliced, and impaled the wooden soldier. Ringing sounds of steel on steel clanged around the room. Shards of wood, metal, and leather flew into the air. Rocking fiercely on its swivel, the wooden figure looked totally defeated. Gently Master Lamedh set the blade, clearly unharmed, back on the table in front of Beth, who was wide-eyed and impressed.

Master Lamedh bowed his head briefly toward the sword. "The sword, your highness, as all your armor, is divinely powerful. With them, you will be able conquer a fortress." He paused, looking over her new outfit. "Now, Milady, you must learn.

"I know," Beth replied. "I know nothing of real warfare, and I am not particularly strong, but—"

"Your weakness," began Lamedh with his first lesson,

"will be your strength."

And so it was. Each day Kaphet, would arrive at some early hour, help Beth put on her armor, and lead her to the training room where Master Lamedh would work her until perspiration dripped down her face through the mail and into her boots. Other trainers gave short lessons on specifics, like the use of shield, bow and arrows, fighting on horseback, and unusual weapons. On occasion a group of gray bearded elders observed her training, commenting on various finer points of attack and defense.

Because she returned at the end of each session sore and bruised, Kaphet would lead her to the hot springs, then accompany her to the sleeping quarters while meekly asking questions along the way. She shared her fears, need of affirmation, and found encouragement in the words and phrases Beth would quote from her book of letters. Beth's heart bonded with this simple, childlike young woman who might never know a man who would love her. Perhaps never have a wedding, certainly no Prince would ever write love letters for her. As Kaphet would leave each evening. Beth would embrace her and wish her happy dreams and peaceful sleep.

‡ ‡ ‡

"SKILL COMES WITH repetition and wise training," quoted Master Lamedh often, and he gave her the opportunity for both. Beth worked hard and her efforts paid off. While resting between the fierce physical lessons involving nimbleness of foot, accurate positioning of the shield, swiftness and precision with the sword, Kaph, sitting at her side, would insert brief words of wisdom. She spoke little, but what Beth garnered was insights into fighting the internal battle and the healing of soul-wounds.

Aleph, still the quiet presence, was always in the background. On rare occasions, as the training went on, their eyes would meet and, with a smile that at times seemed flirtatious, he would nod in approval. Always under the scrutinizing evaluations of Master Lamedh, Beth wondered, *Am I working harder to please Aleph than my teacher?* Her instructor pointed out the flaws, mistakes, and the finer points of attack and defense. Whenever Aleph spoke, it was words of encouragement and approval.

The war, Beth heard from chatty Kaphet, was still confined to skirmishes. Sometimes they prevailed, sometimes were defeated, but significant victories were being won in Beth's soul. Each day without fail, Beth would read and reread the words that brought her faith, hope, and love. Each night, without neglect, by lamplight she would write how she was learning, growing, and healing. Even after the weariness of training, she would also study the leaf-letters copied carefully from the flickering shadows of her spirit-charm. No new letters in the mystical alphabet had come to light, but the belief in some deeper meaning remained.

‡ ‡ ‡

THE DAY CAME when she could wait no longer. As the session finally ended, Beth approached her mentor.

"Master Lamedh, I think I am ready," Beth said with confidence.

He gave a rare smile. "You have learned much, Milady, though there is much I could still teach you. A student subject to the teacher and obedient to the training can continue to learn." The smile vanished. "One who is impatient can no longer grow." He paused, "I am not yet sure. Perhaps it is time for you to face your fears."

A quiet *ahem* from behind him caused Lamedh to turn.

"She has worked hard, Master," Aleph said. "More can be perfected in the actual battle."

Lamedh nodded his agreement at Aleph. "Well said and true. And the battle is even now almost at our door." Surprised that Master Lamedh would acknowledge her stable hand, Beth looked toward Aleph hoping to catch his approving eye, only to find him stooping to retrieve some dropped weapon.

After putting aside his own weapons and armor, Master Lamedh called for the tailor, who approached carrying a decorated box with both hands. From the box, he withdrew a colorful, silk banner bearing the symbol, the crest of the kingdom of the Prince. With great ceremony he draped it across Beth's shoulders. Then he tapped his well-used sword on first one shoulder, then the other, finally on her head. Quoting an ancient warrior's blessing, he said, "O, protector of the weak, who humbles the arrogant and gives the outcome in every battle, I plead, surround this chosen young warrior with your protection and give her the victory you have prepared." Walking backward in honor and respect, Master Lamedh bowed his way out from the room. Aleph, Kaph, Kaphet, and Beth traced their way back to the upper caves to the animal barn and the cavern where Beth slept.

That night, Kaphet embraced Beth long and tightly, wishing her victory. She awkwardly pleaded one thing. "Y–your highness, I would say, w–would ask please, that you would not forget us, when y–you are queen, would you return and grace us w–with, a visit to your hum, I would say, humble servants?"

"Of course, dear Kaphet, if there is any way I can return, I will." Yet as Beth spoke the words, there was no confidence in them. Tearfully Kaphet pulled away, leaving Beth alone. Before allowing her tired, aching body the rest it needed, Beth walked outside into the clear night. Stars shone, bright, sharp and so close they could almost be touched. The sparkle in the eyes of Tzaddi had shone like that as she spoke of the Prince. Feelings of awe at the beauty of it all, and fear for what lay ahead, were mingled with the long-delayed desire to find her Prince.

She stood, face upward toward the heavens, watching the night sky ablaze with stars. Weariness resting heavy on her shoulders and weighty questions on her mind, she rejected memories of the past and nervousness about her future. Then, knowing it was late, she slipped back to her quarters. With tender hands, she took her precious book, now showing significant wear on the cover and sides, and penned her thoughts, knowing the real battle would begin soon.

Your eternal word, O Prince,
stands firm in the heavens.
Your faithfulness extends to every generation,
as enduring as the stars and earth you rule over.
Your regulations remain true to this day,
for everything serves your plans.
If your instructions had not sustained me with joy,
I would have died in my misery.
I will never forget your commandments,
for by them you gave me life.
I am yours; you will continue to rescue me!
For I have worked hard at obeying your teachings.
Though the wicked hide along the way to kill me,
I will quietly keep my mind on your laws.
Even perfection has its limits,
but your commands have no end.

Chapter Thirteen

Mem

BACK ON THE trail, Aleph in the lead with his donkey loaded with food and armaments, followed by Beth on her majestic Friesian mare, they left behind a small band of well-wishers. Lamedh, stern with his arms crossed. Kaph, beside him waving a lace handkerchief, her lanky assistant behind her winding thread on a spool as if totally disinterested. A clump of serious blacksmiths and metalworkers stood in the back, looking on with wonder.

Then Kaphet, out front, bouncing up and down on her toes, waving with both hands, tears in her eyes, saying over and over, "P–please come back, p–please, c–come b–ack!

Embarrassed by the fanfare and unnecessary send-off, Beth smiled dutifully, waved, and promised, mostly for Kaphet's sake, she would return.

Soon, out of sight of the cheering throng, Aleph pointed

upward toward the peak he had referred to as Mount Shin. "That, Milady, is the end of our journey. The place of struggle, the final battle and ultimate sacrifice, and if victory, the promise of lasting peace." He seemed to say it with a somber tone. "A desert, a lake, and a mighty chasm are still between us and the summit, but the end is in sight."

"It honestly is a relief to at least have a destination we can see. Is the Prince already there, Aleph?"

"His highness the Prince will be there soon, Milady. He also needed to embark on a journey to be humbled and tested before reaching Mount Shin. It is there where everything will be revealed. All will be made clear."

Those words were a bit unsettling to her, but just the reality of having the destination in view gave her a thrill. She felt ready. Strong, rested, healed of her wounds, Beth had been trained in the way of war and was bringing weapons and armor with her. She wanted to spur Ashes to a faster pace, to fight whatever battles needed to be fought, defeat the enemy and meet her Prince. A jolt of energy shot through her from her head down to the fingers of her sword-wielding arm clenched on Ashes's reigns. As if sensing her mood, Aleph picked up the pace. His donkey, though heavily burdened, *clip-clopped* a bit faster, with Ashes moving smoothly behind, ears pricked with anticipation.

All day they traveled. Rising up the far edge of the bowl-shaped valley full of stones they could see a vast, red desert landscape. It contained no vegetation. No outcropping. No ridges or gullies. Nothing alive or dead on this broad expanse of sand. In the far distance, the mountain Shin rose from the flatness to the peak standing upright like a three-pronged fork. Aleph paused at a small brook to fill the leather containers strapped to the donkey's saddle and soak every bit of clothing and fabric they had with them, then tied everything tightly as possible, including the travel cloaks covering all but their eyes.

"From here, Milady, we travel at night. Surviving this wilderness in the day is impossible. It would also help, if you are able, to walk and lead the mare. She is strong, but this desert will test her as well. The winds are often fierce enough to blow you from the saddle. It is for safety." Without complaint, Beth determined to be the good soldier prepared for battle.

The sun, sinking below the high range of mountains, shone for an instant through the three broken pillars called Shin, then winked out. Darkness fell like heavy drapery. Aleph stopped briefly, pulling the brass and silver lamp from his donkey's saddle bag. Placing a few carbide stones in the bottom section, he dribbled a precious amount of water in the top. To Beth's amazement, the stones caught fire and burned with a bright light. *How can stones and water create fire?* she wondered.

Then they moved forward into the sandy expanse, leading their mounts into the darkness of the night. Still intense heat from the desert radiated upward, searing any living thing. Their feet, protected by heavy leather boots, survived the burning by stepping quickly across the scorched landscape.

Very soon, every soaked article of clothing and fabric was sucked dry. Sips of water from the leather bags were never enough to quench their thirst. Sand sliding under their feet clutched at their shoes and made each step like two. On and on and on they trekked. How Aleph knew where he was going, Beth did not know. Her guide was the light from the bronze lamp with silver trim which he held high. A haze of dust or clouds covered the sky from horizon to horizon, blanketing any sight of stars or moon.

Then the wind came.

With it, flames of dust whipped them in an inferno of burning red sand. Beating against them, the four pilgrims struggled against the fiery furnace. Beth could only blindly follow the dark silhouette created by the dim light of the lamp barely visible ahead.

Stories were told of those who were lost in this endless oven by walking in circles until they fell, and heat sucked all life from their bones. Hour after hour the trek continued. Once during a brief respite did they stop to drink sparingly. Still the dim figure holding the lamp aloft led them through the furnace.

Well after the midnight hour the wind began to subside. The heat began to lessen. With each step Beth fortified herself with words from the Prince. Words that had become embedded in her memory. Strength flowed from the words. Hope found in those phrases watered her seedling faith. Love in the letters written for her, gave her greater love in return for him.

Beth also rehearsed the lessons Master Lamedh had drilled into her head. Skills she had practiced, repeated over and over again, gave her confidence that she was prepared to face her enemies. Even the Prince's words encouraged her: *Your learning surpasses even some of those who have instructed you.* The motivation to fight alongside her Prince energized her. Successes in training gave her confidence she would not fail. Even when the last drop of water drained from their bags, she knew they would reach the other side.

‡ ‡ ‡

BEHIND HER, GRAY light began seeping over the horizon. Many miles of walking in the fluid terrain sucking at her feet continued to drag her down. Yet in the growing light, on the far horizon, she could see a narrow sliver of blue, an aqua ribbon stretched across the barren wasteland.

"Aleph", she croaked through dry lips, "what is that I see ahead?"

"That, Milady, is Loch Mem," he answered, focused on reaching the life-giving water ahead. "The waters of Loch Mem are pure, fresh, and salvation for the thirsty desert traveler."

Indeed it was.

Falling gratefully face first with a splash into the cool clear water, Beth drank until she could drink no more. Horse and donkey also slaked their thirst. But Aleph, reserved and patient, seemed unhurried. Down on one knee, his eyes open and alert, looking cautiously from one side to the other, he scooped the clear water with his hand, sipping without a sound.

The desert heat almost immediately dissipated in cool breezes coming off the crystal blue lake. Pushing her wet hair back off her face, Beth began looking around. Aleph had moved the animals into the shade of a rock outcropping to protect them from the daytime heat. Patches of grass gave them something to munch on. Tired as they were, hunger inspired them to put together a small breakfast in the shade while looking out upon the teal waters of Loch Mem.

"What now, Aleph?" Beth asked through a mouthful of rice cake. Pointing upward she asked, "I can see the prongs of Mount Shin. How do we get there from here?" The pressure to move onward was tempered by the fatigue of walking all night. Still longing to get to the battlefront and find the Prince, she said, "I mean, how do we get across the lake? Surely, we can't swim?"

"In due time, Milady," Aleph said calmly. "You are correct. It is considerably too far to swim for either of us, and I am sure the mare and the donkey would not survive. We will summon our transport tonight. We must wait here until then."

"Tonight?" Beth responded with a tired sigh. Growing self-control prevented her from saying what she was thinking, which was, I have come all this way. I have struggled, suffered, and been abused. I have trained and learned how to fight. I don't want to wait.

"Yes, your highness, there are seasons when we struggle and make haste. There are seasons when we must wait. The seasons of waiting, can be used to rest, refresh in preparation for the battle ahead."

Puzzled she wondered, *how did he do that. It almost seems at times, as if Aleph knows what I am thinking.*

She sat peering out across the flat expanse of water. "How, then, do we summon this boat?"

"We signal with three fires on the shore. The craft will then arrive in the morning."

"Oh, they arrive tomorrow?"

"Yes, Milady. Now, I would advise you to sleep."

There it was again. Aleph telling her what to do. It had been a long time since she had been irritated at him. Under the weight of her fatigue, it was a struggle to not let it irritate her now.

"I am sorry for being anxious, Aleph, I think you understand." He was right, he had her best interests at heart. She just let it go.

In her precious letters, the Prince had encouraged her to be still and know. He admonished her to have a quiet heart. She would rest.

The morning passed slowly but as the sun came overhead, Beth noticed the sunlight, shining through a crack in the rock she leaned against. The conditions seemed right for examining the shadow-runes made by her charm. Taking it from around her neck she twirled it above a blank page in her book. Now in full daylight the shadows multiplied. The bent rune, split at the bottom, was *gimmel.* Then *vau*, *zayin*, and *heth*, from the evil kingdom, became clear. She shuddered at the memory of that experience. Her father's lessons began returning in bursts that surprised her. *Teith* was the sad, white face of the countess who made the wrong choice.

How quickly the understanding of the images came! These were the letters she had been taught during childhood, but never understood. *Lamedh*, the Master Teacher, and *kaph*, who had instructed her about the inner battle. An image then appeared that sparked some joy. It was *beit*, or Beth, her own name. But as the shadow image spun in the sunbeam, it combined with other letters to quickly form, house, home, creator, artist, and finally the name of her father, Baruch.

Strong emotions came unbidden. Sadness at the loss of her kind, gentle mother. Fear and sorrow for her stern father. All were mingled as they rose up on this stream of memories flowing from times she listened to her mother's songs sitting with her father at his art table, learning the shapes of letters that were now making sense.

It slowly dawned on her that all of life was light and

shadow. A reality and silhouette. The letters connecting her story, in the same way, each had meaning and a reflection. Dark needed the light. Grief would drag you into depression if there was no hope of reciprocal joy. Compassion grew when identifying with someone else's sorrow. Satisfaction increased corresponding to the size of the struggle overcome.

She had learned that victory would be sweeter if the battle was fierce. Ahh, the battle. Yes, there was warfare ahead, but victory was the goal.

The day had been restful. Meditating on the truth of the letters had cleared her mind. Thinking about the fight to come, her body twitched slightly with involuntary movements, repeated hundreds of times under the tutelage of Master Lamedh. The other instructors had trained her to a point, but she had surpassed them.

She felt strong. She felt ready, yet much of the perseverance to endure had come from the letters of the Prince. What I am reading about; his stand for truth, the compassion he shows to his own subjects, all blended with his wisdom, really do inspire me, she thought.

The Prince told of returning to the castle after being wounded in battle and recuperating as he gazed down at her from the nursing ward. His love for her, he claimed, was healing and strength. The battle was still raging as he wrote, and he longed to claim final victory. *All this time*, thought Beth, *he was writing these letters, binding them, and impressing upon Tzaddi to faithfully deliver them to me.*

The last few hours of daylight were spent reading from them again. It left her with few chapters unread. With quill in hand, new thoughts of love were recorded on the next page.

Oh, how I love your precious story,
I think about it all day long.
Your powerful words make me stronger than
my enemies,
for they are my constant guide.
Yes, I have been given more insight than my teachers,
for I am always thinking of your answers.
I am even wiser than the elders,
for I have kept your admonitions.
I will not walk on any evil paths again,
so that I will remain obedient to your word.
I haven't turned away from your regulations,
for you have taught me well.
How sweet your words taste to me;
they are sweeter than honey.
Your declarations give me understanding,
no wonder I hate every deceitful way.

As the sun settled at the far end of the quiet waters, Loch Mem deepened to aquamarine, dark-blue, navy, to black. Busy collecting wood as Beth wrote, Aleph soon had three piles on the shore stacked ready for a flame. Scrub trees were abundant along the desert and driftwood littered the beach.

Looking out over the inky waters, he stood silent for a long time, as still as one of the stones on the shore. Beth finished her writing and watched as his shadow lengthened, blending into the darkness. After relighting the brass lamp, Aleph handed it to Beth, then lit the first fire. Pulling a flaming brand from it, he then lit the second two.

"We must keep the fires lit through the night," he instructed, "to signal our need for conveyance to the other shore." Then wrapped himself in his travel cloak and sat before the middle fire, bowed his head on his knees, and slept. The rest of this band of travelers slept also: two slept on soft sand covered by their cloaks, two standing like sentinels on either side. The lamp burned brightly late into the night. As each awoke in turn, Beth and Aleph tossed more wood on the fires and stoked them into flame. When the fires flared up, they slept again.

Chapter Fourteen

Nun

THREE BLACKENED RINGS were all that remained of the signal fires lit by Aleph, and the brass lamp had gone out as well. Already up, Aleph was preparing the animals for travel, peering over his shoulder occasionally at the horizon. A cool blue mist drifted off Loch Mem. Soon a long, pointed craft could be seen, approaching at a surprising speed. Three gossamer sails held wide and high by booms and masts propelled it toward them. In the stern, balancing in a canvas sling, sat one of the strangest figures Beth had ever seen.

It was mostly his clothes that set him apart. Pieced together from dolphin skins, covered with colorful fish scales, stitched with patches of canvas at knees and elbows, his outfit was topped off with a fin of white hair swooping upward from his forehead. He looked very much the part of "Nun, the fish man," as Aleph introduced him.

With the agility of a spider crab, scuttling from stern to bow, he dropped the sails, swung the tiller to starboard, easing the low craft to the beach with hardly a ripple. The fish man extended a ramp to the shore, then he scuttled off the boat, falling prostrate before Beth, laying his spiked, white-haired forehead on the sandy ground. "My humble craft, my feet, my hands, my head, and my grateful heart are at your service, your majesty," he said.

Even though she had experienced some of this royal treatment before, Beth was still unnerved by such an overt exhibit of humility and respect. "We outcast folk have heard with great excitement of the selection the Prince has made in his choice of a bride. Rumors of your coming, and fears for your safety have thrilled and terrorized us." His voice was muffled by the sand. "Now, the beauty of your countenance is more radiant than I, your humble servant, could have imagined. Welcome aboard my craft, your highness. My request would be that you remember us when you come into your kingdom."

Blushing at the abundant praise, Beth reached down, to take Nun's hand and lift him up. Her Prince, she thought, would have wanted her to do that. Instantly she realized why they called him the fish man. Between each finger clung webbed membranes, very much like frogs she had played with as a girl in the little creek running through her town. Almost dropping the clammy, webbed hand in revulsion, she strengthened herself in the admonition of her Prince, grasped the hand tighter and lifted the fish man to his feet. Between each toe hung the same amphibian webbing.

Overcoming her embarrassment, Beth stammered, "This, this is not necessary, Mr. Nun. I am just a girl from the foot of the castle. Perhaps someday I might find my Prince, some day, he might decide I am not too damaged to marry him and someday I might become queen. It is a tiny arrow, a distant target, and a small bow. But if all of that happens, Mr. Nun, I will remember you and your people."

"Thank you, most kind sovereign, I will treasure the day."

Ashes and her donkey friend climbed the ramp and were tied by their leads to the rear mast. Aleph and Beth stepped to the bow, and Mr. Nun hoisted the astoundingly large sails, scampered to his canvas perch, pulled on the tiller, and they were under way.

Silence but for a whisper wind flowed around them for a long time. It was so peaceful on the glass-smooth loch. It would have been more than wonderful to be enjoying this serenity with her beloved. How would the Prince look? What would he say to her? Would he reach out, take her hand . . . look into her eyes?

A few inches separated her hand from Aleph's, draped casually over the ship's rail. For a moment, reaching out and placing hers on top of his seemed like a good idea. Flushed with the thought, she instantly looked away toward the horizon, ashamed. Surely, the Prince could not read her thoughts, yet her mind was already framing some sort of apology.

There was no room for distractions from her mission: Find the prince, fight the war, win it, have a big wedding, and move into the castle.

Finding the Prince was first. With him she was sure they could win the war. The rest would follow. While floating placidly on the still waters, it was hard to imagine they were headed to a battle where blood would be shed, many would die, and their strength would be tested to the limits of their endurance. For the entire journey, questions and troubling thoughts had floated around in Beth's mind. Looking down deep into the clear water, she was sure large leviathans and all manner of sea creatures swam in the aqua depths. It was a reminder that although the surface could appear serene, doubts and insecurities often roiled underneath.

"Aleph," Beth whispered so Mr. Nun could not hear. "How did the fish man get that way? Can it be treated? Who are his people? Why did he call them outcast-folk, and what did he mean by asking me to remember them? What is it they want? Is this something I need to prepare for?" She knew she was beginning to babble.

"Nun was born with that affliction, Milady. As with many physical anomalies, it happens rarely and without pattern. Many who live on the far side of the lake have been sent across, because of their handicap or disease. Some were sent because of an amputation or wound, others because of a lesion or color of their skin. They are former slaves, the halt, the blind, the lame. The outcasts of this land. All the kings, potentates, and leaders have approved the banishment, forcing them to leave home and find shelter here. For some, the rocky cliffs on the shores of Loch Mem are the only homes they have ever known. Kaphet would have been sent here, save her mother, fierce warrior that she is, defended her and took her to hide in the safety of the mines."

"What!" Beth clenched her fists, then lowered her voice. "They were going to send sweet Kaphet away from the kingdom? For what?"

"It is for no fault of her own, Milady, merely that she, like others, is different like the feeble or damaged. The faint hope of being welcomed back to their own home is if the ruler speaks out in their favor and welcomes them into the kingdom." Looking back at Nun, Beth felt a great weight settle on her heart. *Why should these people be ostracized?* she thought. *If there ever is a way I can change that, I will!*

Most of the day, they sat in the bow. With Aleph's encouragement—"Rest now, Milady, for we travel again by night to remain hidden from the eye of the enemy"—and the smooth rocking of the boat, Beth drifted off to sleep.

The grind of gravel when their boat reached the shore woke her. She sat up. What she thought was waves murmuring on beach stones turned out to be hundreds, no, *thousands* of people standing row upon row, all down the beach, up into the stony hills and cave-pocked cliffs behind them. As she stood, a wave of *ah*s swept over the crowd. A silent applause.

Looking closer, she could tell each one was in some way different or damaged. Split lips, missing limbs, red welts, patchy white skin, missing eyes, ears, or noses. Thousands of sad faces. Had she not been given a hint of what she would find on the far side of the loch, the overwhelming impact might have caused her to faint. Never had she seen suffering like this. The mass of damaged, dejected people was staggering. She felt lightheaded. Heat radiated from the stones and cliffs. The cool of the water was behind them. Her travel cloak felt sweaty so she removed it, folded it, and placed it in her bag.

With the words of the Prince in her mind giving her fortitude she did not possess, Beth stepped onto the bow of the ship looking over the throng. In the very front of the huge crowd of people was a sorrowful mother holding a baby girl with a deformed leg. Not having a shred of an idea what she could say or do or even *think* to help these people, she kneeled and reached out her hand to touch the child's cheek. In that instant, her arm was exposed. Obvious to all.

Pale tracks crisscrossed from the wrist to the elbow. Puckered scar tissue still red, white translucent skin not quite healed, was laid bare. Blue veins, clearly visible under the paper-thin tissue, pulsed with her heartbeat. For the span of five, perhaps six beats, the entire crowd was silent. Then with a choked, mouselike squeal, the mother impulsively reached out her hand to touch the tortured flesh of Beth's wounds. A rush of sound, not unlike quivering dry leaves, whooshed across the gathering, followed by wide eyes, gaping mouths, babbling words, pointing fingers, shaking heads. They were struck with wonder. Scanning the mass of broken people, Beth knew they were connecting, identifying with her scars. She was one of them. As swiftly as Mr. Nun had done, the entire congregation dropped to their faces, hands spread wide, foreheads touching the ground.

"No! No, please don't. Stand up, all of you! I am not a . . . I am not what you think." Beth wrung her hands. "Oh, Aleph, this is not right," she said. She stood and turned to him. "Tell these people they don't need to do this."

Behind her, Aleph placed his hand on her shoulder, and his patient voice calmed her. "Your presence here is healing for the wounds of their souls, your highness. No king, no leader, no shepherd, has ever come to see them. They are affirmed by your presence. Yes, and your scars show them you understand. Perhaps if you read them a portion of the words you carry, they would be lifted up."

By now tears were flooding down Beth's face. Shivering despite the heat, Beth found her precious letters, opened to one of her favorite sections, and with a voice choked with emotion, began to read.

Words of hope and encouragement flowed from her pages. Most of the fractured, wounded bodies pushed toward her until the prow of the boat became her pulpit. Strength returned to her mouth and lungs, attempting to have the words reach the ears, damaged or not, of those at the very back. Mr. Nun sat the closest, right at her side on the bow of his boat. Raptured expressions infused every face. When the strength that sustained her began to fade, the young mother stepped to the gang plank, took her by the hand and led her to a sheltered table with food, drink, and every form of sustenance.

Without pushing or shoving, as if having had food enough for themselves, the people shuffled out of the way with deference, allowing her to eat. For the rest of the day, moving from group to group, family to individual, parent to child, Beth wandered through the people of this barren, forsaken strip of land, speaking words of comfort. Most of the time the words were taken directly from her memory of the love words the Prince had written to her. These forgotten, neglected broken people were being transformed by those words. Whatever food Beth and Aleph had brought with them was distributed and multiplied to eager hands. Written all over their faces was gratitude, a depth of appreciation she could not understand. It was wonderful. It was miraculous.

Aware that Aleph also followed, tending to a wound, repairing a crutch, crafting a sling for a withered arm or merely standing beside someone with his hand on their fevered forehead. She noticed it all. His tenderness exceeded her own and increased her respect for him.

By nightfall, both were weary and had it not been for

Aleph's quiet insistence, they would have stayed the night. But they moved on. Both horse and donkey with a much-lightened load, set off.

‡ ‡ ‡

CLEARLY MARKED, THE smooth trail wound upward toward Citadel Samekh.

The bronze lamp with silver trim was held by Beth, who was in the lead. Aleph had instructed her in how to place a handful of carbide pebbles in the bottom compartment, then pour a cupful of water in the top. It was still amazing to her that just rocks and water could produce fire and light. She held the lamp high, illuminating the steep path ahead. Switchbacks were necessary on the steep mountain. Soon the trail became rock strewn.

Turns and ascents required clambering on hands and knees. The nimble donkey scrambled easily over the rough patches, but Ashes, with her large weight and massive hooves, struggled to make it up the stony scrabble. She was sweating before long, with white lather on her muzzle, strips of foam where harness and tack chafed. Altitude was with them. The temperature dropped the higher they climbed, cooling the dripping sweat. Needing a break, they reached a plateau where enough room allowed them to water the animals and sit on the stones.

"We will rest here for a time, Milady. Then you must put on your armor and holster the weapons to be prepared in case of a battle. We will make the last part of the climb just before dawn. Shin, the threefold peak, will be visible from there."

"I am curious, Aleph," Beth said, still breathing heavily. The darkness beyond the glow of the lamp pressed around them.

"It is not surprising, your highness," Aleph answered with a touch of humor, which Beth considered pointing out, but decided to ignore.

"How is it you seem to know this journey so well? Have you been here before?" *How does this castle stable hand know so much about the land, and the people, and, I might add, the doings of the Prince*? "You don't say much, but you must be more than just an ordinary stable hand."

"Milady, I am nothing other than a humble servant. But I have two good eyes, two ears, and an interest in what is spoken." That said, Aleph began unloading the donkey and the mare, rubbing them down and checking the mare's hooves.

Beth was not satisfied at all with his answer, but this intrigued her all the more. Yet knowing she would not get anything more from him, Beth set the lamp on a boulder behind her left shoulder, took out her book that she had missed reading, and buried herself in the profound words.

She picked up the Prince's story where she had left off, reading of plans being made to face the enemy and the temptation to remain in the shelter of his fortified home.

Belial the deceiver had sent messages offering bribes and treaties enticing him to relinquish power, to share his throne and end the battle. Yet his stalwart commitment to a kingdom of peace and righteousness remained firm. He longed for a place where they could all come together. In words lofty and exalted, the Prince described a wedding feast like no other had ever been. The beauty of his description rose off the page, setting her heart on fire.

Before long, she became so full, she began to write.

Your word is like a lamp to guide my feet and a light
for my path.
I've promised it once, and I'll promise it again:
I will obey your righteous regulations.
You know I have suffered much, my Prince;
I pray your words will heal my body as you promised.
Lord, accept my offering of praise, and teach me
your regulations.
My life is constantly hanging in the balance,
but I will not stop obeying your instructions.
The wicked are setting traps for me,
but I will not turn from your judgments.
Your missives are my treasure;
they are my heart's delight.
I am determined to keep your decrees to the very end.

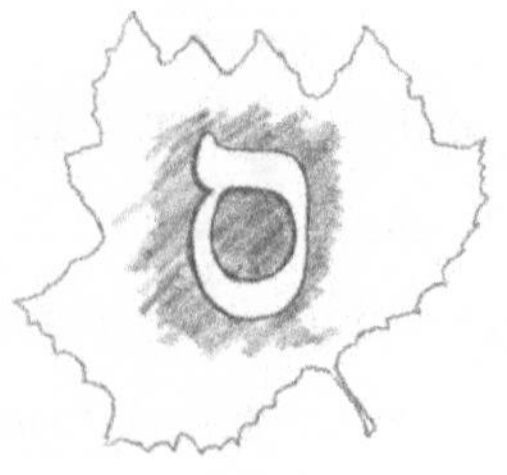

Chapter Fifteen

Samekh

BETH WAS TIRED. Her feet hurt. They had walked all the night across the hot desert, all night climbing toward the Citadel Samekh, and what had been general soreness on her feet was now a stabbing pain. Resolved to not complain to Aleph, who had carried a pack, tended the animals, prepared food, endured criticism, and answered endless questions, mostly, she would face the Prince with joy in her heart once the search was over. If and when it was . . . over.

It was colder the higher they climbed the mountain. Still dark, the light from the lamp had grown dim. She sloshed it to make sure there was enough water, dropped a few more rocks into the base and watched it grow to full brightness. Aching in every joint, pain in each step, they climbed upward. Other trails began to intersect. In the stillness of dawn, the sound of other feet, clanking of metal and whispered voices began to meld with their own.

The trail widened, leveled off, and opened onto a broad plain. In the mountain air, frosty plumes rose from the ground, burst from the nostrils of horses, armor bearers, and soldiers. Above it all loomed the peak called Shin. It did look as if three flames were rising into the sky. As the mist cleared, Beth became aware of thousands of troops massing in the level field around her. Set in orderly ranks of squads, troops, and battalions, they stood facing the pair with their two steeds. She, with Aleph following, had somehow limped right into the center of them all. *Not again*, she thought.

As if emanating from the ground beneath her, a deep resonant voice she recognized immediately, spoke out of the mist: "Your highness."

Gimmel! What a relief, thought Beth, to hear a familiar voice through the fog. "We have gathered to follow you into battle."

"Don't follow me, Gimmel, I don't even know where I am going."

"It is only to care for your many needs we serve," Gimmel said with a wink.

Then a roar of sound made up of clattering swords, shields, armor, swept the plain, washing up at her feet. Every fighter, lackey, armor bearer, and servant, as far as she could see, had dropped to one knee and placed their head on the hilt of their weapon. Beth was different now than when this happened for the first time, however, she still felt awkward in her role.

"My friend," Aleph said, placing his hand on the giant's shoulder, "you have fought well and faithfully. We now face the greatest challenge of all." Gimmel rose from his knee, with all the legions copying him.

"The army has been tested. They are loyal, yet not all." Aleph did not look surprised. "Some," Gimmel continued, "are yet double minded. Some are lukewarm in their commitment to the battle." He ended with disdain in his words.

"Berate them not, Gimmel," Aleph said kindly. "You can be victorious with many, or delivered by the hand of a few."

Gimmel bowed his head, then turning to what appeared to be his leaders, he spoke with them briefly and directed them to speak to each battalion. As the message was passed along, some broke ranks and slunk, as if ashamed, back into the mist. The number of soldiers was diminished.

"Where are they going, Aleph?" Beth asked with concern in her voice. "Why are they leaving? I thought the battle was just going to start?"

"It is not of great concern, Milady; the outcome of this conflict is already assured." Since he had spoken with the confidence she had come to expect from him, she knew not to argue. "Nevertheless, your highness, I can see you are walking in pain. I must tend to your feet." Trying to pull away, Beth resisted his gentle pull, then relented as he sat her on a convenient stone and began unlacing her new warrior boots. They had, no doubt saved her feet in the trek across the dessert, and probably prevented a sprained or broken ankle on the stony trail, but they were stiff, not well broken in.

The damage to her feet was obvious, as the boots came off. Two open blisters on each foot, were red, oozing, and inflamed. Aleph immediately knelt, poured water from his leather bottle to soothe and clean the open wounds, then applied oil that miraculously relieved the pain. Tender hands caressing the oil into the blisters began to elevate her blood pressure, bringing a flush to her face and misting her forehead with droplets defying the cold air. *This is not right*, she thought nervously. *The Prince would definitely not approve*. Gauze bandages also came from his pack, which he used to wrap each foot and finally replace each boot.

While lacing the last one, Beth became aware of the soldiers closest to her looking on with obvious astonishment on their faces. She could imagine their surprise. It was either that she, a woman, or perhaps a princess, someday queen, was allowing a servant to clean and bandage her feet, or perhaps some of these soldiers had never seen a delicate young woman's foot, ankle, and leg before. *Do they feel as I do, that it might anger the Prince? But I do think Aleph has become enamored with me. How can I make it clear that I am taken, my heart belongs to someone else?*

Well, he was done—finally.

Feeling a little awkward under the gapes of the soldiers,

she curtly thanked Aleph and tried to put a little distance between them by asserting her position in the face of all these soldiers.

"Squire, you need to care for my horse and check the tack and saddle," she announced a little stiffly. "I assume I will be riding into battle. I don't think you will be able to keep up on your donkey. Perhaps I will summon you after the battle is done." She rubbed Ashes's muzzle, handed Aleph the reigns, and turned toward Gimmel. Looking up at his massive frame, it occurred to her that if she had to face anyone like him in battle, she was doomed. But with unflagging confidence, and a mischievous smile, she said, "I may not be much as a soldier, Gimmel, but with you to provide for my many needs, I will do what I can."

The same quiet *ahem* she was getting used to came from behind to let her know Aleph was not going to stay behind. Still rattled by the feeling of having him caress her feet, she gave a chilly reply. "Yes, Aleph, what do you need to say?"

"Milady, there is yet a barrier we must cross—a great chasm between us and the battlefront on the approach to the triple peak Shin. The hanging bridge protected by the Fort Samekh reaches across it. It will be the point of attack. There is safety in the fort for a time, a place to prepare for the battle and plan a strategy. We must meet with Gimmel and the leaders in the tower of Ayin."

"Oh, Gimmel." Beth rolled her eyes at him. "What am I going to do with this appendage clinging to me like a limpet from Loch Mem? I have endured his warnings and cautions for this entire journey. Is he going to follow us all the way into battle? I guess he has served me well, no doubt he served the Prince, but is he able to fight? How will he do in warfare? I didn't see him doing any training back in the caves of Master Lamedh."

Gimmel looked down at Beth with a touch of mirth in his eyes. His meaty shoulders rose and fell slowly in a deep sigh. "Your Highness," he rumbled, "the, uh, stable hand, Aleph, was given watch-care over you. Breaking faith with the commission given him would not be possible. Where you go, he must go." He then lifted his shoulders, turned, and began leading the troops toward the fortress before them.

Across the chasm they began to hear sounds of conflict. Clanging of steel against steel, the *twang*, *hiss*, and *thunk* of arrows hitting their mark, the shouts of command and orders to advance or retreat, the underlying moan of the wounded spread toward them. The fortress Samekh was anchored to the edge of the deepest abyss Beth had ever seen. Over the abyss, a slender bridge reached to the cliffs on the other side. There was no chance of crossing the gorge without the bridge. Built on a pinnacle of rock jutting over the chasm, the fortress was strategic for the defense of the crossing.

The narrow way to enter the fort was an ironclad draw-bridge, chain lowered across a moat surrounding the tower wall. When they finally reached the entrance, everything slowed to a crawl. Skirmishes were fierce on the far side of the chasm. Defending the bridge, a small band of soldiers was valiantly keeping the way open. The suspension bridge was narrow. The pathway on the other side was the same. *It is going to be a tight fit getting my horse, Ashes, across the bridge,* thought Beth.

Inside the fort, welcome smells coming from the galley down at the base of the fort reminded her she had not eaten since some time the night before and now made her mouth water. She couldn't ignore the hunger, even though the adrenaline rush of being close to the fighting had kept her going.

"Come, your highness," Aleph said. "It is good the enemy has been prevented from crossing to this side of the chasm. Here we will be safe, but it could some time before all our fighters will be able to open a way for us to cross. We can strengthen ourselves with food and drink until then."

They descended to the lower level, where many of the soldiers were feasting as if there would be no tomorrow. For some, Beth realized, there might not. It was a raucous bedlam that assailed them as they entered, but as soon as they were spotted, an island of calm and reverence encircled them. Beth nodded and smiled to the soldiers, who were displaying their deference with much bowing, removing of helmets and caps. Together, she and Aleph took some food from the loaded tables and tried to find a quiet corner. They were guided to an alcove, where a door opened into a room prepared for them. They settled on a convenient bench, where a low window allowed the slanting sun, well past noon, to warm the small room.

"Who"—wondered Beth out loud—"does all this preparing of meals and cleaning up, Aleph? I mean, this is probably more food than they were fixing at the palace of Vau. Do they have some tyrant in the kitchen, whipping them to cook those sides of beef and scrub those pots?" She shuddered at the thought.

Aleph had a mix of feelings behind his eyes at her growing awareness of others serving her. "Nay, Milady, they are willing servants, supporting the Prince."

"How amazing!" Beth's eyes widened in astonishment. "They are serving for the good of others." As they finished up, a rotund woman came by to collect their dishes and leftovers. Beth thanked her profusely. Finally, with nothing else to do, Beth took out her charm, opened her precious book and set all the leaf drawings in a row. Aleph leaned against the stone wall and slept. As the sun dropped lower in the sky, the twisting shadows of her pendant became clear. Beth again began to see patterns in the shapes.

"Look, Aleph." Beth nudged him. "The letters are taking shape! I have discovered fifteen letters in the shadows formed by my charm. See?"

She pointed, pushing the book in his direction. "Each shape is a letter, the letters are in a sequence, it is forming an alphabet. There must be a story they are trying to tell." She looked up at him. "I think it is a story about me. Perhaps it is my story. Could that be possible?"

She pointed now at the leaf drawings of the shapes. "Look, this is the letter *zayin*; he was the serpent adviser to king Vau I told you about. And *heth* stands for the ogress in the kitchen. Look here"—she underlined it with her finger—"this is *teith*, which represents the countess who never followed." Excitedly she pointed out *mem*, for the loch, and even *nun*, for the fish-man."

What secret do they hold? She wondered. *What are they trying to tell me?* Aleph looking over wide eyed, revealed nothing.

Then with a touch of respect and a sly nod, Beth began to coax. "I think you know what I am talking about, Aleph. You must have some aptitude in reading runes and drawing letters. I studied the directions you traced in the sand during our trek through the swamp. Those symbols kept us safe." Beth looked up at him; Aleph was looking at her with what appeared to be rapt adoration. It made her shiver and look away.

He smiled briefly and dipped his head. "Words, Milady, and the letters that form them are powerful."

To Beth what he was saying sounded so like the letters from the Prince. Would the Prince ever have revealed his letters to someone from the stables? Aleph is probably about the same age as the prince. Could they have spoken? Might they have even been friends?

"It is good that you are discovering the secret letters and

how they combine," Aleph said. "For it is in the words that powerful truths can be revealed to the heart. I was schooled as a boy in all the letters of the *aleph-bet* and how to combine them. They have guided me during my journey as well."

Beth wanted to know more about Aleph. He spoke seldom but with such authority. He knew more about the Prince than she did, but continuing a conversation with him was risky. Her feelings could lurch out of control.

Looking back at her drawings as a willful distraction, Beth knew she was tantalizingly close to some revelation, a source of guidance or wisdom that lay just beyond her thoughts. It gave her some measure of hope. Squinting carefully at her leaf-drawings, at their shapes and then at the slowly spinning charm, she was trying to squeeze the answer out by sheer power of her will. But they would not be squeezed.

With the last rays of the sun, Beth turned to the book. The next chapter brimmed with tender descriptions of their eventual meeting. Even describing a longed for, gentle kiss. She imagined facing the Prince and flushed. The thought terrified her, but his passionate words gave her hope.

She would write while still safe behind the fortress walls of Samekh. Therefore, with the memory of soldiers deserting their troops and the evil men who strayed from their duty, she wrote words of submission, devotion, and faithfulness to him.

I hate those with divided loyalties who desert you,
but I love your instructions.
You are my refuge and my shield;
your word is my source of hope.
Double-minded people may just leave,
but I intend to be loyal to my Prince.
Sustain me as you told me in your promises,
that I may live! Do not let my hope be crushed.
If you sustain me, I will be rescued;
then I will meditate continually on your decrees.
You have rejected all who stray from your leadership.
They are only fooling themselves.
You will skim off the wicked of the earth like scum;
no wonder I love to obey your laws!
I tremble in fear of what you can do;
I stand in awe of your wisdom.

Sleeping accommodations for Beth were comfortable but limited in the round fortress of Samekh. They were safe for the time, as Aleph had said, but the citadel was filled with fighters. Every room was bristling with the tools of war and those who wielded them. The alcove, small room, and bath were a concession to her future royalty, and had been reserved even in the press of bodies, spears, swords, and shields. The padded bench in the bedroom, she assumed, had been placed for Aleph. But he set her bag on it, spread her travel cloak on the bed, stepped out, closed the door, then stretched out on the floor in the alcove. Soon they both slept.

Chapter Sixteen

Ayin

SNORES, HEAVY BREATHING, rattling weapons had not bothered the sleepers. They awoke to a cloudless sky. Sunlight streaming through tall windows, as transparent as the waters of Mem, painted the floors and walls with radiance. Smells from the kitchen indicated the cooks had been up even earlier. The experience with the ogress, queen of the kitchens of Vau, made Beth profoundly grateful for the workers volunteering to serve in a war they had not started. After breaking their fast, Aleph led Beth to the highest point of Fort Samekh. A tower so high, with visibility so broad, it was called Ayin, the Eye.

It was from that zenith that every corner of the realm could be seen. Beth was amazed at the panorama lying before her. Close at hand was the aqua-blue of Loch Mem, home to Mr. Nun and his community of damaged outcasts. The sandy desert beyond, reached all the way to the brown bowl of stones where the mines were, also hiding the caves, weapon factory, and training school of Master Lamedh. There, too, lived Kaph, mentor of the soul, and sweet Kaphet. Far to her left she recognized the dilapidated, crenelated walls and spires of King Vau's party empire next to the grim palace of Lady Teith. Dark forest-green trees were interspersed with the shining aqua water-canals leading into the marshes where the swamp people paddled their boats. Somewhere beyond lay the cozy village of Daleth, singing its melodious songs.

Off on the far horizon, more remote than the high dark-green forest, gray in the distance, she could see her home. The King's palace. In those turrets and spires resided thoughts of safety, security, the images of her childhood, the memories of her mother and father, even the dreams of a Prince. A palace and a very far away, might-not-ever-materialize wedding. Beth felt moisture beginning to puddle in her eyes, but she was a warrior now. Steeling herself, taking a breath, she knew perhaps someday in the future, she could allow herself the freedom to weep again. Too much time and effort, learning and training, too much difficulty had been endured to fall apart now. Of course, Aleph was also watching. Somehow that mattered to her.

Turning due west, the scene changed. Peering across the divide, up to the three flames of the mountain volcano Shin, she knew, was the goal: the place of the final battle. Covering the entire slope of the great volcano, reaching all the way down to the crevice dividing them from the base of the fiery peak, moved a mass of warriors. A grim blanket of the enemy cascaded down the slope like ants devouring every green and living thing. The Fortress Samekh, protected by the chasm, looked so vulnerable. Rising up from the canyon floor on a pinnacle of rock, it speared dangerously toward enemy territory. And there, tethered to that dark side by the long suspension bridge, it was defended valiantly by a terrifyingly insignificant band of brave warriors.

Looking full circle, Beth became aware of what was at stake. It was not just winning a bloody victory. It was not about power or control, certainly not about fancy robes, banquets, golden jewelry, or crowns. It was not even the vision of being ushered into the castle, lifted up to the high tower and sitting enthroned next to her very own Prince.

Her eyes had been opened. She saw the people who wanted, who needed a kind and just leader to protect them. To give them freedom to live their lives in safety. A leader who inspired them. That was the man she had grown to love. She now believed all the words that had sustained her, those words of love, care, patience, hope, and grace could also inspire anyone who would follow the Prince.

Pivoting again to view the entire scope of the kingdom laid out in clear view, she could visualize the suffering and anguish so many endured under the heel of Belial and his cruel taskmasters. Those hungry, poor, and enslaved who were forced to endure cruel punishment needed to be released from bondage. She could see those ostracized because of being damaged or just different. *If I am queen to all these lands and people, I will set them free and rule them well. I know the Prince from his letters would be able to instruct me.*

She turned again, her eyes falling on Aleph, standing patiently waiting. Even Aleph. *He is just another servant, given the difficult task to care for me, a young woman who aspires someday to be queen.* He would probably return to the stables to live out his life in anonymity, in the bowels of the castle. She felt a great kindness for him. *No,* she thought, *I have come to feel a great deal more than that. I am deeply grateful for his sacrifice and as queen, I could allow him to live out his servitude in safety, perhaps give him a plot of land for himself and family.*

The way Aleph's head was cocked to one side, looking down at her affectionately, unsettled her. The thought of standing beside him on the porch of a small cottage, his arm around her waist, made her blush. She swallowed a lump in her throat. That would not work. Being kind to him for his sacrifice was one thing but . . . *If everything does fail,* she thought, *kind and faithful as he is, could I really have him as my husband?* She nervously looked away.

"Aleph, I really like it up here. It is an inspiring and terrifying view. I would very much prefer to stay for a time alone. Could you please bring me up some lunch when they have it prepared?"

"Of course, your highness." Aleph bowed his head, touched his hat. "It would be my pleasure."

"Thank you, Aleph."

After he was gone, Beth wiped her moist forehead on her sleeve and took a few shuddering breaths. *I just can't let this be happening. The Prince would not approve.* With lips tight against her teeth she forcefully pulled out her book and charm, sat on one of the stone benches that circled the parapet, and began looking through her leaf collection. She shuffled them and began placing them on the bench beside her. Counting out loud rendered fifteen different letter drawings. Seven blank leaves remained.

Wondering if there were still seven shadows to be cast, with the pendant hung from one hand she moved the leaves around beneath it. Direct sunlight made the best shadows. *Yes! Here is another one, and now two.* Amazed at the variety of shapes the shadow took, Beth kept tracing them, moving the leaves, until twenty leaves were laid out, each with a letter clearly drawn on it. Only two remained blank. Beth was so excited she couldn't sit still. Crouching on the stone pavers in front of the bench made the most sense as the leaves, spread out before her, could then be studied more clearly. Sliding them around first in one order, then changing them back. Sometimes scrambling them all around, they slowly began to fall into the pattern she remembered from her father's teaching. The significance of each letter began to return as well. She found Gimmel, her gentle warrior, placed it next to

Dalith, the door, the gateway into selflessness and humility.

Now they were all coming back to her! It was like finally discovering her purpose in life. The story was starting to make sense! Hei, the gentle shepherd at Dalith, then . . . she shuddered, moving the leaf with the letter *vau* with *zayin* next to it, followed by *heth*, shaped much like the turban of orange hair the kitchen ogress always wore. After was . . . of course, the Countess Teith. As the story continued, Beth saw more and more how her story had been mapped out ahead of her. Each letter had a purpose. There was no random chaos to her journey. Order was twined into it with every letter. Could it be the letters spelled out everything she would endure and perhaps be victorious over?

She kept organizing, finding joy in the meaning of each letter but also the wonder that they spelled out the story of her life. At the tenth leaf she paused and pondered which one went next. *Oh, of course*, she thought. The little dot. The point. *yodh*, which formed the shape of the silver charm from which all the other shapes had come. Almost all of the other leaves became obvious. *kaph*, was the bowl shape of cupped hands and the hands of her healer. Learning from Master Lamedh, the trainer, came next. *mem*, the blue lake, *nun*, the fish man, *samekh*, a place of safety, then finally, *ayin*, the eye, where she now stood seeing the whole kingdom she lived in. Here on the eye, she had been given a vision of the needs that lay around her. Only seven leaves remained.

Five had runes on them she could not place. Two were

blank. Bringing all the leaves out, arranging them in a row, in sequence, challenged her to imagine what lay ahead. Before her journey began, she lived one day at a time. No thought was ever given to her place in the wide sweep of history. Perhaps briefly wondering what she wanted, and how to get it, was the extent of her musings about the future. Now, even though nothing was perfectly clear about what tomorrow would bring, Beth understood she had a place. There was a purpose for her in the vast breadth of this story. Her life was a valuable part.

Caught up in the images on the leaves, her swirling imagination attempting to visualize what the future might hold, had filled up her morning. The soft shuffle of feet alerted her to the return of Aleph. Carrying a tray with lunch, wafting the fragrance of soup, freshly baked bread, and fruit was more than enough to move Beth to scoop up her leaves, align the edges and slip them into the back of her book. She looked up at the sun realizing she was quite hungry, and it was way past lunch time.

"Aleph," Beth said, "it is long past the lunch hour. What took so long with the food?"

With a humble dip of his head, Aleph responded kindly, "The food has been ready for some time, Milady. I merely was waiting until you concluded your thoughts."

"You have been standing there, for this whole time?" The old Beth would have rolled her eyes and chastised him. The words formed in their place now had become tender toward her patient servant. "Oh, Aleph, thank you for your kindness. All you had to do was say something!" Her heart and her eyes were tempted to say more, much more, but held back. Purposed to be gentle with this faithful servant, kindness was appropriate but she guarded herself, fearing to say what might be growing in her heart.

"Your highness," he said again softly, "your thoughts were elsewhere. I would never want to intrude unless asked. I am always ready to wait."

Beth shook her head. "Well . . . I am grateful. You are incredibly patient. I am trying to be more patient myself. Thank you again for the food." Accepting the tray, her hand inadvertently brushed against his. More than just warmth, an electric discharge went up her arm, almost causing her to jerk back. His cordial expression might mask his feelings but hers seemed to be spilling out all over. Pulling herself together she sat back on the bench facing the mountain Shin, distancing her eyes from Aleph and looking beyond him to the great gulf.

The tray was loaded with more than she could eat. Several varieties of fruit, nuts and vegetables surrounded some very creative looking crackers with slivers of meat beside.

As she took her first nibble, Aleph standing attentively reminded her to ask, "Have you had food, Aleph?"

"Yes, Milady, thank you kindly for asking. I had a portion in the kitchen as they prepared your tray."

"Well, next time . . . you could perhaps bring it with you

and we . . . we could eat, you could join me. Why don't you go back down, finish eating, and I will come later?"

"Very well, Milady, I will collect the tray after you have returned."

"Uhh, no . . . no, I will carry it down. It is the least I can do."

Aleph slipped down the stairs, leaving Beth alone on Ayin's spire. She sat in silence, picking at her food until she had swallowed all her nervous stomach could handle. *I must do better at controlling myself around him*, she thought.

In time, the sun sank toward the horizon, releasing a cool evening breeze to wash down the peak, across the chasm, and around the tower to chill anyone watching. With it came the sounds of war. The spectacle Beth could see, far, far below, was dreadful. The dark hordes continued to sluice down the slopes, surrounding the treacherous foothold on the far side of the canyon, threatening to spill across the narrow bridge and engulf everything good. With that image in her mind, she opened her journal.

Don't leave us at the mercy of the attacker, O Prince,
for we have tried to do what is just and right.
Please guarantee our safety.
Don't let the cruel enemy overcome us!
Your people long to see your rescue,
to see the truth of your promise fulfilled.
We are willing to listen; show us your unfailing love,

and teach us your wisdom.
Give me, your beloved, your heart;
then I will understand everything you say.
My Prince, it is time for you to act!
These evil people are invading your land.
Truly, I love your words more than gold,
even the finest gold.
Each of your guidelines is right.
That is why I hate every false way.

Very pensive after her clarified view of the kingdom she lived in, Beth hid her book away, collected the food item and descended into the citadel.

Each level she reached rattled with the tense bustle of preparations for war. Sounds of grinding stones, flying sparks, and acrid smells of sharpening oil hung in the air. Racks of weapons and machines of war filled the great halls. Much was being made ready for an assault into the stronghold of Belial, the prince of destruction. On the main level, where the draw bridge opened on to the plain, she could see throngs of mighty workers, dragging battering rams, long ladders, and siege towers toward the fortress in preparation to move them across to the battle.

Out on the plain she noticed a skirmish, a struggle going on between armed soldiers and a group stripped of their weapons trying to escape. Reinforcements arrived, led by Gimmel, to quell the uprising, bind the rebellious group, and force them at sword point toward the drawbridge and into the open portal.

Marching into the fort, Gimmel noticed Beth. Speaking to her directly, he said, “Your highness, a tribunal has been called in the throne room. Your attendance is most humbly requested.”

Flanked at once by two soldiers almost as big as Gimmel, she had to drop the tray on a convenient table and was escorted across the great hall and through the high doors swung open into the throne room itself. Two thrones sat side by side on the dais, three steps above the polished marble floor. Her cortège turned to face her, bowed, and then backed off the raised platform. Beth was left standing alone in a bit of a panic, in front of the gold and red velvet thrones.

Gimmel forced the group of rebels to kneel before her. He turned to one side, nodding to what appeared to be the judge and a group of counselors. They walked solemnly up the steps to stand on one side of the platform. The judge stepped to a podium, banged the lectern twice with a black stone, then holding up a large scroll, turned anxiously toward Beth, as if waiting for her. Beyond him at the edge of a great tapestry, she gratefully noticed the shadow of Aleph. His appearance produced a now familiar lurch in her heart. She desperately wished it would not interfere with her responsibilities.

He indicated with a pantomime; she was to be seated. Taking the cue, she sat. Beth, suddenly realized, at this moment, the Prince might enter. He would take the other throne, turn to her, smile and reach out his hand for hers. She almost swooned at the thought. But looking around the great hall, no Prince appeared. For a long time, she searched the room, then with a sigh, turned to the judge and nodded. She would not see the Prince today.

Relieved, the leader unrolled the parchment, turned toward her, and begin to read.

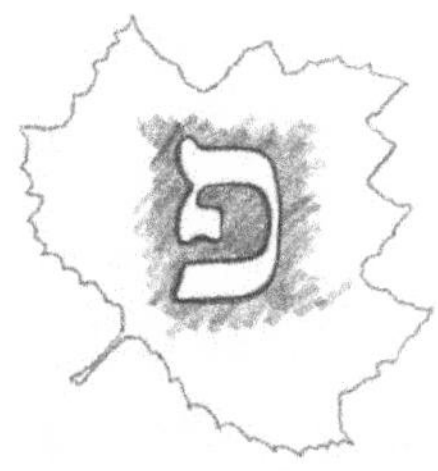

Chapter Seventeen

Peh

So many strange situations had been thrust on Beth. Her confidence that all was going to work out had grown in small ways, but there seemed to be no plan. No concrete battle plan at all. The letters from the Prince and the story revealed to her by the shadow letters, gave her hints of some things to come, but she had no assurance that any of it would work together for the satisfactory completion of her story. All might be well. Or not.

Sitting on a throne in a courtroom filled quickly with warriors, soldiers, dignitaries, and a crowd of onlookers, swam in her vision, but the words of the Prince stiffened her spine. Smoke from torches lighting the hall and pungent odors from the anxious throng made her lightheaded. In truth, there was also a clench of fear, knowing that unless the Prince showed up, she might have to render some kind of verdict.

What was happening around her was in a small way like the hometown court sessions held in the stone hall at the foot of the castle. The local magistrate and two arbiters were usually presiding. But the issues generally involved a misappropriated pig or minor land dispute. This looked like a grievous breach of military protocol. Spies. This was serious. This was beyond her level of comfort. She was working hard not to panic.

"Be it known today in the presence of these dignitaries, these callous fellows have plotted to undermine and defeat the armies of the Prince," read the judge, his voice echoing among the rafters of the cavernous throne room. "With malice and wicked intent, these scurrilous deceivers have mortgaged their eternal souls for gold. They have sullied their integrity for wealth. Cooperating with the vile enemy, they were apprehended in the very act of attempting to deliver damaging information to the wicked leader of the foe. It is therefore requested that they forfeit their very lives for their transgressions." He rolled up the scroll and nodded to one of the counselors standing in line.

He stepped forward, cleared his throat, and spoke in Beth's direction. "Your highness, honorable judge, fellow counselors," giving a nod toward them, the rather drab, fidgety counselor continued in a whiny, high-pitched voice. "These men have been accused of a serious offense of treason. There is clear evidence they were attempting to carry secret plans to the enemy. We have witnesses and assurance they were caught in the very act of scaling the walls to leave the citadel with documents taken from our senior command. I would have them declared guilty as charged and sentenced to death." His statement completed, he returned to his position in line.

A second counselor stepped forward. Long silver hair and tall in his elegant robes, he had an unassailable air of dignity and poise. He turned and bowed toward Beth, nodded to the judge, the other counselors, and began in a voice as deep and resonant as that of Gimmel's, but with greater polish.

"Who," he spoke with smooth confidence and authority, "who is their accuser, and what evidence do they," waving a hand decorated with bracelets and rings, "what evidence do they offer of this crime?" He spoke casually without notes. *The spies have chosen wisely in finding someone to defend them*, Beth thought.

"I would submit to you, your highness and most honorable counselor, these men were accused of crimes to cover the crimes of others. Who are the accusers? Are they hiding a crime of their own?" His words came out so smoothly that Beth did wonder, perhaps they were framed. A soft rustle beside her caused her to turn her head slightly to see Aleph, standing almost hidden behind her throne. He had slipped unobserved between the tapestries and the wall to arrive at her side.

Beth leaned toward him and whispered, "Who is that counselor defending the prisoners? I think I have seen him before."

"It is Counselor Peh with the golden tongue," Aleph whispered back. "It is not always clear where he places his loyalty."

Again, the counselor for the prosecution stepped forward. "Twelve men of the regiment led by Gimmel apprehended this cohort, who were in the act of scaling the fortress wall after stealing military plans they were attempting to deliver into enemy hands." He paused briefly, then held his hand palm up toward Gimmel. "Who will voluntarily attest to these accusations?"

As if rehearsed, twelve men stood to their feet behind Gimmel and with one voice shouted, "We do!"

"Let the record then show," responded the prosecutor, again facing Beth, "the honest testimony of twelve loyal soldiers has been given as evidence against these men guilty of the crime of treachery and sedition!" He turned for one last look at the defense, who stood implacable, and returned to his place.

His haughty look stirred Beth's memory, as Counselor Peh returned to stand before the throne. "If I might ask?" the baritone voice smoothly requested. "If I might ask, what business did the cohort of soldiers led by Commander Gimmel . . . what business did they have outside the fortress walls?" He paused, taking a deep breath in through his long nose and gave Beth a disdainful glance. "Were they not seeking illegal spoils of war? Plunder by law is to be gathered into the coffers of the Prince. Is that not the reason for their exploration beyond the walls?" His voice rose at the end, giving an accusatory look at Gimmel.

The response from Gimmel was swift and loud, directed to Beth. "Yes, your highness, my men and I were collecting the spoils, yet only for the purpose of bringing them into the storehouse, and—"

His words were cut short by the judge striking the stone on the podium. "Silence! Silence, Gimmel, your time will come to present your rebuttal. Counselor Peh, you may continue."

"So he says," sniffed Counselor Peh. "Every man caught in transgression lies to protect himself. Are they not displaying better weapons, armor, and clothing than your average soldier? Perhaps we would do well to search their quarters to find what other spoils they have appropriated?"

The debate went back and forth with each side claiming the other was guilty until Beth became totally confused. When time was given for a defense made by Gimmel or his men, Counselor Peh would casually interject a reasonable doubt. He was so smooth Beth began to feel a little uncomfortable with his polished arguments. She still could not remember where she might have seen Counselor Peh before, but she was still nervous about his well thought out arguments and reasons.

Finally, the stone on the judge's podium banged twice. "The evidence has been presented." He looked toward Beth. "It is time now, your highness, to render a verdict."

Now was the time to panic, thought Beth. Such a mass of accusations and defenses, blame and justification. She really had no idea what was expected of her. The entire room up to this moment had been filled with a low undercurrent of mumbling and finger pointing. It now went still. All eyes turned to Beth. She turned toward the only one she could think of . . . Aleph.

There was a measure of relief as she looked to her friend behind her. She whispered intensely, "Aleph, what do I do now? How can I even decide? What would the Prince do? What would He want me to do?"

"Merely speak to them," whispered Aleph softly enough so no one could hear. "Speak to them from the Prince's words that are in your heart, Milady."

Her mind began to fly through passages from the letters lodged in her memory from many readings. Give discernment to me, your servant; then I will understand your laws. You have made me wiser than many counselors, your laws are just and right. More and more wonderful words came to mind. With some of the best on her lips, she stood.

Aleph whisper, "You may sit, while rendering the verdict."

So she sat.

"Judge, counselors, accused and accusers, hear these

words from the Prince." She began to quote some of the phrases about good and evil, light and darkness, truth and error, wisdom and folly. "Good people, those words are valuable for us all." A soft murmur of approval permeated the room. In that moment, a flash of insight as if from the spirit of the Prince himself and the power of his words entered her mind. "Could I, would it be . . ." she hesitated, trying to make a request she was not sure was proper. Then taking confidence in the words already spoken, she went ahead boldly. "Gimmel, speak honestly, have you and your men ever taken spoils to the storehouse?"

"Of course, your highness," Gimmel said with a tiny mischievous tone in his voice, as he bowed humbly to her. "We have delivered much in the way of spoils, many times."

"Tell me now," Beth said to the entire room, "is there a guardian or keeper of the storehouse in the courtroom?" She looked out across the crowd, not sure of what to expect.

A frail old man wearing a clerk's visor raised an ink-stained hand. He lifted his chin and spoke, but Beth could not comprehend the quavering words.

Growing in strength she said, "Speak louder, ancient one. The verdict is in your words." Two soldiers helped the old man to the front of the room. "You, sir, are the keeper of the storehouse?" Beth asked.

He bowed deeply before answering, "Yes, your highness, I have served the Prince for many years."

"Thanks to you, sir, for your loyalty. Now tell me," Beth

said, "has Commander Gimmel ever brought spoils to the storeroom?"

"Many times, your highness."

"And at any time, was there ever a shortage, or any indication that Gimmel or his men had kept anything for themselves?"

"Never, Milady, I know they have always been loyal to the Prince."

She looked over at Counselor Peh, who was looking sinister but a bit uncomfortable.

"And what would you say to Counselor Peh concerning his accusations?"

Regardless of his age and frail appearance, the keeper of the storehouse pulled himself up as straight as his aged frame would allow and spoke with quavering clarity. "It is a lie!" A growl of satisfaction rolled across the crowd.

Beth sat back, smiled inwardly, thanking the Prince for his insightful words. Confidence flowed through her as she chose her words carefully. "Thinking about this very carefully and considering all the facts, I would like to give the guilty men an opportunity to confess to their crime. If they do, and renew a vow of loyalty to the Prince, I might consider giving them leniency.

"Loyalty to the Prince! Bah! Never!" the leader of the accused gang shouted, then spat on the floor. Gimmel immediately placed his giant sandaled foot in between the man's shoulder blades and mashed his face into the puddle on the floor.

"Well, then, I would declare these men guilty as charged," Beth said with authority.

Humphing in disgust, Counselor Peh turned away from the throne, stepped off the dais, and strode from the room. In a flash, Beth remembered where she had last seen him: giving counsel to king Vau! A different throne room. A different verdict. A long-ago time and place.

The case was now over. Soldiers and counselors alike began streaming from the throne room with a consort of soldiers escorting the condemned to their fate.

Beth sat until almost all had gone. *How did Counselor Peh get here. What is he doing? I need to know more about him,* she thought. Her head was full of accusations, defenses, and questions. The lofty view from Ayin would clear her mind and renew perspective on her journey. It would also remind her to focus on finding the Prince. She could ask him about Counselor Peh. He would know. Asking Aleph what he knew would help too.

Turning to speak to Aleph, she discovered he had gone. Still on the dais with her friend Gimmel was the old storehouse keeper, speaking in quiet tones.

He turned to her eyes cast down, "Great wisdom have you spoken, your highness. Truth has won out today."

"It is not I, ancient one, but the words written for me by the Prince that have been planted in my mind and in my mouth. He deserves the praise."

"Aha, but you, most humble and noble lady," Gimmel said with a slightly exaggerated bow, "have chosen to trust and obey those words."

"Do not mock me, Gimmel." Beth laughed with great relief that the affair was over. She gave him a playful shove with the same effect she would have shoving one of the granite pillars. "If you tease the future queen, she might have to send her stable hand to thrash you." The old storehouse keeper made a noise that was obviously stifled laughter.

"Nay, Milady, my respect for you is absolute," replied a stern, overly serious Gimmel.

Finally alone, she sat for a time in the empty throne room that had been used for a judicial court. The curtains rustled behind her, and she turned, expecting to see Aleph. It was not. The elegant form of Counselor Peh stepped up beside her.

"Your highness," he spoke, his words as smooth as oil, "if you will excuse my intrusion into your meditations, I have words of apology from an ardent admirer."

"You! You were advising wretched king Vau at that miserable pile of rocks he called a palace. I am still so angry with him, he gives me nightmares."

"It is for that very reason he sent me, your highness. He was in terrible anguish when he returned to ask for your merciful forgiveness and discovered you had gone. It was recently the treachery of the wicked Zayin was discovered. Zayin hated you from the start and banished you to the scullery under the cruel lash of his minion, the ogress Heth. The king is so grieved he sent me here with a gift to show his repentance." Then lifting a box from his side opening it he offered it to Beth with a look of genuine sorrow on his face. Within lay a robe so like the one displayed by the marsh people it shocked her. On top was a velvet box which Counselor Peh opened with a flourish displaying a jewel encrusted ring of stunning magnificence." *Does this smooth talker really think I am going to fall for this?* Beth wondered.

"Do you even know what that evil man did to me?"

"Your highness, he did confess this terrible mistreatment done at a time of great weakness and under the influence of strong drink. He begs that you would return ever so briefly that he might display his sincere repentance."

"I would not go back even if he offered me all his wealth and a seat on the throne at his right hand!" Her voice was tight with anger. She stood to get away from this slimy, smooth-talking emissary of king Vau.

As she turned to leave, the tall counselor lowered his lips to her ear. "It would be a good choice, your highness. You will still face the battle but there will be no reward. For I have spoken to your beloved Prince. He revealed to me his knowledge of your defilement. You have been rejected as his choice. You will never be his bride."

Kicked in the stomach by Ashes her mighty horse would easily describe the blow she felt. "You filth!" she snarled, turning and running from the throne room. Up the broad staircase she fled. Without stopping to breathe, she ran up Ayin, the very top of the tower. Throwing herself on the stone bench, her heart rent with pain. Heaving sobs shook her as she wept and wept until she could weep no more.

Never would she return to the misery and debasement she experienced at the palace of Vau. Never! But the fears she had hoped were gone darkened her mind again. Even the desire to return to her old life raised its head.

The resolve that had sustained her was now melting into misery and defeat. She wanted to find her horse, abandon the quest, leave Aleph behind, and go home.

‡ ‡ ‡

IT TOOK TEN paces to cross the wide stones of Ayin's tower to the steps leading down to the keep. But her stride was blocked. There, with a face more stern than she had ever seen, was Aleph. She moved to pass him. He moved to block her.

"Your highness, you cannot leave."

Shocked by the stern command from her servant brought her to a standstill.

Eyes always kind and gentle hardened into coal-black stones.

"Lies, deceptions were conceived with the desire to steal what has been planted in your heart and destroy all the good that has grown there. You cannot uproot that to throw it all away."

"Do you know what Counselor Peh told me?"

"Every word," Aleph said, softening his tone. "All of them are vipers. King Vau, Counselor Peh, Zayin, and their minions. Serpents who load their followers with burdens they are not willing to bear themselves." Then with the steel restored to his voice, he repeated, "You cannot go!"

She had failed. The fear that her beloved had heard and rejected her, loomed large. She had been lied to, deceived, and Counselor Peh was maligning the Prince she loved but did not know. But the hasty decision to forget the quest, the battle, and dreams of royalty began to wither under Aleph's rock-hard stare.

Dropping her eyes to the stone pavers at her feet, Beth shook her head and muttered through clenched teeth. "Then what am I to do Aleph? What can I do?"

"It is not far from you, Milady, it is within you, in your very heart." Softer, a tone stately and poignant, Aleph continued. "Be reminded again of what is planted there. Take up the letters, true words, sincere words written from an honest and loyal heart. Read again, trust those words." As a quiet afterthought he whispered, "Most tragic of all, if you turn back, sweet Beth, the Prince would be broken hearted for all time."

After a long silence, Beth spoke. "I believe you, Aleph. I will believe the words of the Prince." She sighed. *Dear Prince, I pray you will forgive my unbelief.*

She looked up and was alone. The day was far spent.

settling down with a clear evening sky, a cool breeze, and solitude. Perhaps it was just what she needed. *I cannot believe the anger I saw in Aleph's look. No . . . it was not anger, it was conviction. And he is right.*

Sitting where she could see the castle far off in the distance, her home for all her life. She pulled the well-worn book out and reread some of the passages that had come to mind so forcefully in the courtroom. *I am amazed again how powerful they are. These messages and encouragement are so open, practical, and so soothing to my heart. They really did give me wisdom and direction.*

They struck like a clear bell to the masses in the courtroom. The wise judge and counselors, all the soldiers, even the uneducated workers had been moved and inspired by those truths. *All but one evil, deceptive defense attorney.* After pondering the words for a long time, Beth, exhausted by the emotional whiplash, chose gratitude. She took the quill from its hidden case and wrote words so soothing to the confusion within.

Please forgive me, Lord. Your words are wonderful.
No wonder everyone wants to follow them!
Proclaiming your standards give light,
so even simple people can understand.
Everyone gasps with expectation,
longing for your instructions.
Please come to us and show us your mercy,

as you say you do for all who love your name.
We need your words to guide us,
so we will not be overcome by the enemy.
Rescue us from the lies and deception of evil people;
then we can obey your commandments.
I long to look into your eyes of love;
I need to hear your voice.
Rivers of tears have gushed from my eyes
because nobody can speak like you.

Chapter Eighteen

Tzaddi

ALL THE VALLEY faded to dark ochre, even on the tall tower Ayin, she was in shadow. The last filtered rays of sunset, clung to the very pinnacle of the fiery volcano of Shin. From the peak, three flames in the gloaming sky blended with the final blaze of the sun to give a hellish scarlet glow to the mountain. Beth shivered, not so much from the cold but a touch of foreboding.

This was not anything like she imagined at any time in her journey. It did not turn out to be the little jaunt in the woods as she had visualized at first, nor the challenging trek, which would give her the satisfaction of reaching the summit. The painful suffering, the lies, the deceptions were never expected. Even her determination to join the battle and become a warrior was not what she had originally prepared for.

The all-out war against the hordes of Belial looked like impossible odds. He was powerful, but his rebellion against the Prince, cruelty to his own people, the murder of innocents, all disqualified him for leadership. Furthermore, she hoped, doomed him to destruction. That evil power knew she existed, yet he would consider her insignificant and dispensable. *His might seems overwhelming,* she thought. *Those who have believed his lies and followed him are without number. Is victory hopeless?*

Even the battle within, against insecurity, despair, doubt, and darkness, was something she was not sure she could overcome. Fondling these gloomy thoughts like a gray blanket allowed them to take hold in her mind. Like the dampness of the cold ground she had slept on at times, it crept into her bones. Brooding on the darkness could easily take her even deeper. It was easy to slip into the bottomless well of depression, but in the fading light, she looked down at the open book in her lap.

The dove, hanging near her heart warmed. Her skin began to prickle. The fine hair on the back of her neck stood up, even the scars on her arms tingled at what she read. The chapter, now toward the end of her book, described something unbelievable. The Prince, her Prince had been captured, betrayed, abused, beaten then rejected by his own. At the lowest most dejected place in his life, he had thought of her. Lifting his eyes to his attackers, he granted them forgiveness.

If he forgave them, I know he will forgive me!

Stunned, Beth stared at the page, written in her beloved's own hand.

Forgive.

It happened every time. Words speared off the page, pierced her heart, dividing her soul and spirit. Words of hope and encouragement. Words of strength, direction, and power. In them, she became confident again in victory. Words of faith. Words of duty. Beautiful words. Wonderful words. Wonderful words of life.

Words of forgiveness.

Then, as if to confirm the light in them, bobbing up the stairs came the cheerful, golden glow of Aleph's lamp. Weary, cold, emotionally wrecked, Beth was ready to leave her high perch and descend into the warmth and security of the citadel to find sleep.

"Your highness." Aleph bowed. "There is one who is longing to speak with you."

Her thoughts toward Aleph had so changed. He was doing what he had done all along. Serving her with kindness, speaking out with authority and, yes, even love. He was tenacious, caring for her in ways that proved he saw himself as far more than a servant. She wondered if he truly loved her. *How do I handle those feelings?* she thought, avoiding his eyes, trying to smile without revealing more.

"Oh, Aleph, I am cold and so tired," she said, trying not to plead. "I really don't want to speak to anyone right now."

"It is distressing to see you uncomfortable, your highness. But the righteous one, your most true, humble servant, has come a far distance to pray a blessing over you."

Behind him, limping slowly up the steep steps, came a figure she did not immediately recognize. Shrunken, hunched over, halting as if in pain, up one step at a time, came the shadow. Finally shuffling into the glow of the lamp appeared the one who had started it all.

In the same raspy croak that had echoed often in Beth's dreams, she spoke. "Ahh, your highness, it is I, your humble servant, Tzaddi." She approached, bowed deeply then lay her wrinkled hand on Beth's head.

"Tzaddi!" cried Beth. "I can hardly believe it is you! How on earth did you get here?" Jumping to her feet, she embraced the old woman. Genuine affection came over her. Tears formed in her eyes. "This the most amazing reunion. I really thought I would never see you again!"

Taking Beth's face between her two wrinkled, crooked-fingered hands, Tzaddi had tears in her eyes as well." Milady, my queen. I was not sure myself these tired eyes would ever be blessed with the sight of your countenance." It was not lost on Beth that this nursemaid to the Prince was no longer speaking to her as a child. She was being addressed as royalty the way Aleph and so many others on her quest always had.

"Tell me," Beth said, "what is happening at home? Have you spoken to my father? How did you get here? I am amazed you even made it!"

"Yes, it has been a long perilous journey. Sometimes by cart. Sometimes by donkey. Sometimes by boat. At times, although very slowly, even walking. All the while you were captive, or in training, or healing, or resting, I traveled. Your father sends his love. Much fear has overcome the castle, but the message that you have arrived at the battlefront will encourage many." She paused, breathing heavily, and continued. "There is much I still need to say to you."

"Oh my, could you not have said it before I left? It would have saved you many miles."

"You would not have listened. You would have not heard. It was not time."

"Well, I am truly sorry you had to come so far and endure so much. Perhaps I am ready now. I will admit, I have changed."

Tzaddi took one of Beth's hands and slid the drape of her sleeve up to her elbow and peered at the wounds and scars. Anguish creased her already wrinkled face. "Yes, Milady, you have been transformed by what you have suffered. Sometimes there is no other way." Then looking deep into her eyes, she said, "Always give thanks for your wounds."

Although distressed by that comment, Beth said nothing. She was still glad to see the old nursemaid.

"Tell me then, Tzaddi, what have you come this far to say? Do you have wisdom to share before the battle? Perhaps a prediction as to the outcome? I most assuredly need it. I will listen."

Tzaddi shuffled to the bench and sat wrapping her cloak about her shoulders to ward off the cold. Beth sat beside her, wrapping herself also. Aleph stood quietly to one side holding the lamp, occasionally adding fuel and adjusting the flame to keep it bright.

After a long silence, Tzaddi asked, "What have you learned on your journey? What has given you strength to continue? Where hope? Why persistence? When courage?" Not expecting an answer, she continued. "It was the words. The letters of the Prince. His love scribed on parchment that gave you the strength to go on. Those thoughts, written for you, have power. They can be more precious than gold or silver. As one speaks, the words transform the listener. They give value, worth, significance, inspiration, which cannot be easily taken away. But words emanating from your mouth with carelessness do damage, wound, destroy. Harsh words can twist another for life. For that reason, your lips must be guarded carefully. Your words will change you and those who hear." She paused for a moment.

"The book you have carried all those miles." Tzaddi pointed to the book of letters lying open on the bench. "It has been wisdom, strength, and hope for you. It has been light in the darkness and fire to purify. Direction in the wilderness is found in those missives, even guidance for the lost. Those insights have been protection, a sword for battle, a hammer that breaks asunder. Even nourishment as milk and bread for hunger. Those instructions were seeds for planting and the rain that nourished them for growth. It became a salve as medicine, healing for your wounds. Every word was breath for your soul."

Thinking back over the months of her perilous journey, Beth knew everything Tzaddi was saying had proven true. This amazing book had taken her heart captive, because of the love written into each line. It had proven to be so much more. Very thoughtfully she asked, "Tzaddi, how can this be, that words on a page can change a heart, heal a wound, direct your feet, give you victory, hope, and strength in times of weakness? Is this really possible?"

"Yes, your Highness," Tzaddi said, nodding her ancient head. "It can even transform a lowly peasant girl into a queen. Ink on a page cannot change anything. It is the spirit within the writer and the open soul of the reader. The love of the speaker, the hunger of the listener. This combination can then ignite a fire, light the way, heal the wound, give strength, and win the victory." Her voice began to grow softer with weariness, but she was not done. "What is most important about the power of the letters is as they changed you, now your own words can become all those things for others."

This truth was almost too incredible for Beth to believe. Would she be able to share love and affirmation in the same way the Prince had written of his love and encouragement to her? She had needed it. But she had also met many people on her journey who needed it more than she did. It did not change her intense and deepening love for the Prince, which had grown almost daily through the letters.

Tzaddi continued, whispering about the power of words. She began telling stories of her own difficult and painful childhood. Of brutal pain, rejection, damage she had suffered. Then how she had been lifted into the royal family as a servant. How kind words of love had transformed her. It was amazing to hear how her miserable years had been redeemed by the power of words.

Beth noticed Tzaddi's frail body was beginning to shiver from the cold. Wrapping her arms around the old woman gave her the warmth she needed to go on. The stories continued.

The story of Gimmel, violent, angry, a danger to his family and any who provoked him because of his size and strength. Yet after meeting the Prince during his military service to the kingdom, he was redeemed and changed into the loyal, gentle giant who had rescued Beth more than once. Kaph, slave to Belial in the valley whose name she bore, set free by the Prince to become a loyal follower. Others in the palace and the countryside who had been converted by love and kind words.

Tzaddi told of the downtrodden lifted up and damaged people restored by the power of those words. Prisoners who had been set free. The weak had been made strong. Broken ones had healed. The wicked had been made holy. The stories tumbled off her tongue one after another. It seemed as if this was a never-ending volume. The stories slowed with longer pauses between them.

"Tzaddi, "interrupted Beth gently, "is there any significance to the seven stones on the cover of this most wonderful book?"

"Aye, Milady, the precious stones are the seven miracles on your journey to find your Prince."

As her energy finally started running low, Tzaddi ended with a brief admonition, in a final whisper. "You, Milady, will soon be queen. To rule well you must be holy. The words will purify you. The greatest gift you can give to yourself and all who wrong you is forgiveness. Then you will be set free to love and be loved. Treasure his righteous words forever."

Tzaddi went silent. Aleph, holding the lamp over them, was silent as well. Beth continued to embrace Tzaddi, resisting the cold. Her shivering finally stopped with a long sigh. She slumped against Beth as if asleep. Holding the old woman close to her chest, Beth felt the fragile body relax. Slowly Tzaddi's body grew cold, as cold as ice. Beth knew Tzaddi had given her last admonition.

‡ ‡ ‡

ALL THE CROWD had finally left the high tower of Ayin. Another death, another corpse, another preparation for burial during this endless war, was for them, a never-ending ritual. Blue frost from the mortician's and porter's breath, still hovered in the cold air. Beth was alone. Her book, a cold sliver of moon, a black night scattered with stars and Aleph, still holding his lamp, were all that remained. The cold of Tzaddi's body clung to her and the shivering returned. Beth tried to clear her thoughts, a fog like death that clung.

The other impression that did not leave was the tenderness of Aleph's embrace. As the porters carried away Tzaddi's empty shell for preparation, he stepped alongside her and without any awkwardness, reached his arms around her, holding her in the warmth of his embrace. Grief saddened his countenance. Tears spilled from his eyes and bowed head exposed more than just sorrow at Tzaddi's death. His grief spilled over into his affection for Beth. Falling, trembling into his embrace she clutched him as a human lifeline. Punctuated by sobs, her words choked out "Why . . . why did Tzaddi have to die?"

"Milady, I weep with you," Aleph whispered stroking her hair. "We know all must die, but the sting of death has been taken away. As you have read in the letters, soon even the victory of the grave will be overcome."

Her tears mingled with his as they coursed down her cheek into his beard. A great comfort soothed her in Aleph's strong arms. As close as she felt to Aleph entwined in his embrace, Beth knew Tzaddi was right. The words of the Prince had sustained her. She had to remain loyal to him, to his words. *Here I am trembling in the arms of my servant. Would the Prince be shocked if he knows? Is it possible for me to remain loyal to an absentee Prince? I see loyal followers doing it even without his words. Soldiers are giving their lives in defense of his kingdom, Even Aleph, kind, faithful Aleph, is serving him by serving me.*

Beth pulled Aleph even tighter. It was inconceivable that many had turned away from the Prince after hearing his words. How could anyone reject his words? Would she?

Embarrassed by her thoughts and the warmth she felt clinging to Aleph for so long, Beth finally disentangled herself from the comfort of Aleph's embrace. Tearfully she shooed him away.

So much more had become clear in the tumultuous journey of the past months as she had contemplated them from the cold stone bench. The enslaved people she imagined looking down from the tower reminded her of how the words of the Prince could make a difference. Hungry looks on the faces of shepherds, soldiers, slaves, and servants who listened enraptured as she read. They were people of the Prince. They had become her people. Even all those transformed in the stories Tzaddi had told. Yes, and she, too, had comfort in her own broken heart because of the loss of sweet Tzaddi. Finally, she took up the Prince's letters and smoothed a blank page with shivering fingers.

O my Prince, even though I have not seen you,
you are good, and your guidance is fair.
Your teachings are perfect and completely trustworthy.
I am overwhelmed with indignation,

for the wicked enemy that has rejected your words.
Your promises have been tested;
that is why I love them so much.
At times my heart has been divided and tempted,
but I can't forget your faithfulness.
Your justice is eternal, and your instructions
are perfect and true.
As pressure and stress bear down on me,
I find joy and strength in your letters.
Your laws are always right;
help me share them so others may live.

Chapter Nineteen

Qoph

HEAT RADIATING FROM the roaring fire in the keep still had not completely calmed the shivering or thawed the cold in Beth's chest. Even the covers Aleph had laid over her shoulders and the hot cider he had urged her to drink did nothing to quell the shivering. Letting go of Tzaddi was a hard reminder of the loss of her mother, the estrangement of her father, and the distance she was from home. Tzaddi's death also highlighted the seeming futility of her journey. So many miles, days, sorrows, and she still felt no closer to finding her Prince.

Hope kindled by his words dwindled with the death of Tzaddi. Many of the other deaths around her were unknown, unnamed soldiers. It was easier that way. In Beth's mind, Tzaddi's passing felt like the end of the journey. *But this cannot be the end?* She moved a bit closer, trying to soak in the heat from the blaze in the fireplace. Folding herself into a knot, she closed her eyes, pulled the blanket over her head, and pressed her palms to her ears.

Cocooned by the heavy blanket, ears covered, eyes squeezed shut, she allowed grief to flood in. Along with it, came the darkness. The swirling night was all about her.

The weight of loss, fear of the future, pain of rejection, guilt of failure, voices of mockery, thoughts of worthlessness, desires to wound herself and end her life, dragged her down into a nightmare. Darker yet she descended into the blackness. In deep sleep she remembered. Beth had been there before. It was the long dark hallway in the shrine of Countess Teith. Painting after painting, image after image paraded past. Each an idol to herself. Looking closer at the portraits and carvings, they had transformed to become tributes to her. A temple to the goddess Beth. I can abandon my quest, forget the Prince and think of myself instead. *I think I better understand the Countess Teith,* Beth thought in her dream. *This darkness is all about me. I hurt because of those who have hurt me. I feel sorry for myself, the girl that did not get her own way. Pity me. This weight is familiar to me as well.*

The darkness had not appeared often but when it did, escape seemed impossible. Time became meaningless. It felt like death.

Then words came into the dream. *Holy* is what Tzaddi had said. It echoed in her darkness. Holy, holy, holy. Who can be holy? she wondered. Was forgiveness a part of that?

Safe in the Citadel called Salah, would she be able to forgive?

Into the darkness, came a small light. Very much like Aleph's lamp. There was light but a tiny surge of warmth came with it at the reminder of her kind companion. The light shone at her feet and illuminated a pathway. Steps ahead, the path split in two. To the right, a narrow rocky path that headed upward. To the left, downward, a wide smooth highway, became even darker still.

Standing at the fork, the voice of Kaph, the seamstress, healer of the wounded and mender of broken things, spoke in her ear. "Much of the real battle is fought in the hidden world of the soul. This battle is against powers and authorities in spiritual places. It is a battle of choices, decisions of thoughts and feelings. A choice must be made to change direction. You are to be set apart for an extraordinary purpose." At that moment, the impossible word came out of the mouth of the healer, "Forgive."

This is the fork in the road. This must be the place of choice, thought Beth. She had read of this place in the letters. The path leading to a place of wholeness, a place of freedom; being set apart for a unique and beautiful dwelling. It was here she must claim a victory already won for her, or reject it, descending the dark road of self-centered obsession. Living for herself alone. This was the road to sorrow and defeat. In his own hand the Prince had written, "Forgive, even as I have forgiven you." *I cannot do this,* was all Beth could think.

Then the struggle began.

In times past, as a young girl she had given in to the dark moods. Her mother grieved during those moods. Silent, not knowing what could be done, her father, would drift farther away. With time the gloom would lift, but the darkness always left wounds.

Now memories of the evil forced upon her, enlarged the darkness looming to crush her.

That word, spoken by the healer, gently advised by her faithful servant, whispered by Tzaddi, hovered over, around her, and the words of the Prince pierced her soul. *Forgive. It is not for my enemy*, Beth said to herself. *It is for my own freedom.* In an instant it was done. The decision was easy when the power came from the words of the ultimate forgiver.

For the first time, there was light, there was hope.

Even in her nightmare, hope had not been snuffed out. The tiny spark of light became her locus. It captured her vision. Reaching towards it ignited more light. The surge of darkness began to give way. It was the words of her lord, the Prince! Lines she had memorized. Those sentences, phrases, quotes from the passionate love the Prince had poured from his heart to her, swung about her, lighting up her gloom with a brightness she had never known. The word appeared written as if in gold ink, began to glow in the dark. FORGIVE.

The battle centered around believing the words and looking at, looking for, the face of her Prince.

An explosion of pure light burned away years of depressive memories. The more she focused on the words of her Prince, the image of his face, the love in his eyes, the brighter the light. Gradually, strength flowed back into her cold limbs.

First a crack, then a rending of the dark crusted cocoon, and the gloom around her broke open, sooty pieces slaking off as she reached toward the light. Released from her prison, the shell that confined her melted. Floating upwards, delivered, she was confidently aware her mind, her thoughts, her body were set free! Nothing could have prepared her for the freedom she felt.

Drifting upward from the darkness, was the feeling of rising slowly through warm honey. It calmed her palpitating heart.

Floating beside her, carried upward by some invisible current, was her wonderful book. From the open book swirled leaves, each marked with the letters of the mystical alphabet. Dreamily drifting upwards, she recognized each letter as they glided past. The last five of the leaves came into view. Each meaning became clear. *Peh*, the mouth, smooth talker, and next, *tzaddi*, the just and righteous nursemaid who had died hours ago in her arms. Following it was revealed *kaph*, a place of forgiveness and holiness. The one which floated next became clear: *reish*, a banner of leadership and authority. The last of her drawings floated past. It was the round circle of safety. *Samekh*, Aleph had said, also called Salah, the place of forgiveness. *In forgiveness, I am free!*

Only two blank leaves remained.

Released from the nightmare, waking from her dream, Beth sat up. Gulps of fresh air dispelled all darkness. Beth found herself, arms and legs stretched out on the couch before the fire. Her head was clear infused with a sense of euphoria. The internal battle had been won. Recalling the darkness and struggle, she realized other soul-battles might come. But now, the memory of darkness no longer enslaved her. She would struggle, perhaps for years. Or even her whole life, but she was confident the light she carried within would always prevail.

A timepiece on the mantel over the fire, chimed out the stroke of midnight. Beth was not tired. The precious letters on a table in front of her were clearly legible by two torches and the light of the fire kept burning all night. She read again, written as if in gold, of the passion, the love and the hope the Prince offered her in his words. She meditated on the promises contained in the letters. His claims of faithfulness. Beautiful scenes unfolded: a joyful wedding, a kingdom at peace, lavish joyful banquets, singing choirs, children—*perhaps our very own*—playing in gardens overflowing with lush blooms and fountains.

The hours passed quickly. Each hour the timepiece chimed was a reminder of the privilege that was hers enjoying those night hours with the Prince. She envisioned him standing before his throne, golden crown on his brow, clothed in royal finery. *I can imagine him reaching out his hand to me, bedecked with jewels. I see a welcoming smile on his face.*

He would speak. The silent words on the pages she had carried, protected, and meditated on for months would come spilling from his lips.

Chimes indicated the hour just before the rising of the sun. Beth arose, wanting to see the dawn from atop the spire of Ayin. It would be glorious. Running up steps recently climbed in broken-hearted grief, now refreshed, energized, believing perhaps tomorrow she would see the face of her beloved. The sunrise, always symbolic of new days, new hope shone with the promise of new life.

Arriving at the *ayin* at just the right moment, breathless with anticipation, sun rays sliced through the gray dawn painting the stray clouds, the tower, the lake, the forest, the mountain, the entire kingdom, with saffron, pink, and gold. *Tzaddi is to be praised*, Beth thought happily. *She introduced me to the quest. Her hand offered me the words of the Prince. Her encouragement convinced me to follow him. According to his words she lives on forever.* And the aged nursemaid would always be enshrined in her memory as the giver of the good gift.

Facing the sun, Beth allowed its warmth to melt away the last few traces of chill in the morning air and in her heart. Breathing deeply, she felt ready for whatever lay ahead. She had pursued the Prince with her whole heart. Forgiveness had set her free. There were no regrets.

Lighthearted, with sunbeams shining down on her precious letters, her fingers took up the pen.

She paused to focus her thoughts. Leaning forward to write, the silver dove swung forward into the sunlight. The shadow cast on the page was instantly recognizable: *tav*. The End. A mark, a seal, an omen. *It is finished.* Echoing as if down a long hallway, her father's voice came back to her: *Tav signifies perfection, completion, the culmination of all things.* Just before she began to copy the final letter, she realized there was still one leaf. *If Tav, is the final letter, what do I draw on the remaining leaf? What is it for?*

It was the only blank leaf remaining. Twenty-two leaves had found their way into her hands, she was convinced, not by accident. She remembered that was the total of the letters taught to her by her father. Tav was the last letter. *Is the story coming to a close? Will I lose my life in this battle? What, then, is the letter on the blank leaf?* Studying the shadows again revealed no new shapes. *And what about this passionate love that has grown up to encompass my entire heart?*

As the sun rose into a cloudy sky, the shadows faded. Although the story was not complete, nothing further would be revealed today. She longed to reach the end, where she would be united with her Prince. That time would come. But in a desire to be steadfast, she prayed. Her eyes closed and this time brought the peace beyond all measure. Invocations, prayed often over the past months, gave her comfort. Comfort and the assurance she would soon be with her

Prince. Yet the battle still came first. Standing against the foe, defeating the lawless was necessary. Then victory. After many supplications, she opened her eyes, quill still in her hand.

I pray with all my heart; answer me, my King!
We will embrace your edicts.
I am crying out to you; give us victory,
And because of that we will cling to your words.
I rose early, before the sun was up;
I called out for help and turned my eyes on you.
Through the night I stayed awake,
thinking about your promises,
in your faithful love, O my Lord, hear my cry;
I have been revived by following your advice.
Liars and lawless people are coming to attack us;
they don't understand and live far from
your declarations.
But you are near, O Lord, and all your affirmations
are true.
I now know now from the beginning; your utterances
will last forever.

Chapter Twenty

Reish

SHE CLOSED HER book and set it on the bench with her fingers tracing the gems on the cover. Hunger began to remind her the day was moving on. On cue, with every indication of prescience, Aleph had appeared on the spire with milk, pastries, and fruit.

"How did you know, Aleph?" Beth smiled. "You seem to always show up at the right time, which I am convinced is the perfect skill of a servant; to anticipate the needs of the one you are serving. Well done, friend."

With his typical smile, Aleph bowed, placed the food beside her. "Thank you, Milady."

"Oh, and did you hear me ask Tzaddi last night about the seven stones on the cover of my book? Beth asked. "Do you know what the seven miracles are?"

"I did hear your request and know they all will be revealed in due time, Milady. Now, you have time to eat without haste, but then your presence is requested as preparations are made for the burial of your servant, Tzaddi. Also, your highness, with your permission, the horse Ashes has been requested for service in the team pulling the bier."

"Oh, that would be so special. Of course they may use Ashes, it is fitting." As Beth finished eating, Aleph cleaned up and followed her down to the main fortress gate.

In the great hall entrance, colorful drapes had been festooned from one pillar to the next, creating an archway of color over the hearse hitched to the team of horses. Beth felt proud to see her powerful Friesian harnessed with the company of five other horses. Ashes dominated the others by her size and majesty. A band of musicians, dancers, and singers began a lively melody as the crowd clapped in rhythm.

Aleph had vanished into the eating hall, so Beth followed the horse-drawn carriage out into the plain and across to the stones near the cliff. There niches in the stones had been carved out for burials. There were many. They came to a halt before a flat-topped stone. The body of faithful Tzaddi, as small as child, wrapped in linen, was laid on the stone by two soldiers. After a songlike invocation was sung by one dressed in the humble robes of a monk, another humble spokesman gave a heartfelt eulogy of the righteous and just nursemaid to the Prince. *It is obvious,* Beth thought, *Tzaddi was well known and beloved to many who knew her.* The band played another joyful tune, Tzaddi's body was placed in one of the carved openings with a stone rolled in front and they all returned to the fort.

Back in her chamber Beth located her friend. "Aleph, why was there so much happiness and joy going on? I thought this was to be a funeral. It was more like a party."

He smiled, looking up at but beyond the ceiling, "It is simply this, Milady: Tzaddi, the just and righteous one, was a loyal follower of the Prince. She has been translated into a better place for all eternity. It is a time of joy."

Beth nodded. "I guess that is the best way to look at it." Beth sighed stifling a yawn. "It was brief, cheerful and in a strange way very satisfying. But now, I think, having been up most of the night, I must get some rest."

A cloud crossed his face. "I regret to inform you, Milady, but your presence is requested again in the throne room."

Not eager to be a part of another trial, she asked "Are there more prisoners needing to be sentenced, or is this some other kind of big assembly?"

"All the troops are in place, the generals are assembled, and final plans for the attack must be made. But it has reached my ears that a messenger arrived moments ago with an announcement of great import."

"What announcement, Aleph?" When he seemed hesitant, she pressed him. "Tell me, I need to know!"

"It has come from the castle. Beyond that I can say no more."

There was no question of resting now. If there was news from the castle, she needed to hear it. Turning, she headed for the throne room.

Over her shoulder she said, "Come along, Aleph, it's news from home. We have heard nothing from the castle—this is exciting." But there was no need for concern about Aleph. He was in step right behind her. Beth remembered the way to the throne room, arriving as the last few crowded into the room she had been in before. The doors were beginning to swing closed. Her arrival stirred up some confusion when those recognizing her began to chant, "Make way! Make way for the princess." Instantly a path widened from the doors, clear to the throne.

She was ushered and flanked on either side by the same guards from the day before. A quick glance behind the throne revealed no sign of Aleph. He had been right behind her but now had disappeared. By the time she was seated, a low rhythmic pounding of spears, shields, and feet began, until all were caught up in the cadence. Then with unexplained precision, at the exact beat, the pounding stopped. The meeting was now in session.

A group of generals and dignitaries formed the military council, standing on either side of the thrones reserved for Beth and, she assumed, her Prince. In the middle stood Gimmel, a head taller than any of the others. A military leader of some sort stood at the podium. When the silence was complete, the leader took a parchment scroll, sealed with the royal red-wax emblem, broke the seal and unrolled it before the crowd. A breath of anticipation was inhaled across the throne room.

With a grim voice reverberating in the rafters overhead, the general read: "From the official advisor. This letter is to inform you that all leadership, all authority, all divine power, is now transferred to the Prince of the realm. The imperial standard, the banner *Resh* belongs to him. The crown, the royal scepter, the robe of power, and the gold ring bearing the royal seal are all his." A pause in the reading brought the room to almost silence. Peering at the document in unbelief, the general coughed softly and continued. "With great sorrow we regret to inform you, the King is dead." A wave of noise crashed into the room. Everyone was shouting a comment.

"He has been sickly." "The King has waited too long." "I knew death was close." Where is the Prince?" Who will lead us?" "Can the battle begin without a leader?" What do we do now?"

The entire time, the general in charge was banging the stone on the podium. "Silence! We must have silence!" The banging continued until a measure of quiet was gradually restored.

Comments still being whispered by the multitude gave the entire proceedings a feeling of unrest. The general's stentorian voice spoke over the murmur. "Silence, all. We must choose one to carry the banner Resh. One to be our temporary leader until the Prince reveals himself. Tomorrow the battle will commence, whether we are prepared or not. Who, then, can take our standard and carry it into battle?"

Around the room various names were shouted out. It looked as if confusion and uncontrolled chaos was going to reign. Then the name Gimmel was repeated. "Yes, Gimmel, he can lead us!" Shouted another, "We want Gimmel!"

Beth, feeling weak and confused, looked over at him. She could tell he was decidedly uncomfortable. Shuffling his large, booted feet, he lowered his head, shaking it slowly from side to side.

"Quiet. Let him speak!" shouted the general.

"Yes! Let him speak!" yelled someone in the back of the room.

Hesitant, Gimmel stepped to the front of the platform, and out of respect a measure of quiet was granted him. In the deep rumbling voice so familiar to Beth, he spoke briefly, yet with clarity and confidence.

"Leaders, fellow soldiers, all people loyal to the Prince. I have not been given the imperial banner. I have no authority. I cannot lead you. We have known for many months of the choice made by the Prince of his bride-to-be. The woman selected to be our future queen. *She* must carry our standard. We have no option but to appoint her as the one to lead us into battle."

Every eye in the throne room turned toward her. Heart pounding, brain reeling, gasping for breath, wide-eyed, uncomprehending, Beth almost fainted and nearly fell off the throne.

The entire crowd went into bedlam. "Yes, the Queen!" "Hail Beth!" shouted some. "Boo!" "No, we will not be led by a child." "She has no authority," shouted others. Many looked at her with compassion and shook their heads, no. Many looked away and cursed under their breath. Others still shouted, "Gimmel! He can lead us!" There was no consensus. No agreement. The arguments were heated and contentious.

The general, speaker in charge, wisely waited as the shouts died down and dissension began to fade. But it was clear, many were not happy with Gimmel's statement. After banging his stone gavel for some time, the noise settled into a tense grumbling, and the general spoke.

"Here me! Listen all of you! This is what we know. Here are the unassailable facts before us. This is what we face. First, Gimmel has declared he will not lead us. It is assured that no one is able to change the mind of Gimmel. Second, word has been given by the Prince himself that the princess Beth is to be our queen." Discontented rumbles went across the crowd. "Lastly, all our sources confirm the enemy will invade tomorrow and overwhelm our defenses, unless we strike first. Or surrender and run for our lives." A universal grunt of discouragement resulted from that statement. "I then propose we place the choice of our leader before the military council and accept their decision without question."

Again, the entire room erupted. Some were in favor,

shouting, "Yes, we must have a vote!" Some, not as loud, but with deep conviction, said, "We will not fight without Gimmel!" "We will not go into battle under a queen!" "We must be led by the Prince!"

This is not happening, thought Beth. Her unfocused eyes were flicking from the speaker to the crowd and back. Heart pounding, mouth dry, hands clenching and unclenching in her lap, she glanced again at Gimmel, who had stepped back into the ranks. He did not meet her gaze. This was terrifying. Looking over her shoulder and around the room, she hoped to see Aleph, but his peaked hat and humble figure were nowhere in sight. Dependence on his steadfast presence had become a rock, a stable place. To panic and run for the exit was impossible, but it crossed her mind. What was absolutely clear was that she was just a humble scribe, an artist. She was not a princess, certainly not the queen. There had been no wedding, no royal decree, and there was no sign of the newly appointed King!

Ignoring the noisy crowd, the speaker turned to the military council on the stage. "How, then, do you vote? Yea, the princess Beth will lead us. Step forward! Nay, we surrender to Belial, the prince of destruction—stand as you are." The entire room, for the first time since they entered, descended into whisper quiet. Beth had her eyes locked onto Gimmel, keeping the rest of the military council in her vision. She held her breath.

The silence extended longer than could be imagined. Every single member of the council, hesitated, looked left and right, frozen in place, until each one turned their eyes to Gimmel. With courage gained from many years as a soldier, he lifted his face to Beth, gave her a tight-lipped smile, a deep nod of respect, and what could have passed as a tiny wink, took a giant step forward. As if one man, the entire council followed.

There was no controlling the crowd now. Crashing the giant doors open, a stream of soldiers obviously angry at the decision, were leaving the room, a few even dropping their weapons in disgust as they left. To Beth it looked like the entire army was deserting in anger. Noise, frustration, and chaos left with them. Those remaining, stood in solidarity, firmly committed to the choice, and to the leadership of the queen-to-be.

Her ears ringing from the shouts and heart pounding tension of the moment, Beth was frantic to find Aleph. When she could not, she reached out to the only one in the room left in whom she had confidence. "Gimmel," she called, trying to control the panic in her voice.

Without hesitation, in one giant stride he was at her side. Kneeling before her he respectfully addressed her. "Your highness, it was our desire, those of your servants loyal to the Prince, to inform you of this development. There was not time." Under his breath, he continued, "Gain confidence in this, we are all here to serve you."

Just the deep rumble of his voice quieted her somewhat.

"What, oh Gimmel, what do I do now? I have no authority, and I cannot carry the royal banner. The imperial Resh was granted to the Prince. The King alone can carry the standard."

Her hand touched the massive shoulder, remembering the kindness and encouraging words he had spoken on the journey. Gimmel would make a noble Prince. I wish he would stand and take the throne next to me. Where, oh where is my Prince when I need him?

Gimmel looked at her. "Milady, you have the authority to carry the banner, because you hold the words of the Prince. That alone gives you power and authority to speak. Merely stand and read a portion befitting your new royal status. All will be well." Taller than the throne, he stood, bowed once again, and returned to his place with the councilors.

It had worked before. The power in the words, Tzaddi and Aleph had both assured her, would be appropriate for any occasion. With quaking knees, trembling hands, and quivering lips, she stood, took courage from words which had taken permanent residence in her heart, and began to speak.

"Only be strong and courageous," she read. "One will chase a thousand, two will be victorious over ten thousand." As she continued to read promises from her letters, the warriors in the throne room grew in confidence. It even appeared they grew in number as some who had left in anger returned slowly in repentance to hear the affirmations found in those powerful epistles.

As she ended her reading, she sat. The general stepped again to the podium. "You have heard the words of the

Prince. Go! Prepare your troops now for the battle to come."

‡ ‡ ‡

AFTER ALL HAD gone save the general and a few of the council, Beth wearily rose, turned to Gimmel, and asked, "Well, friend, can I really do this? I wonder, how many have abandoned the fight? It sounded to me like some of those leaving were out for blood. My blood."

"They are traitors, Milady, wicked men who may persecute you. They may bring trouble, as some before them who were never truly loyal to the Prince."

"All right, Gimmel, go prepare your troops for battle. Will I see you after the fighting has begun?"

"You, can rest assured, I will be by your side as long as I am able to stand."

With the stealth of a shadow, Aleph slipped from behind a tapestry unseen and followed her down the stairs. Knowing the call would probably come early, Beth headed to her small room behind the alcove to get some rest. Groups of soldiers huddled at different floors and hallways during her descent. She could hear their furtive comments as she passed. Most respectfully turned to face her and bow. Some cursed and spat, threatening her well-being and even her life. Rounding the last corner, she was relieved to reach the seclusion of her room.

Her silent shadow finally spoke. "Shall I bring food, Milady?"

Beth almost jumped out of her armor. "G—gosh, Aleph! You scared me halfway to Mount Shin! Where were you hiding? Did you hear? The King is dead!"

"Yes, Milady." Aleph hung his head, speaking with a quaver in his voice. "The news had reached here before the announcement was made. My grief is deep. I cannot imagine being forsaken now." He sounded so tragically bereft.

She wanted to reach out and embrace him. Strong feelings of great affection came upon her. What had been an internal skirmish threatened to become a full-scale civil war. Aleph was here, now offering to be with her and care for her! She could sense the strength of his quiet unspoken love for her. Aleph was here. The Prince, for all his passionate words, was not. For all this time, throughout the entire journey, all she had been given was words, just words. The longing—for Aleph's embrace, real arms, genuine care, the sensitive look in his eyes—was strong. Those eyes settled on hers. She could see nothing else. Blood rushed to her face. She could feel nothing but her pounding heart. His mouth opened to speak but the ringing in her ears made it impossible to hear.

"Love me with all your soul, love me with all your mind, love me with all your heart, even as I have loved you. It is the only thing I ask."

Words from the Prince broke the spell.

Rushing to the window across the room, away from Aleph, Beth composed herself. Outside the low window she could see the chasm, the far side of the bridge, and imagine the battle beyond. Without turning around, she voiced the first thought in her head.

"How, then, can we go forward with the battle, Aleph?" Sensing the same conflict in him as tormented her, she hurried on, not waiting for his response. "I am terrified at the thought of having to carry Resh. Gimmel, he should carry the standard and lead our soldiers into battle. I am fearful many have left us."

With infinitely more self-control than was hers, he answered the way he always did. "The craven troops that rejected your leadership will be held accountable for their treachery. But the vote was taken, and I am pleased to see it was united."

Still shaky, her eyes unable to leave the sight out the window, she tried to give a measured response.

"Well, it was not an enjoyable experience. But back in the valley of Kaph, I determined to follow this quest to the end. So I shall! You and Tzaddi, have assured me I will find the Prince. I have no other option but to trust him, to believe in his words."

In the alcove with the small bench and room beyond, Beth turned and bravely looked Aleph directly in the eye. Emotions she had carried for so long but could never express tried to surface again. His eyes, clear and innocent, revealed true devotion, his servant's heart—and even love.

She looked down, trying to break the strong attraction and choked out the words, "And . . . yes, I would like some food and tea to drink, if you don't mind."

"With pleasure, my queen." He bowed his head and slipped away.

My queen roared in her ears. Aleph had never given her that royal designation before. Others had hinted, even Tzaddi. Perhaps this was all going to happen after all. Before Aleph returned with food, Beth, still astounded at the events in the throne room, sat down at the desk and wrote these pleading words.

Look upon my indecision, my King, and rescue me,
for all I have is your letters.
Come hold me; please come to my side!
Be with me as you promised.
Many have moved far from your instructions,
for they do not want to listen to you.
My King, how great is your mercy;
I now need your strength and wisdom to lead.
Many have turned away and rejected my leadership,
yet I have not swerved from your edicts.
Seeing these traitors makes me sick at heart,
because they care nothing for your instructions.
You know I love you, Lord.
Strengthen me with your unfailing love.
The very meaning of your words is truth;
all your encouragement will uphold me forever.

Chapter Twenty One

Shin

AN ORDER, SHOUTED at the top, was repeated down each floor until it reached them in the lower level. The hall began to empty out as soldiers regathered their armor and moved toward the stairway up from the bowels of Samekh. They climbed high toward the tower, across the bridge to the war beyond. Followed by Aleph, Beth collected her weapons and climbed the wide stairs leading upward.

The number of soldiers had dwindled. She thought of the many who had defected the day before, rejecting her leadership. More left from fatigue, second thoughts, or perhaps craven fear. Disdain and anger at their possible cowardice irritated her. *What if we lose the war and then the kingdom because of the shortage of warriors loyal to the cause? Will the new King have to flee into hiding? Will I need to run with him? What if we are captured and killed?* These thoughts and more worrisome ones started to nibble away at her courage and loyalty. Her feet began to slow on the stairs. Aleph moved ahead of her, then looked back with a worried expression on his face.

"Your highness, have your wounded feet begun to cause pain again?" he asked with concern.

She shook her head. "No, Aleph, I am just thinking of all those cowards who left the ranks yesterday and this morning. Maybe, in the thick of the battle, I might give way to my own fears as well."

Aleph smiled, a poignant look in his eyes. "The time for that has passed, Milady. The bridge and the crossing are before us." And so they were. The landing ahead opened on to the parapet holding the uprights of the bridge. "There can be no turning back now, the narrow path allows for only those moving forward. There is no room for return, your highness. Your hand is on the plow." Courage in his voice surprised her. She had these strong feelings for him but had no confidence in Aleph as a warrior. Serving her, helping her, leading her, comforting her in trouble and caring for her mare and the donkey had been the extent of his experience. Oh, and giving advice. He seemed to dispense that a bit too often for a stable hand. Looking him over, she hoped he would not become a hindrance. With the early morning light shining around him, he did look more mature. His peaked hat was gone and during the journey, his smooth, boyish face had developed a rugged beard and mustache. He might have even grown taller. *If someone gave him a sword, he might be helpful in the fight,* she thought. But that was all she had time to ponder.

Now for the first time, Beth became aware of the real battle. Noise began to increase in volume and tempo. Standing patiently by the bridge was Ashes. Beside her Gimmel stood holding the staff of the bright red standard Resh. Leading the way with the banner waving over his head, he stepped onto the narrow way. Beth followed leading her horse. Ahead, she could see the heave and push of the King's soldiers, slashing and thrusting their way up the mountain side. The enemy forces had the overwhelming look of a slow-moving avalanche of grim stones. Even the acrid smell of blood, wounds, and death struck her in the face. She began to gag on the taste of it in the back of her throat.

The pace increased too. Gimmel lengthened his stride, causing her to run to keep up. His mass, like a shield before her, gave her some comfort. Over the top of his helmet, she could see the mountain Shin. More broken, more malevolent than ever, the three flames appeared to have a white core with a putrid scarlet-stained hue surrounding each flame. Intense red tinged everything with the look of blood. Shivering at the gruesome appearance, Beth forced her eyes away. A final step and they were across the bridge.

Clang! The blow came unexpectedly, knocking her to the ground. Trained reflex lifted her shield almost too late to ward off a slashing ax-swing aimed at her neck with the clear intent of severing her head from her body. The shield did its work. Dull from much fighting, the enemy ax glanced off the steel protection, but quickly raised again for a death blow. Leaping nimbly to her feet, her training began to flow. Her left arm and shoulder were numb and tingling from the strike. The pain would set in later.

Her attacker looked as evil as the volcano itself. Low brows hung over beady eyes with a mashed-in nose and barred yellow teeth. Gangly arms ended with hands gripping the weighty ax in both hands. Leather armor covered the muscular body. Harness and belt studded with metal spikes pointing in every direction. Beth was convinced the next swing would slay her. It never fell. With a deep grunt, Gimmel swung his massive sword, severing the creature in half.

"Thank you, Gimmel," she muttered, hoping he had heard, but not wanting to say it. To be chopped in half in the very first skirmish of the battle would have been humiliating. Not to mention she would be dead.

Before the next attack, Aleph hoisted her into the saddle of her giant horse. Gimmel handed her the banner of Resh. With a whinny and snort, Ashes revealed the horse admired for her beauty had also been trained for war.

Rearing, kicking, and thrusting forward, Ashes gave Beth every opportunity to strike from above. Fear crossed the face of many a soldier as a massive hoof knocked them from their feet or trampled them into the gravel beneath. With the endurance bred into her lineage, Ashes forged her way into the lead, with Beth holding the banner unfurled revealing the image and colors of the kingdom. She became the tip of the spear, the rallying cry for the soldiers of the Prince!

The sight of the charging horse urged on by the future queen with the royal banner whipping in the wind inspired cheers from the soldiers, strength for the fainthearted, and courage for the fearful. Onward the entire army charged, pushing the enemy off the cliffs into the abyss and forcing them back on every front. The size and strength of the forces against them was staggering, yet they fought courageously onward.

Gravel and stones made the climb more difficult for Ashes. After hours of fighting up the slope, even the mighty horse began to tire. Finally with an arrow hanging from her withers and wounds in many places, a serious limp hampered her upward climb. As the day wore on, it became obvious to Beth, Ashes could no longer continue. She was left, head down in a small gully, defended by a few wounded soldiers who vowed to keep her safe.

The battle continued on foot. Now Beth had no overwhelming advantage over the enemy. She had to fight, one on one. Each victory came at a huge cost. One spiky-haired soldier not much bigger than she was, came screaming down the slope with her sword held high. For almost an hour they traded blows, till finally, down on one knee, Beth scored a devastating slice at her attacker's thigh that dropped her to one side.

Hoping to rise and finish her off, she found no strength in her legs to rise and strike the final thrust. It was left to Gimmel, her loyal protector, to finish the job. Time after time, she would make a valiant effort to deliver the final overcoming blow and yet the victory came from Gimmel and the legions surrounding her. More often as the day wore on, she found herself being helped to her feet by Aleph, who was always at her side offering assistance and tending to her wounds.

Advancing up the mountain, one brutal clash at a time made slow progress, but ground was won at a serious price. Fatigued, covered in mud, soot and dried blood—other than size, Beth was indistinguishable from any of the other warriors. She would fall, but she would not stay down. Each stumble would make her more determined to not give up.

As the first day ground down toward dusk, Beth became aware of what her mentor, Kaph, in the cave school, had warned her about: the conflict within. What raged on the outside was often mirrored in her soul. Thoughts, urges, pressures, and fatigue from within continually urged her to stop and rest, to give in, to flee down the mountain to safety. In her head, voices at times strident, demanded that she give up, mocking her worthless feeble attempts. No King would take a second glance at this mud-covered, sweaty, wounded, and scarred woman. Nor would she be considered for a bride. Fears that haunted her before returned: *You are not worthy. No one will ever love you.*

But energy from the determination within strengthened her with unassailable joy and courage without. Again and again the words of the Prince fought the unseen battle for her. She would recall a word, a phrase, a paragraph from the letters becoming fuel for her fire.

At times she leapt up the stones, carving her way toward an assured victory. Then at times she fell, weakness holding her implacably with thoughts of failure. Yet each time she arose. Each delight, each joy, each victory claimed only by a miracle.

When the voices were too loud, shouting the words of the Prince cleared her mind. In the full darkness of the first night, Aleph drew her gasping into a shelter beneath a boulder. He lit the lamp he still carried. Sorrow creased his face.

"Your highness has fought valiantly and well," he murmured, handing her a used bandana to wipe her eyes and face. "I am grieved, no food or water is to be found anywhere on this stone carapace. I could attempt to return to the bridge at Samekh for supplies, but I would hate to leave you alone and my safe return would be almost impossible. We are surrounded by the enemy. No word of supplies or reinforcements has reached us. If you turn back, Milady, as have so many others, I would go with you."

His offer stood. She could perhaps survive, return home, and lead a quiet life with the humble stable hand who had demonstrated his love and loyalty. But that was impossible. She was committed, she was marked, Belial would never allow it.

An unanticipated smile crossed Beth's mud-covered face. "We were warned it would be a fierce battle. My whole heart is at stake. I have committed it completely to my Prince, my King. But you, faithful Aleph, have been every bit as much my sword and shield." She gave him a playful punch on the shoulder. "However long it takes. With whatever strength we have. Because of love for the King, we will fight to the end."

By the light of the rock-burning lamp, Beth pulled her now bent and dirtied book from the pouch in her cloak. Opening to one of the few blank pages left, she wrote.

A powerful enemy attacks us without ceasing,
but my heart trembles only at your word.
I rejoice in your letters
like one who discovers great strength.
I hate and abhor all evil, but I love your instructions.
I will praise you seven times a day
because all your regulations are just.
Those who love your instructions have great peace,
if I stumble, I will rise again.
We long for your rescue, O King,
we long for your coming.
I have followed your instructions,
for I love them very much.

Yes, I obey them because you are with me, in everything I do.

Even in the blackness of the night, the clash and shouts of skirmishes continued. There was no silence for sleep, no reprieve from the sounds of war, there was no food or water for refreshment.

A feeble sun dawned on the second day of the major battle. The conflict, powered by grit and tenacity, sucked every ounce of will from friend and foe. Yet the fighting went on.

By dawn of day three, Beth could not speak, because her mouth was utterly dry. Her parched lips were caked with dried spit, her throat raspy and parched. There was nothing to say. Only the will to continue the fight. Many times, she wondered if it would ever end. Hope was as dry as her lips. Victory had been stolen, not by a blaze of strategic brilliance or overwhelming military strength, but by the moment-by-moment grind of endless small losses.

No mighty frontal attack had taken them down, merely a million seemingly insignificant skirmishes. Daily drudgery became the continual, unremitting, slog of defeat. The battle was now being fought entirely from within. Only the will to push beyond the strength of muscle and sinew would keep them moving upward.

Her dwindling but faithful troops, had carved their way to within steps of the summit. Many lay scattered down the mountain, sacrificed in the conflict. All appearances showed the war had been lost. Bodies lay among the stones as far as the eye could see.

After forty hours without food, water or rest, her body and her mind, her soul could go no further. No shred of strength remained. Without warning, one of few remaining enemy soldiers recognized her as the chosen one. He stood between her and the top. Facing him, shoulders drooped, shield hanging down, sword notched and broken, she knew it was the end. Evil written clearly on a distorted face, the soldier raised his sword to end Beth's life.

The blow never landed. Prying her cramped hand from the damaged sword, ever present Aleph parried the downward stroke and pierced the enemy soldier's armor with a final slicing blow. Beth, draped in the torn banner of Resh, slumped where she stood. Before she could hit the ground, her savior reached beneath her fall and lifted her in a strong embrace. Cradled, her scarred arms compassed his neck, face buried against his throat. Her cheek felt his heartbeat and lips brushed by his beard. There had been no safety since the war began, till now. Even in the midst of death, surrounded by chaos, she felt secure.

The war, it seemed was over. They had lost. No Prince, no King had come to rescue them. Who had written the letters, the passionate words, she did not know. If they were false, she had been deceived. Cruelly manipulated by lies. Led on a journey that ended in defeat. Outrage and pain threatened to pull her under. But being carried to safety by her faithful companion, other emotions welled up; gratefulness, comfort, along with what she felt was genuine love for this humble man who had stayed with her during this entire quest.

"Have faith, your highness. Hope is not dead," whispered Aleph through lips so close, his breath tickled her ear. "I will fetch the mare, Ashes, who will convey you to safety."

With ease, Aleph carried her upslope, away from the remnants of battle, then gently wrapped in the royal banner, lay her on a lonely patch of withered turf.

"Watch and wait till I return."

Eyes closed, coveting the memory of his strong embrace, Beth tried to find whatever shred was left of her faith. Doubt loomed larger than hope. A sharp cry opened her eyes. Looking up, surprised, she lay at the very entrance to the broken palace of Belial built atop the mountain Shin. A staircase was all that stood between her and the white arched doorway. The fractured marble staircase leading up to the amphitheater still swept upward with a graceful curve only marred by a jagged crack near the top. Growing from the crevice, with knotted roots and bearing a burned mark on its twisted trunk, stood an immense cedar tree.

Confused, Beth tried to comprehend the scene with bloodshot eyes. The symbol charred into the trunk of the old tree came into focus. It was '*Tav*', the final letter. It is finished. The end of the story. As her father had explained her so long ago, this was the end. Her eyes moved past the gnarled tree. Up toward the pinnacle. Then…

‡ ‡ ‡

THERE HE WAS! The future queen of the kingdom saw him! The king. More handsome than she had ever imagined. Magnificent. Powerful. Elegant in full royal attire. Crowned with a bejeweled, golden crown set at a rakish tilt. A casual drape of raven-black hair curled on his forehead. He was draped with a long red cloak, trimmed in white ermine and black piping that cascaded down across the crack, nearly to the foot of the staircase. With bandolier, sword, and chest filled with a regalia of medals, he filled her vision. He looked truly regal, all framed by the elegant marble arch.

His right hand was casually lain on a table brimming with food and drink. His left, holding the regal staff of power. On either side, stood fierce and finely dressed guards. Behind him in obsidian elegance stood his stallion. Liveried in the same black leather and silver studs, he was the replica of her mare, Ashes. Panting in short gasps, Beth's heart began pounding with enough strength to explode from her chest. She tried to cry out to him, but no sound came.

Gazing over the entire battlefield, the newly appointed king, confident of victory, was not even aware that Beth was there. Right in front of him. Within feet of the end of his cloak. Moisture began pooling in her eyes, but dehydration prevented tears from running down her face. With an impossible show of strength, on her hands and knees, she began crawling up one step at a time. Finally reaching out, she clutched at the hem of his royal cape.

Something tugged at his cloak. The prince looked down and finally saw Beth with one hand on his robe.

"Aha, look who has finally joined us. It is the princess." His dark eyebrows rose slightly. "It looks as if you have had a difficult time, Milady?"

Forcing the words from her mouth, Beth croaked, "Yes, my Lord, I have searched for you with my whole heart."

"Well, good for you. Has it been a long journey? You certainly sound thirsty, and perhaps hungry?" He spoke cheerfully. "Come up here and enjoy some of this delicious fruit and wine."

A little confused at his response, Beth, famished and thirst-driven, crawled up two more steps.

"Yes, you may have all you can eat, lady." Then bending slightly forward, he extended his right hand. "Give me those letters you have been dragging around all this time."

She slowly reached for the book of letters. Her thoughts muddled from fatigue, hunger, and thirst caused her to move slowly. Something was wrong. She pulled the book from her pocket and began to offer it to the king. They were, after all, his letters.

"Come, come now, just give me the book and you can have all the food and wine you want." The king reached lower to grasp the book. Then as Beth looked up, the figure beside him came into focus. Counselor Peh! The smarmy advisor to the king of Vau. The smooth-tongued defense attorney to the traitors. *Why is he here?* The words echoed in her brain. With great difficulty she slowly shook her head.

"No," she croaked, pulling back her hand. "You wrote them for me. I cannot let them go."

"Well, no matter," he said breezily, "you will relinquish them eventually. Come, get yourself up here and enjoy the feast." He waved his hand over the loaded table.

Beth ran her tongue across her cracked lips. The thought of a cool drink and delicious food energized her enough to pull one foot under and then the other until, swaying dizzily, she stood. Climbing slowly, dragging the frayed banner draped on her shoulders, each step excruciatingly painful, she reached the crack in the stair. It was not wide, but looking down, she could see it was dark and so deep it seemed bottomless. Dizzy and exhausted, it appeared to be a mile across.

"Come, come, your highness," chided the king. "Don't worry, if you can't cross it, my guards will help you, they can catch you if you fall." There was a mocking tone in his voice.

She hesitated for a moment while memories swirled in her head. Overcoming fear had become a daily occurrence now. Just squeezing her eyes shut and stepping across, even in her weakened state it was not so far. What was troubling her, though, was the mocking tone in his voice and the evil presence of Counselor Peh whispering in his ear.

Was this a final test of her loyalty? Did she still have one last challenge to overcome? Bothering her just as much, was being told she could *not* do something. Even in her feeble state she would not ask for help. Not being able to say anything, she merely shook her head again.

"Well, fine," said the king with a tinge of frustration. "Look around you, you grubby little coward, you can see the entire kingdom from here. Don't you want to be able to rule over all that?" He pointed to the vast land below them.

Beth continued to gaze at him, trying to puzzle it out.

"Here, show a little respect to your king." Extending his ornate staff across the gap, the king held the sharp point to her lips. "Just reverently kiss the tip of my scepter," he said condescendingly. "Worship me, and I will personally come and escort you to your throne."

A combination of betrayal and confusion oozed like acid up the back of Beth's throat. Her voice, driven by anger she couldn't contain, came out raspy but strong. "You said you loved me! Your words convinced me to come on this misbegotten journey because they were kind and gentle! Because of your letters, I fell in love with you! I worshipped you for your goodness." The tears now began to fall. Her voice shaky, choked up but determined, continued. "I can see now you are cruel and selfish and demanding and . . . and mean! I will not kiss your worthless stick!"

The handsome features darkened. Jaw muscles bunched up and his face began to contort until it was a hideous mask of anger and cruelty. Eyes narrowed, voice saturated with hatred he shouted, "Take this, you prideful, arrogant, insignificant worm!" He drew back the massive, ornate staff with both hands and swung forward in a deadly thrust aimed directly at the heart of the young scribe, princess, warrior, and now queen.

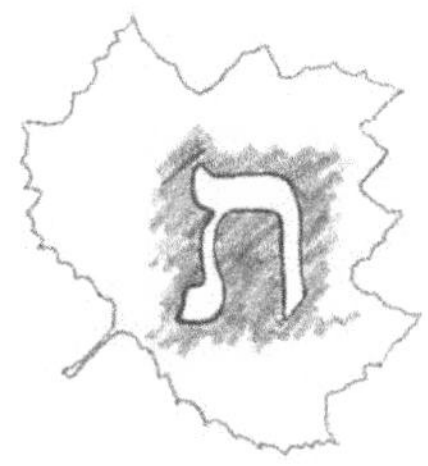

Chapter Twenty Two

Tav

WHAT HAPPENS IN an instant, looking back at times, is seen in meticulous detail, moving in painfully slow measured increments. Almost inert pieces gradually coming together. So it was now for Beth.

Standing before the king—wavering, tired, confused, and angry—the young woman could see the vicious pointed steel scepter moving inexorably toward her own heart. Behind the spear, clasped in white knuckled hands, grimaced the terrible, brutal face of the king. There was no time, no weapon, nor opportunity for deflection or defense.

Beyond imagining, strong hands gripped her shoulders, moving the intended victim slowly to one side. Impossibly, the lethal blade did not even graze her arm, but caught the hem of the royal banner. Turning to follow its path, Beth, in horror, saw it cleave Aleph's chest. In the last possible moment, she had been thrust aside, rescued by her noble and faithful companion and friend, Aleph.

With ruthless force, the scepter speared the center of his chest, piercing his heart and lifting him bodily above her head, impaling him on the very tree bearing the burned symbol tav. A tattered scarlet banner hung bloodlike from the shaft in his side.

Collapsed, falling again to her hands and knees, leaves and letters cascading in front of her, Beth cried out, "No! No, no, no, not Aleph!"

The charm, hot around her neck, swung free. By the light of the three flames behind her, she could see the shadow clearly on the final blank leaf between her two hands. The dove turned slightly, and the shadow became clear. It was the letter Aleph.

The only one missing and the very first letter in her aleph-bet.

In that painfully slow, immeasurable cadence of thought, the truth shone through.

Aleph was the Prince!

He is the King!

She was shocked by a fury so powerful it jolted her to her feet. The object of her wrath stood smirking down at her from under the white arch. She turned to face him. Proud imposter, pretender, slayer of the one Beth now knew was the rightful heir to the throne. The lover of her soul. He who had served her, cared for her, and sacrificed his own life to save her, was gasping his last breaths impaled on the massive cedar behind her.

In one bound she leapt up and across the chasm separating her from the monster standing arrogantly above her. Divinely empowered by the words penned for her by Aleph, Beth tugged at her side and yanked out the bloody, well-used but still sharp sword that hung from her belt.

Amusement crossed the deceivingly handsome face of Aleph's slayer. "Oh my, the queen bee still has her little stinger."

Turning to counselor Peh on his right, he said, "Does this little insect still annoy us, counselor? I can't be bothered. Just shove her into the pit." Counselor Peh moved but not quickly enough.

Beth, sword in hand, reached the dais upon which Belial stood.

Righteous indignation exploded in her chest. Peh tried to intervene by shoving her to one side. As Beth fell to one knee, every ounce of that passion drove the sword in a backswing that completely severed Belial's achilles tendon. A bellow of anger and pain spewed from his mouth.

He fell.

Landing on top of counselor Peh, both tangled in his robe. In the struggle to break free they rolled to the edge of the precipice. Scrambling for purchase on the marble steps, they fought each other hopelessly. Still bellowing, they dropped headlong into the abyss.

Adrenaline coursing in her veins, Beth in three strides reached the base of the massive tree and kneeled at the feet of her servant-king, Aleph. Gathering up her treasured book, lifted her eyes to meet His. All the love was there. Each and every kind word. All of the wisdom, instruction, and guidance contained in her letters was true.

"My beloved Prince," Beth whispered without releasing his eyes so full of pain, "I looked for you with my whole heart. Your words will remain there forever. I promise to read them aloud to encouraged any who listen." Words from the precious letters began to form on her lips.

O Lord, you heard my weeping
and gave me the discerning mind you said you would.
You heard my prayer; you rescued me as
you promised.
Praise will flow from my lips,
for you faithfully taught me your decrees.
I will sing songs about your word,
for everything you wrote is true.
You helped me at the worst time,
I chose to follow you to the end.
O my King, I longed for your salvation and it came.
Telling that delightful story will be my endless delight.
I now must live so I can praise you,
your message of hope will help me.

As the words sighed out of her parched throat, eyes still fettered to his, she became aware that he was murmuring them along with her. Words that tethered her heart to his in life were now tying them together in death.

I wandered like a lost sheep;
but the entire time you were right beside me,
Now I will never, never forget your sweet Love Letters
to me!

Drops of blood from the mortal wound dripped down onto the book in her hands. His final sigh wrenched her heart as if she were dying with him.

Clutching the Love Letters to her chest, she knew he would live through them forever.

Epilogue

TALL ON THE marble steps framed by the palace arch, the royal banner whipping victoriously above her head and wind-blown hair streaming behind, Beth stood in pain, tearful but proud. At her feet lay the forever still body of Aleph her love. Blinking away tears, she could see the faithful assembled before her. Spreading far down the slope of Mount Shin, some standing, the wounded sitting or kneeling, all mingled among the bodies of the fallen. Those of the enemy who still lived had skulked away to escape from the victors.

The mighty giant Gimmel had limped to her side at the foot of the ancient cedar, removed his battered helmet, and, as sorrowful as a mother with a stillborn child, released the faithful servant-prince, lying his body at the top of the marble steps. Taking food and drink from the banquet table of the enemy to the new queen, Gimmel pressed her to eat and drink.

"Dear Gimmel," Beth whispered, looking up at the gentle warrior. "You knew?"

Nodding his massive curly head still drenched with

sweat, he answered apologetically, "Yes, my queen, only I and your just and righteous servant Tzaddi knew."

Then as some measure of her strength was restored, Gimmel escorted her to the top of the stairs, helping her stand gripping the seven-jeweled banner which had been hastily tied to the confiscated scepter, the deadly spear of Belial.

She was now hailed as the royal Queen. Her courage had won the loyalty of them all. A swell of cheers came from tem thousand throats. She was humbled but proud, yet there was no arrogance in her. Tears of pain were flowing freely from her eyes, but she stood as straight as her scepter.

No, the pride was for the brave and loyal throng of subjects who had fought so valiantly and were now crowding the base of the steps; the pain was for those fallen who sacrificed all; the tears were for the loss of her beloved servant-prince.

Amazed, she looked across the throng and recognized Master Lamedh, her trainer, with more than a hundred sturdy blacksmiths and metalworkers standing with an abundance of armor and weapons. Dressed in white, the gentle shepherd, Hei, was there with soldiers from his village. Beyond them a band of emaciated slaves who had broken their shackles and climbed the trail to join the battle. Coming slowly up the steep mountain were a few of the damaged people led by Nun the fish man. Closer still were Kaph and Kaphet, tending to the burial preparations for her beloved Aleph. Then striding up the slope with military bearing was her father, Baruch. He stepped to her side and embraced her as only a loving father could.

How they all had come to be here she did not know, yet they all looked to her as their new Queen. Perhaps more awestruck and hesitant than ever on her arduous journey, Beth knew that with guidance from the words, she would lead these wonderous people with dignity and justice.

Your words make me stronger than my enemies.
They give me more insight than my teachers,
even wiser than the elders.
They will be my constant guide.

"All mankind is of one author, and is one volume; when one man dies, one chapter is not torn out of the book, but translated into a better language; and every chapter must be so translated; God employs several translators; some pieces are translated by age, some by sickness, some by war, some by justice; but God's hand is in every translation, and his hand shall bind up all our scattered leaves again, for that library where every book shall lie open to one another."

—John Donne (1572–1631)

Cartography

Notes for the Wise

I HOPE YOU have discovered by now that what Beth writes is the actual text taken from Psalm 119. The word of God, His testimonies, statutes, laws, and commands contain everything we need to know about Him. With 176 verses, this is the longest chapter in the Scriptures and mentions His word in every single verse. Also, each section of eight verses is an acrostic starting each line with the sequential letter of the Hebrew alphabet.

Two things on earth are eternal: His Holy word and the souls of His beloved people.

I beg your indulgence for altering Psalm 119 in my story to conform those words to the growing heart of Beth as she writes of her love for the Prince and the transformative power of his words. A lifelong passion for the word of God will transform you. I pray that you will believe and incorporate the words of this wonderful Psalm into your own life, and that you will seek Him with your whole heart.

Many deep and wonderful truths can be mined from this Psalm, and some of the best are included in a Wisdom Guide available for personal or group study:

LoveLetters/joecastillo.com

Free Bible Version

Psalm 119

Aleph

1. Happy are those who do what is right, who follow what the Lord says.
2. Happy are those who keep his commandments, who sincerely want to follow him.
3. They don't do what's wrong; they walk in his ways.
4. You have ordered us to follow your instructions carefully.
5. May I be reliable in the way I keep your rules!
6. Then I won't be ashamed when I compare what I do to what you have said.
7. I will praise you sincerely as I learn from you the right way to live.
8. I will observe your laws. Please never give up on me!

Beth

9. How does a young person remain pure? By following what you say.
10. I worship you sincerely; please don't let me stray from your commands.

11. I keep what you say in my mind so I won't sin against you.
12. Thank you Lord! Teach me what to do!
13. I repeat out loud your instructions.
14. I enjoy your laws more than having plenty of money.
15. I will think deeply about your teachings, and reflect on your ways.
16. I will take pleasure in following your directions; I won't forget what you say.

Gimmel

17. Be kind to your servant so I can live and follow what you teach.
18. Open my eyes so I may discover wonderful things in your law.
19. I'm only here for a short time—don't let me miss what you have to say.
20. I'm always so keen to know your instructions.
21. You reprimand those who are arrogant; those who don't follow your commandments are cursed.
22. Don't let me be scorned and insulted, for I have kept your laws.
23. Even leaders sit down together and slander me, but I, your servant, will think seriously about your instructions.
24. Your laws make me happy—they are my wise advisors.

25. I'm dying here, lying in the dust. Keep me alive as you promised.

Daleth

26. I explained my situation to you, and you answered me. Teach me to follow your directions.
27. Help me understand what your laws mean, and I will meditate on the wonderful things you do.
28. I'm weeping because I'm so sad; please encourage me as you promised.
29. Stop me fooling myself; kindly teach me your law.
30. I have chosen to trust in you. I always pay attention to what you say.
31. I hold on to your teachings, Lord. Don't let me be ridiculed.
32. I run to follow your commands, for you have expanded my mind!

He

33. Teach me the meaning of your laws, and I will always keep them.
34. Help me to understand so I can be totally committed to doing what you want.
35. Lead me to follow your commands, for this is what I love to do.
36. Help me to concentrate on what you say rather than on making a profit.

37. Don't let me focus on things that are worthless. Help me live in your ways.
38. Please keep your promise to me, your servant, that you made to those who worship you.
39. Take away the shame I dread, for your law is good.
40. I always want to do what you say. Please let me live, for you do what is right.

Vau

41. Lord, please love me with your trustworthy love; please give me the salvation you promised.
42. Then I can reply to those who mock me, for I trust what you say.
43. Don't ever prevent me from being able to speak your words of truth, for I place my complete confidence in your just judgments.
44. I will continue to follow your teachings, forever and ever.
45. I shall live in freedom, for I have committed myself to obeying you.
46. I will instruct kings about your laws—I won't be embarrassed.
47. I'm so happy for your instructions. I love them!
48. I lift up my hands in prayer, honoring your commandments. I will think deeply about all you say.

Zayin

49. Remember your promise to me, your servant. It's my only hope.

50. This is what brings me encouragement in my misery—your promise keeps me going!

51. Arrogant people mock me terribly, but I don't give up on your teachings.

52. I think about the instructions you gave long ago, Lord, and they reassure me.

53. I am angry with the wicked because they have rejected your law.

54. Your instructions have been music to my ears wherever I have lived.

55. At night I think about the kind of person you are, Lord, and do what you say.

56. For this is how I live my life—by following your principles.

Heth

57. Lord, you are mine! I have promised to do as you say.

58. My whole being wants your blessing—please be kind to me, as you have promised!

59. As I think about my life, I turn to follow what you have said.

60. I hurry to keep your commandments without delay.

61. Even though wicked people try to tie me up, I won't forget your instructions.
62. I get up in the middle of the night to thank you for your good laws.
63. I identify with all those who follow you, those who do what you tell them.
64. Lord, you love everyone on earth; please teach me what to do.

Teth

65. Lord, you have been so good to me, your servant, as you have promised.
66. Now teach me wise judgment and discernment because I believe in your instructions.
67. Previously I was suffering, wandering away from you, but now I do what you say.
68. Since you are good, everything you do is good. Teach me your ways.
69. Arrogant people smear my reputation with lies; but I whole-heartedly follow your commands.
70. They are cold and unfeeling, but I love your law.
71. The suffering I went through was good for me, so I could think about what you have stipulated.
72. What you tell me to do is worth more to me than much gold and silver.

Yod

73. You created me and made me what I am; help me to learn and better understand your commandments.
74. May those who worship you be happy when they see me, for I place my confidence in your word.
75. Lord, I know that what you decide is right; you brought me down in order to help me because you are trustworthy.
76. May your trustworthy love comfort me as your promised me, your servant.
77. Be compassionate to me so I may live, for I love your teachings.
78. Bring down those proud people who wronged me with their lies. I will spend time thinking about your instructions.
79. Let those who follow you turn to me, those who understand your laws.
80. May I be innocent in the way I keep your rules so that I won't be ashamed.

Kaph

81. I'm exhausted waiting for you to save me, but my hope is in your word.
82. I strain my eyes looking for you to keep your promises, asking "When will you comfort me?"

83. I've become like a wineskin that's been shriveled up by smoke, but I have not forgotten to do as you say.
84. How long do I have to wait before you punish my persecutors?
85. These arrogant people have dug pits to trap me, these people who don't care anything about your law.
86. All your commands are trustworthy. Help me against these people who persecute me with their lies!
87. They have almost killed me, but I have not given up on what you say.
88. Since you love me with your trustworthy love, don't let me die, so I can go on following the instructions you have given.

Lamedh

89. Your word, Lord, lasts forever. It stands firm in the heavens.
90. Your faithfulness lasts for all generations, as permanent as the earth you created.
91. Your judgments stand—they are as true today as ever—for everything serves your will.
92. If I didn't love your teachings, my suffering would have killed me.
93. I will never forget your instructions, for through them you give me life.

94. I belong to you, so please save me! I am committed to following your rules.
95. Even though wicked people are waiting to ambush and kill me, I will focus my mind on what you say.
96. I recognize that human perfection has its limits, but your law is limitless.

Mem

97. I really love your law! I meditate on it all day long.
98. Your commands make me wiser than my enemies, for I'm always thinking about your instructions.
99. In fact I have a better insight than all of my teachers because I spend time concentrating on what you say.
100. I even understand more than the elders because I follow your directions.
101. I avoid any course of action that leads to evil, because I want to remain faithful to your word.
102. I have not disregarded your instructions because you yourself taught me what to do.
103. Your words taste so sweet to me! They are sweeter than honey to my mouth.
104. I gain understanding from what you say, so I hate any way of life that's just a lie.

Nun

105. Your word is a lamp that shows me where to walk, it's a light for my path.

106. I've made a promise, and I will keep it: I will keep your rules that are always right!

107. Lord, I'm really suffering! Please let me live, as you have promised.

108. Lord, please accept my offerings of praise that I freely give you. Teach me your rules.

109. My life is always at risk but I will not forget your law.

110. Wicked people have set a trap for me, but I will not stray from your commandments.

111. I will always hold on to what you say for your words make me really happy,

112. I have made up my mind to follow your instructions to the very end.

Samekh

113. I hate people who are two-faced, but I love your law.

114. You keep me safe and you defend me, your word gives me reason to hope.

115. Leave me alone, you evil people, and let me keep the commandments of my God.

116. Support me, Lord, as you promised, so I can live. Don't let my hope turn into discouragement.

117. Support me, so I can be saved and always pay attention to your instructions.

118. You reject all those who don't follow your instructions—they're fooling themselves by living a lie.

119. You treat the wicked people on earth as something worthless, to be discarded; therefore I love your laws.

120. I have goose bumps thinking of you—I'm in awe! I'm scared of your judgments!

Ayin

121. I have done what's fair and right, so please don't abandon me to my enemies.

122. Please promise you'll take care of me, your servant. Don't let these arrogant people mistreat me.

123. I strain my eyes looking for your salvation, watching for you to fulfill your promise to make everything good.

124. Please treat me, your servant, according to your trustworthy love. Teach me what you want me to do.

125. I am your servant. Please give me discernment so I can understand your instructions.

126. Lord, it's time for you to act, for these people have broken your laws.

127. This is why I love your commandments more than gold, more than the finest gold.

128. All of your rules are right in every way, and so I hate any way of life that's just a lie.

Peh

129. Your laws are truly wonderful—that's why I keep them!

130. Studying your words brings light so that even the uneducated can understand.

131. With keen desires I long for what you have to say.

132. Please pay attention to me and be kind to me, as you are with those who love you.

133. Tell me by your word the way I should go, and don't let any kind of evil control me.

134. Save me from cruel people so I can follow your instructions.

135. Please look favorably on me, your servant, teach me what I should do.

136. My tears stream down as I weep for those who don't keep your law.

Tzaddi

137. Lord, you are right, and what you decide is just!

138. You have given your instructions which are fair and totally trustworthy.

139. My devotion is burning me up inside because my enemies ignore your words.

140. Your promises have been proved true, and that's why I, your servant, love them.

141. I may be unimportant and looked down on, but I don't forget your commandments.

142. Your goodness and justice last forever; and your law is the truth.

143. When I have problems and sadness, your commands make me happy.

144. Your laws are always right; help me to understand what they mean so I can live.

Qoph

145. My whole being is crying out! Lord, please answer me! I will follow your instructions.

146. I pray to you, asking, "Please save me!" so I can do what you say.

147. I get up before dawn, and call out to you for help and put my hope in your word.

148. During the night I stay awake, meditating on your word.

149. Listen to what I have to say, Lord, because of your trustworthy love. Keep me alive, Lord, because you always do what's right.

150. Evil people come running to attack me—they totally disregard your law.

151. But you, Lord, are close beside me; all your commandments are true.

152. Long ago I realized that your laws will last forever.

Resh

153. Please look at my suffering and save me! I have not forgotten your teachings.

154. Plead my case, and save me as you promised! Let me live!

155. Wicked people can't be saved, because they don't care about what you say.

156. Lord, your mercy is so great! Because you are always fair, please let me live!
157. Despite the many people who persecute and mistreat me, I have not strayed from your laws.
158. Watching these unfaithful people disgusts me because they take no notice of your word.
159. See how much I love your commandments, Lord. Please let me live because of your trustworthy love.
160. Your word can be summed up in one word: truth! All of your just laws will last forever.

Shin

161. Leaders persecute me for no reason, but I am in awe only of your word.
162. Your word makes me so happy—I'm like someone who discovers immense treasure.
163. I hate and detest lies, but I love your teachings.
164. I praise you seven times a day because your laws are good.
165. Those who love your teachings have wonderful peace and nothing trips them up.
166. Lord, I look forward to your salvation. I keep your commandments.
167. I obey your laws and love them very much.
168. I keep your commandments and laws because you see everything I do.

Taw

169. Lord, please listen to my sad cry; help me to understand, as you promised.

170. Please hear what I have to say to you, and save me, as you promised.

171. Let me pour out my words of praise, for you teach me what to do.

172. I will sing about your word, for all your commandments are right.

173. Please be ready to help me, for I have chosen to follow your instructions.

174. I long for your salvation, Lord; your teachings make me happy.

175. May I live my life in praise to you, and may your instructions help me.

176. I have wandered away like a lost sheep, so please come looking for me, for I have not forgotten your commandments.